R E A D E R S are saying...

"A sequel that's as good as the first novel. Maybe better."

"I want to be a Chianti Girl!"

"I love Norma and wish I had someone like her in my life."

-"I kept wishing I was in Italy."

"So touching. Had to read with a box of tissues."

Barbara,

Hope you enjoy this tale
of love and friendship — They
are the best gifts in life!

Because of Tuscany

A Tale of Friendship and Love

Karen

Karen Ross

February 2016

ISBN: 1499591012
ISBN-13:   978-1499591019

Printed by Create Space, An Amazon.com Company

Cover illustration by Karen Ross
Photography by Judith Black Horn
Graphic design by James Newton

Chianti Girl \kē-ˈän-tē, gər(-ə)l\

Definition:
- Knows the power of love and friendship
- Lives passionately and wholeheartedly
- Recognizes her imperfections and embraces them
- Resists judgment of herself and others
- Sometimes drinks too much wine (especially Chianti)

To all the Chianti Girls I know

(you know who you are)

I hope you will go out and let stories happen to you, and that you will work them, water them with your blood and tears and laughter til they Bloom, til you yourself burst into BLOOM.

-Clarissa Pinkola Estes

CHAPTER 1

🕉️📖

Fayetteville, Ohio

LUKE DAVIS PROPPED the black and white photo of Anna against the Jack Daniel's bottle and stared at her beautiful face. He replayed the memories of the magical four days they had shared nearly thirty years earlier during his military leave in Tuscany. Then he imagined the countless possibilities of what could have happened to her.

Coping with painful memories of Vietnam was difficult, but losing contact with Anna was worse.

He ran his thick fingers through his sandy gray hair and let out a big sigh before emptying the bottle of Jack Daniel's into his glass. Straight up was his preferred way to drink it.

Jack was a constant companion. And so was Scout, the 10-year-old hound mix sleeping at his feet under the table.

The phone rang. It was Caroline.

"Sure," Luke said. "I'll be there in a couple of hours, around eight."

He needed time to shower and stop at the liquor store for a new bottle of Jack.

A warm meal and a night under the covers with Caroline would take care of some of his basic human needs, and hers. In the fifteen or so years since they met at his favorite local dive, they had kept each other company and agreed not to complicate their relationship with commitment. He didn't know why her heart was as frozen as his was because they never talked about things like that.

He studied Anna's face for a minute longer then guzzled the Tennessee spirit. It went down warm like sunshine, but it cooled his aching heart. He let out another big sigh. Scout let out a snort.

He wished he had more photos of her, but this was the only one. And he had carried it with him every day since the sixties, then laminated it in the seventies, but by now the laminated edges were frayed and curled.

He carefully put it back in his wallet and removed the credit card-sized calendar his insurance rep had sent with his annual holiday card. Luke needed to figure out when he could take his next trip to New Orleans.

As a retired firefighter and paramedic, his skills had been invaluable during the months following Hurricane Katrina's wrath on New Orleans. And now his carpentry expertise was equally prized as he helped to rebuild the homes lost in the storm. Since 2005, he averaged two month-long trips a year to the Crescent City, and this year was no different. He had already been there a few months earlier in the spring.

He squinted at the tiny calendar. July was almost over, and he ruled out August because of the Mississippi Delta's sweltering heat and humidity. In September and October, he was booked because he had volunteered to be an extra hand at his friend's nursery and landscaping business. Autumn was peak season in Ohio for selling and planting trees.

At 68, he could still perform heavy-duty landscaping tasks because his back was as strong as an ox. His arms and legs were well built, too, attracting second looks from ladies of all ages – especially when they saw his baby blues. No one ever guessed he was over sixty.

The month of November will be best, Luke thought.

He didn't mind hopping into his Ford pick-up he called "Big Blue" and making the 12-hour drive to New

Orleans with Scout. But he'd call his friend Tom to find out if he wanted to go, too. Same as Luke, Tom was an excellent carpenter, but he would probably want to be home for Thanksgiving with his kids and grandkids.

As a lifelong bachelor, the holiday didn't matter as much to Luke. In fact, he preferred being out of town and working. Then he'd have a good reason for being alone.

CHAPTER 2

ಐಉಐಔಚಚ

Terzano, Tuscany

MARY LISTENED AS Luca made calls to U.S. wine distributors to confirm his upcoming appointments in New York City, Newark, Philadelphia, Chicago, Miami and Atlanta.

"I wish I could make this trip with you," she said after his last call.

Luca wrapped his arms around her waist and gazed into her big, dark eyes.

"I know, and I would like to take you with me. But when I return in the winter for the West Coast sales calls and wine expos, you'll be there."

"I know," she said.

Even though it was Ferragosto - a holiday period in August for most Italians– she needed to stay home. She had to take care of their nine-year-old son Enzo, and there was a never-ending list of work for the art gallery, two vacation rental properties, the winery and the fourteenth-century villa they called home. And her adult stepson Alex had limited time to help because he was busy with his thriving Tuscan tour business. So she knew it was impossible to join her husband on this trip.

"Will the boys be home tonight?" Luca asked.

"Enzo is spending the night with his cousin, and Alex is staying with friends in Siena."

"Hmmm, an empty house. Is this on purpose?"

"What do you think?"

Luca smiled and slid his hands up Mary's back, under her long dark wavy hair. He pulled her closer.

"So dinner in the courtyard?" he asked.

"Of course."

"Mm."

He cradled the back of her head in his hands and kissed her.

The open-air courtyard in the center of their home was their *paradiso*. They savored time together in this sacred place as often as possible, giving in to the rhythm of life and love under the night sky.

This was where they made love the first time. On that wildly romantic night surrounded by warm candlelight, ancient castle walls and a twinkling night sky, Luca had told Mary their souls already knew each other, and it was only their bodies that were new.

Twelve years later and now in their mid-forties, their soulful connection was as strong as ever, and they knew each other's every curve and crevice.

This night was not much different than the first one, but this time they started it with a picnic-style dinner in the courtyard.

Mary prepared a simple antipasto plate of meat, cheese and marinated vegetables, a basket full of crusty bread and their winery's own Ribelli Chianti.

Luca piled cotton blankets on the ground and surrounded them with a dozen candles.

They settled in at sunset and the *cucina povera* nourished their bodies while the Chianti wine warmed their souls.

As the sky grew darker, they lit the candles and it didn't take much longer until their clothes were off. Their bodies exquisitely melded together in the way only the bodies of two people who share a deep love can.

After making love, they fell asleep tangled in each other's arms, not waking until just before sunrise on Saturday by the rooster crows of the Tuscan countryside.

Luca was catching the early bus to Rome's Leonardo da Vinci airport for a New York-bound flight. The bus was efficient, and it was the most economical means of transportation to Rome. This, and other sensible decisions, helped them save money to reinvest in their business.

"The two weeks will go fast," Mary said, as Luca got out of her royal blue Fiat at the bus station.

She was trying to convince herself and even nodded her head as though it would help.

"Stella will be here in a week," she said. "And we'll go to the Palio. She's never been so it should be fun."

"And it might be a good time to work on your novel. You will have some quiet time without me trying to steal all your attention."

He winked one of his soft blue eyes.

"What do you think I prefer?" Mary asked. "Being naked with you or writing?"

"Let me think."

He touched his lips with his forefinger.

"Hmmm..."

Then he winked again.

"Stop it," she said. "You look too sexy. It makes me want to take you back to home with me."

"You better not," he said. "I have some wine to sell."

"Like you always say, wine gets better with age. So the wine can wait!"

"You would not do that."

"You're right. I wouldn't because we've worked so hard for this opportunity. And I have a lot to do this morning to get the apartment ready at the Cielo villa for the German couple who get in this afternoon."

"We need more people like them to rent that villa."

"I know," she said. "We're getting too many cancellations. But it's probably a blessing in disguise since we've had our fair share of repairs to make."

Luca didn't say anything else.

The Cielo villa was a delicate topic. On paper, buying the neighboring property five months earlier was a good idea because it doubled their vineyard size and provided four additional apartment rental units in addition to the six they already owned at their other farmhouse called Ribelli.

The price had also been good. They bought it below market value because the recently widowed owner had to leave abruptly. She was older and unable to care for it alone, so she moved in with her younger sister in Florence.

But since purchasing it, Mary and Luca had dealt with endless repairs, so the new venture hadn't gone exactly as planned.

Luca's only brother Giovanni had even warned them against purchasing it. Giovanni strongly believed a local rumor that there was a hex on the villa by Sardinian ghosts, or the Sardi, as everyone referred to them.

Luca thought it was nonsense and didn't listen to Giovanni because he rarely agreed with his older brother. Luca only saw the villa's potential value to expand their business, and he still stood by his decision.

Mary wasn't sure yet.

"Hopefully, this week will be better," she said.

Luca barely nodded.

Mary held him closely before saying goodbye. Then she watched the love of her life walk toward the bus in his dark tee and faded jeans, pulling a suitcase. He had a black blazer draped over his tanned arm, and carried a weathered saddle brown leather briefcase. The bag was at least twenty years old and was made in the family leather factory they once owned.

Mary never tired of this backside view. His long, dark hair hit the top of his tee, which stretched across his solid shoulders, and his jeans snuggly wrapped his muscular legs.

He was more than a dream-come-true. Her life with him had blended as perfectly as the Tuscan sun and soil do to make wine. And like wine, Luca got better with age, too.

CHAPTER 3

❧❧❦❦

MARY VISITED HER 92-year-old friend Dorotea Turchi every Saturday morning, traveling the kilometer or so to get there either by car or on foot, depending upon the weather.

She decided to stop in today on her way home from the bus station. It was earlier than her usual visits, but she knew Dorotea would be awake. Mary knocked on her front door and Dorotea answered and invited her into the kitchen.

"*Caffé e crostata?*" Dorotea asked.

"Sure," Mary said. "You know I can never turn down a slice of your homemade tart."

Dorotea loved baking cookies, cakes, tarts and bread, and everyone in the hamlet of Terzano benefitted from her incredible cooking skills. Since she couldn't eat everything she made, she always shared her homemade goods with friends and neighbors – even the ones she didn't like – because the delivery of a homemade treat was the best way to keep up with the local gossip.

"It is a peach tart today," Dorotea said.

As Mary was finishing the heavenly slice of tart, Dorotea got a funny look on her face.

"I'm getting a strong message for you. I need your hands."

Dorotea had psychic abilities, but very few people knew this. In fact, Mary was possibly the only living person with this knowledge because Dorotea had outlived many of her friends and family members. She had asked Mary to keep her ability as a secret, because she didn't want people asking her to tell their fortunes. Dorotea only shared very important visions, as deemed by her.

Dorotea placed her hands over Mary's palms and was silent for a minute.

"I have never had such a powerful premonition. Maybe it is because you are in the room with me."

She paused for another half minute or so.

"You are about to have some new people come into your life," Dorotea said. "There is a lady who will come soon, very soon. She is smart, but a devil rides on one shoulder. A powerful angel is on the other. But she needs your help. She is lucky, because she will have you to play a critical role. I must add, you are the only person who can do this for her."

Mary waited for Dorotea to say more, but she didn't.

"What will I need to do for her?" Mary asked.

"Chase away her devil."

Mary raised an eyebrow.

"What? How will I do that?"

"It is for you to figure out. Your heart and soul will guide you, as always."

The answer was vague, but Mary knew Dorotea never said more than she wanted to say.

"There is one more thing I am seeing," Dorotea said. "You can rest your worries. Luca is going to have much prosperity on his trip in the United States."

"I'm happy to hear that."

Mary wasn't surprised, though, because Luca was determined to make their wine a global success. And he worked hard every day to make it happen.

"Can you tell me anything more about the lady?"

"I can only say it is your destiny, too. By fulfilling your role, you will be rewarded as greatly as she will be."

Mary had many more questions, but she knew it was useless to keep probing once Dorotea had decided she had said enough.

"Well, I better head to the grocery store," Mary said, standing up. "Do you have your list ready?"

"Of course. Here it is."

Dorotea gave Mary a small piece of paper with her grocery items scrawled on it and several Euros.

"I'll be back soon."

Mary hopped into her car and rolled down the windows. She headed to the nearest Coop grocery store, enjoying the fresh air before the sun rose in the sky and it got too hot. Mary didn't mind making the trip to the grocery for Dorotea. Her older friend had never driven a car before, so she needed help getting her groceries.

Of all the people Mary had met in Italy, it was Dorotea who had become her closest friend. Dorotea was a lot like an older Italian friend she had known in Philadelphia named Enzo Moretti. He had owned a deli near her apartment and was from Tuscany. Warm and nurturing, Mr. Moretti had become a surrogate father to Mary and shared his love for Italy with her. She even named her son after him.

Mary kept thinking about "the lady with the devil on her shoulder." She had no idea what it could mean, but she wasn't surprised about the premonition that she would meet someone new. In the seven years she had operated her art gallery deep in the heart of Tuscany, a cast of interesting characters had sought out the small haven perched high upon a hilltop.

But this was the first time Dorotea had ever predicted she would meet a stranger who needed help. So Mary knew to be on the lookout, because Dorotea's premonitions had proven to be accurate time and time again.

In fact, Mary often asked Dorotea for guidance about their business decisions, but she hadn't told Luca she did this. He wouldn't have put much credibility in it. The main reason Mary still had some confidence about buying Cielo was because Dorotea wholeheartedly gave her approval of the purchase.

Yet Mary couldn't help wonder if there was more to the story. The problems with the villa were so frequent it didn't seem right. It was time to ask Dorotea about it, but today she was short on time. She'd ask another day.

CHAPTER 4

ဗာၵၰၵၰ

BY WEDNESDAY, Mary missed Luca like crazy. Minutes felt like days and hours like weeks. Their daily lives were so intertwined with running the business together and taking care of their family – and Mary loved it.

She started writing an email message to Luca, but had only typed a few sentences when a solo female traveler walked into the gallery.

The woman wore broken-in cowboy boots and a tangerine sundress that looked like it was from the seventies. A weathered canvas messenger bag was thrown across her five-foot-eight, curvy body. She had long dark hair pulled into a ponytail and bright blue eyes.

It wasn't often young women came in the gallery alone, and if they did they weren't dressed like this. Most tourists wore practical no-iron shorts and shirts in neutral colors. And Mary was pretty sure this was her first visitor to wear cowboy boots, especially with an above-the-knee length dress. She liked this lady's style, and Mary suddenly suspected she was the lady who Dorotea predicted would arrive.

"*Buongiorno*," Mary said.

"Um, *buongiorno*," the visitor said.

"Are you American?"

"Yes. Thank God, you speak English. My Italian is horrible. Are you an American, too?"

"Well, I've lived here many years, but yes. I'm Mary."

She extended her hand.

"Pleased to meet you. I'm Jessica or Jessie."

"Where's home?" Mary asked.

"New Orleans."

"I thought I detected a Southern lilt to your voice. New Orleans is an incredible city, one of my favorites, but I haven't been for so long. I used to love going to Jazz Fest, and I have a couple of framed posters in the house. I need to go back there someday. But welcome to Chianti – it's quite fantastic here, too. Enjoy the gallery and stay as long as you like."

"Thanks, I have about an hour."

Jessie slowly strolled along one wall of photos and then turned back to look at them again.

"These are so beautiful," Jessie said. "And that's quite an understatement. I feel like there's a story with each of these pieces. I'd love to hear them all."

Mary smiled and gazed out the small window by her desk.

"You're right, Jessie, they do tell a story, and it's safe to say they tell the story of my life, or at least its most important chapters."

Mary gave Jessie an appraising look, as if sizing her up.

"Are you an artist, too?"

"Well, yes, a starving artist," Jessie said. "I don't sell enough to make a living at it."

Jessie began to play with her ponytail.

"I work full-time in a coffeehouse where the owner lets me sell my paintings. It's where I met my fiancé, too. His family's law office is next door. But I haven't created much lately."

"Is your fiancé here in Italy with you?" Mary asked.

"Yes, but I left him near Siena to work at an Internet café. The WiFi at our rental villa went out and he had something important to send to his father, who is also his boss. So he's there and I'm here. It's not such a bad thing."

Jessie giggled a little.

"Too much time together?" Mary asked. "Sometimes traveling can be tough even with the best of friends."

"Oh my gosh, yes. He's making me crazy, and I'm exhausted by his schedules. He wants everything to be planned, and I want to throw away the maps and explore. He's such a taskmaster, and I haven't really been enjoying myself. I'm really beginning to wonder if we're right for each other."

Mary's heart skipped a few beats when she heard this last bit about Jessie's fiancé. The story was eerily familiar. Twelve years earlier her own boyfriend Garrett had brought her to Tuscany promising the romantic vacation of her dreams. But he went home after three days to manage an office crisis. Mary chose to finish the vacation alone and this opened the door for her to spend time with Luca who added the romantic part of her Tuscan vacation. This hadn't been Mary's intention at all, especially since Garrett proposed to her before leaving Italy.

She has to be the lady Dorotea told me about, Mary thought. Perhaps her hardworking fiancé is her devil, just like Garrett had turned out to be a devil.

"You and I have more in common than you can imagine," Mary said.

She offered Jessie a glass of Chianti because it seemed like she needed one – and because it would give them time to talk.

An hour later, the two ladies had drowned themselves in conversation and a bottle and a half of wine. Drinking this much in the middle of the day wasn't typical for Mary, but she had to know more about Jessie. And she couldn't help but give her some advice. She wanted to make sure Jessie knew she shouldn't have to talk herself into marrying anyone.

Mary did this subtly by telling Jessie about the difficult relationship with Garrett that led to living in Tuscany with Luca.

By the time Jessie had to leave, Mary was almost convinced that Jessie was Dorotea's lady, but she wanted more time to get to know her. So she invited Jessie and her fiancé, Charles, to return for dinner, and Jessie accepted.

CHAPTER 5

ɮʘɕɔꞇɞ

CHIANTI WINE WAS the reason Jessie wasn't driving to pick up her fiancé herself. She knew better than to take the driver's seat of their rental car after drinking several glasses of wine.

Fortunately, Mary's charming stepson Alex agreed to give her a lift.

Jessie hopped into the passenger seat of his silver Fiat Doblò – a boxy wagon with big windows, perfect for his tour business. But this wasn't a tour. They were only making a 15-minute drive to pick up Charles, who was at the Internet café on the north side of Siena.

Mary had already told her a lot about Alex, so Jessie felt as though she knew him. And since he was a tour guide, he was skilled at making strangers feel welcome and entertained.

While she took in the breathtaking views of the serene countryside, Alex talked about his life in Italy. Then Alex surprised her by warning her to be careful in Tuscany.

Jessie thought Tuscany felt exceptionally safe, and she was used to living in areas that weren't.

"Really?" she asked, surprised. "Why?"

"You might never want to leave," he said with a smile.

He was right. Tuscany already had her under a magical spell. From the moment she and Charles had gotten there, the area's beauty had fueled her creative spirit, and she hadn't felt this happy in months.

"You're not kidding," she said, and laughed. "It sure is beautiful here, and I want to paint everything I see. After meeting Mary and visiting her gallery, I would love to find some of the same locations she's photographed and painted."

"Most of the sites are right there at the castle and on the two properties we own next door," Alex said. "Mary grabs her camera and wanders around taking shots all year. Then she recreates some of her photos as paintings."

"Then I'd like to spend more time there."

Mary's life in Tuscany seemed wonderful, and Jessie wanted to hear more about it. She was so glad to be going back for dinner.

Jessie turned toward Alex. So far, she'd tried not to look in his direction because all she could do was stare. He was gorgeous with sandy blond hair, blue eyes and dark skin. But she managed to keep the conversation going.

"Mary said she and your dad never plan to live in the U.S. How about you? Do you want to move back?"

"I doubt it. I'm happy visiting New Jersey a couple of weeks each year to see my mom, but I prefer it here."

"I can understand why. You're really lucky."

Meeting Alex and Mary at a Tuscan castle was like a reward – a fairytale ending to a challenging journey. The months leading up to trip had been some of the most difficult in Jessie's life.

She twirled her hair, catching a whiff of lavender from the sprigs she had picked outside Mary's gallery. The aroma lingered on her fingers.

She smiled and imagined herself wandering the castle's property and strolling through its vineyards.

At the bottom of the hill, the gravel road ended. Alex stopped and looked both ways before turning, but when he looked Jessie's way, he gave her a bright smile accented with long dimples.

"I am definitely lucky to be living here," Alex said. "And I'm always meeting really interesting people like you."

Jessie smiled back and watched the scenery change as he turned onto the pavement. This scenic route was the same she had driven to find the gallery, but in reverse. She was sure he knew where they were headed, but thought she'd double-check since she was already late.

"You said you've been to the CyberCafé?"

"Yeah, but not recently since we have Wi-Fi at the house."

"You mean the castle?"

She grinned.

"Yes," Alex said. "But it's still weird to say I live in a castle."

He laughed but then got serious.

"Do you want to know a dirty little secret?" he asked.

He tilted his head down and raised his eyebrows as if the answer was going to be really naughty. The look melted Jessie's heart.

"Sure," she said.

He changed his voice to an upper-crust English accent.

"It's not really a castle."

He bit his bottom lip, raised his eyebrows and lowered his voice for the reveal.

"Technically, it's a 'fortified villa,' but the tower makes everyone think it's a castle. It's a bloody fake."

"It fooled me."

She laughed heartily, the Chianti's effect intensifying her reaction.

"Let me guess," she said. "You have an endless supply of wine hidden away in your dusty cellars. Probably some bags of gold, too!"

"Aye, aye."

"What a life!"

Alex laughed and dropped the English brogue.

"Yes," he said. "The stars aligned for me."

"You're superstitious?" Jessie asked.

She was definitely superstitious, and she sometimes even had psychic visions at unpredictable times. At least she thought they were psychic.

"If I wasn't before," he said. "I should be now. I must have done something right in a past life to have this one."

His life seemed remarkable, like Mary's. For so long she had dreamed of having any life but her own because hers hadn't started out easy.

She was the only daughter of a single mom and had grown up in Tremé, a low-income area of New Orleans not far from the French Quarter. She had always wanted to overcome the stigma of it, but it wasn't easy to do in New Orleans with the city's strong class divisions.

She was definitely from the "other side of the tracks," but she had jumped them a bit by moving to the French Quarter. She was a self-described "work in progress."

The only thing about her past that she believed she had turned into a positive was her style. She never had money for new clothes, so she'd always worn secondhand clothing. Now she combed consignment stores for interesting vintage pieces that helped her create a signature Bohemian look.

"Mary said you grew up not knowing Luca was your biological father."

"Right."

"How was it? I mean, what happened when you found out?"

"At first, life didn't change. I was eighteen, about to graduate from high school and start a business program at Rutgers. So I stayed in New Jersey with my mom, stepdad and younger brothers. It was two years before I quit school and moved here."

"Big move."

"It was. I worked in the vineyards for a couple of years and learned Italian, specifically 'Tuscan' Italian. The strong dialect here isn't easy to learn. Eventually, I enrolled at the University of Siena."

"When did you graduate?"

"About three years ago."

He had graduated late, like she had, but she had started going to school part-time in her mid-twenties while she worked two jobs.

"So you're how old?" she asked.

"Twenty-nine."

"When I was twenty-nine, all year long I kept thinking, 'I'm almost thirty!' I survived, though, and today I turned thirty-two."

"No way!" He exclaimed. "Happy birthday! I wouldn't have guessed you were over thirty."

"Thanks! My birthday is one of a few reasons why we came to Italy. It's a present from my fiancé."

Charles had been generous since they met, but this trip was the ultimate gift, and the timing was especially good.

"Did you already have plans tonight for your birthday?" Alex asked.

"Nothing too specific. We were going to tour Siena and then stay for dinner."

"Will your boyfriend mind the change?"

"I'll tell him it's my birthday, and it's up to me to choose what I want to do!"

She laughed, knowing she sounded bratty.

In reality, she would have to convince Charles of the benefit of the new plan. He was the analytical, pragmatic one in the couple, and her spontaneity sometimes upset him. She carefully picked her battles with him and could usually win him over. She knew this one was worth the effort. She had no doubt he would enjoy seeing a historic Tuscan home and chapel.

"I'd let you choose whatever you wanted to do on your birthday," Alex said.

She smiled and bit her lip as she thought about what she might like from him. Then she reminded herself she was engaged. Very engaged.

"A trip to Italy is the best present anyone could receive," Alex said. "Just add a spaghetti dinner and life couldn't get any better."

They laughed because he had earlier teased her, saying spaghetti was his single favorite thing about Italy. He had finally confessed it wasn't only the spaghetti he loved, but all the food and wine, the people and its history.

"With or without spaghetti, I'm happy to be here."

CHAPTER 6

❦❧❧❦❧

ONCE JESSIE AND ALEX left for Siena, Mary took notes about her conversation with Jessie while it was still fresh in her mind. She often did this when customers made witty or quirky comments she didn't want to forget. Or when they triggered a lost memory she was glad to recall, and Jessie had done exactly that.

Mary sat at the old oak table she used as a desk. The top drawer squeaked as she opened it. She grabbed her leather-bound journal and scribbled down some memories from when she was Jessie's age. With surprising clarity, she remembered her late twenties and early thirties and the undying hope - and pain - of finding true love.

> *Idealistic and full of passion, I wanted it all immediately and lived on an emotional rollercoaster. Everything was the best or the worst. Wanted excitement. Little life happened "in the middle." Talked myself into loving the wrong guys because I was impatient to find love and tried to force it. I thought I was following my heart, but I wasn't.*

This collection of notes was one of the resources she was using for her latest creative endeavor, a memoir about living in Tuscany.

The romantic true-life story focused on how fate, or at least inexplicable coincidences, brought her to the Ribelli farmhouse where she met Luca. Nearly everyone who heard the story encouraged her to write a book about it, so in the quiet months of the previous winter she started writing.

After she put away the journal, she remembered to hang the "closed" sign on the door. Grabbing the dirty wine glasses, she left through the rear door of the gallery that led to the secluded garden patio.

Enzo was on the patio, practicing soccer ball bounces off his head and dodging wrought iron furniture and terra cotta planters.

"You're getting better," she said, always encouraging him.

Enzo tried to smile, but he was concentrating and trying not to break his bouncing streak. He loved soccer, or *il calcio*, and at nine years old he was confident he would someday play for the Azzurri in the World Cup, like nearly every young Italian boy dreamed of doing.

She couldn't coach like his dad, but she was his number one fan and watched until he broke his streak.

When she went into the house, he followed her and did a head bounce one more time inside the doorway.

"You can only do that outdoors or in the courtyard."

She spoke English to him and Luca spoke Italian, giving Enzo the gift of fluency in both languages.

"I know. Sorry."

Enzo took his ball to the open-air courtyard in the center of their ancient home. Here he could continue practicing without risk of damaging anything.

Mary headed down the terra cotta hallway to the kitchen.

She couldn't wait to dine with the Americans and hear about their lives in New Orleans, a city she loved. And she could speak English.

She was fluent in Italian, specifically in Tuscan Italian, because Luca had forced her to learn it beyond a beginner's conversational skill level. He told her the locals would never accept her if she didn't speak their language. And he was right, but Italian didn't always roll off her tongue as effortlessly as her native language. She still didn't understand a lot of their jokes and idioms, and they didn't understand hers.

Her American accent caused some of the locals to refer to her as the "stranger." She preferred it when they called her the "*artista*" instead of the "*straniera.*"

As she practiced saying "*artista*" with just the right inflection, she rummaged through their small refrigerator to take inventory for dinner with the Americans.

CHAPTER 7

‪ঽ০ঽ০ৎ৩ৎ৩‬

"I'm really looking forward to spending the evening with Mary," Jessie said.

"She's awesome," Alex said. "And so is my dad. Everyone likes him. Well, everyone except his brother Giovanni. Long story."

Mary had told Jessie about Luca's rivalry with Giovanni earlier that day. All families seemed to have some conflict, Jessie thought, except hers, because it was non-existent.

She paused a moment before she asked her next question. She had made a life-long practice of not asking personal questions about other people's lives because they might reciprocate by doing the same. It was part of her well-honed practice of not letting anyone get to know her too well.

But the Chianti had relaxed her inhibitions and Alex was so easygoing. She knew part of his job as a tour guide was making conversation, so customers surely asked a lot about his life. And she really didn't want to pass up the opportunity to talk to someone who was in a situation similar to the one she was in with her own father.

"What was it like was when you learned Luca was your biological father? Was it hard since you were older?"

"Yes and no. I was shocked, but my questions about my looks and the frequent trips to Italy were finally answered. Did Mary tell you I'm the result of a New Jersey Shore summer romance between my mom and dad?"

"Yes, she mentioned that," Mary smiled. "She told me a lot about your family. We talked for about an hour."

"Yeah, when I was kid my mom brought me here every summer for a week. We stayed at the Ribelli farmhouse next to the castle. She said it was because she had Italian heritage, but we never visited any family. My stepdad came for the first few years and eventually only she and I would come. I always thought it was strange no one else in the family came with us."

"I bet you were bored."

"Exactly. We wouldn't do much but hang out at the pool. I was annoyed because I missed my baseball games. Now I know it was a time for Luca, or my dad, to see me."

Jessie nodded her head.

"And it explained why I'm the only blond in the family. Everyone told me it must have been a recessive gene. I had no idea what that meant when I was kid."

He laughed before continuing.

"What does your stepdad look like?"

"Jeff is Irish, kind of short and stocky with pale skin and dark hair. My mom has dark skin like me, but her eyes and hair are dark. I'm the only one with blond hair and blue eyes."

Jessie had always analyzed her features too. She knew which ones she got from her mother and assumed the different ones like her height and dark hair were her dad's.

"We assume I got my looks from my dad's biological father. The American he's never met."

"Mary told me about that."

"So you already know a lot of this."

"Yes, but keep going. It's interesting."

"So I learned that my dad paid for all of those summer trips when I came to Italy. He and my mom had agreed he wouldn't have an active role in my life until I was older, but he willingly provided financial support."

Jessie knew for a fact her father had never sent money to her mom.

"We have time before we get to the Internet café if you want to know another family secret," he said.

"Only if you tell me with an English accent."

"I'm not that good," he said. "I would probably annoy the hell out of you."

She giggled.

"Okay, no English accent required."

"Well, here's the rest of the story, and I know my parents don't care if I tell it.

"My dad was in a difficult situation when he found out my mom was pregnant. Her name is Angela, by the way. My grandfather Rusconi is a strict Catholic and would have disowned dad for having a child out of wedlock. Dad knew this for a fact because the same thing had already happened to Giovanni."

"Oh."

"Giovanni is nine years older than my dad, and Rossana got pregnant when they were teenagers. My grandfather disowned him until the day he died."

"That's awful. Your grandfather was really old-fashioned."

"Yes, and very Catholic. Dad and Giovanni agreed one of the Rusconi sons had to stay in good grace. Without sounding callous, they had to do this in order to inherit the leather factory and the properties here in Tuscany."

"So your dad had to keep your existence a secret from his father?"

"Correct. And, making it even harder, my dad was adopted when he was a baby and always felt indebted to his parents. He didn't want to be a disappointment.

"Giovanni was always bitter about the entire situation, and to this day Giovanni believes my grandfather favored my dad who wasn't even his own blood."

"Giovanni and your grandfather seem like they have similar personalities, holding grudges for so long."

"It must be in the Rusconi genes, because my dad isn't like that at all."

"What last name do you use?"

"Rusconi. It helps me with my business. No one wants to take an Italian tour with Alex Steele."

"True!"

Jessie giggled. She was glad he was being so open, so she kept asking questions.

"So you weren't ever angry about losing eighteen years with Luca?"

She was up to thirty-two lost years with her dad.

"No, not really. I decided it wasn't worth wasting time being angry. I chose make the most of it."

"Great attitude."

She wondered if she could be so forgiving about her dad, but her circumstance was quite a bit different.

"I'm sure it helped that I already knew my dad. I had seen him all those summers, and he had always been so nice to my mom and me. And my life in New Jersey was good. Jeff treated me the same as my half-brothers, and he never had reason to complain about my dad. It probably helped they rarely saw each other."

He paused.

"But that doesn't mean it wasn't confusing."

Jessie nodded her head. It would have been nice to at least see her dad when she was a kid, like Alex had. But she hadn't. From the time Jessie was old enough to ask questions, her mother, Loretta, told her she'd never meet him. When Jessie was old enough to understand, her mom said her dad was an oil-worker who had been on a short-term assignment in New Orleans. When he found out her mom was pregnant, he said he already had a family up north and didn't want to be involved.

Jessie never understood why her dad hadn't ever wanted to meet her. Her mom consoled Jessie by telling her she hadn't done anything wrong. Her dad was the jerk who made the bad decision.

So to save herself pain, Jessie had trained herself not to think about him. When she did, she gave little credit to the man who didn't even want to know his own kid.

But nine months before she came to Italy everything changed.

She learned her mother had lied to her all those years.

The truth was her dad was a teenage father who most likely never knew Jessie was born. And unfortunately, this news was revealed to Jessie the day after her 53-year-old mother died from complications after a heart attack, so she couldn't ask her mom any more questions.

Hearing Alex's story about meeting Luca made her want to find her dad "Will." For the first time, she realized he could be someone remarkable – someone like Luca and not a heartless thug.

She had been debating about whether or not she wanted to meet him, and now she found herself strongly leaning in the direction of trying to find him.

"I'm glad it worked out so well for you," she said.

He laughed and said, "It's been great."

It wasn't the time to sink deeper into her own thoughts about her dad, so she changed the subject.

"What's it like being a tour guide?" she asked.

"It's interesting. I meet all kinds of people, mostly Americans. And most of them are interested in what I have to share. Others should have saved their money and stayed at home. I'm always surprised by the people who do crossword puzzles and play games on their phones instead of looking out the window."

"That's hard to believe with scenery like this."

"How about you?" he asked. "Where's home?"

"New Orleans."

"Do you travel a lot?"

"This is the farthest away I've ever been. As a matter of fact, until Charles took me to Chicago to visit his sister, I had only been to two states – Louisiana and Texas. But the more I travel, the more I want to see. I love it."

"Traveling is awesome. I live for it."

"I'd be happy to spend less time in New Orleans."

"I've heard it's a crazy city. I've been to Carnevale in Venice, but I'd like to go to Mardi Gras someday."

"Charles and I would show you around if you came to town," Jessie said, as they pulled into a small parking space on the street in front of the CyberCafé.

CHAPTER 8

𐌔𐌖𐌔𐌖𐌂𐌔𐌂𐌔

ALEX AND ENZO weren't going to be home for the evening, and Mary already had enough fresh sausage links from the local butcher for three people. So it was the right amount for her and the two Americans. She had three large potatoes – enough for a full batch of gnocchi. And there was a half-kilo of pecorino cheese.

She made an easy dinner decision – antipasto platter, gnocchi in pecorino sauce, grilled sausage, grilled zucchini and baked pears.

Mary walked through the house picking up Enzo's comic books and model cars, and fluffing pillows. She was going to give Jessie and Charles a full tour, so she wanted it to look nice. Visitors always enjoyed seeing the historic Tuscan home. They especially liked climbing the tower for its magnificent views.

After straightening up inside, she went out on the patio, covered the wrought iron table with a thick white tablecloth and set it with yellow fabric placemats and napkins.

Then she grabbed a basket and shears and went into the garden beyond the patio. She clipped one ripe zucchini and a thick bunch of lavender.

She put the zucchini in the sink and grabbed a clay vase for the flowers. After stuffing the vase, she took it outside and put it on the center of the patio table along with some candles.

Pleased with the setting, she went back into the gallery and switched on her laptop to finish the email she had started writing earlier to Luca. She told him about the day's events and included her plans for dinner with her new friends.

Words were flowing easy thanks to the nice buzz from the wine she'd had with Jessie. So she finished her email to Luca and opened her manuscript.

She scrolled to the end of the document and reread the last couple of paragraphs she had written a few days earlier. It was the section where she recounted buying the magical pocket watch during her one-day trip to Venice – the pocket watch she wore on as a necklace nearly every day of her life. She held it in her hand while she read.

> *As I headed to the train station, I saw the pocket watch hanging on a long silver chain in a jewelry store window. It was old, broken and stuck on the time of my birthday – 7:11. It seemed like it was meant for me.*
>
> *I returned to Tuscany the same night with plans to have dinner with Luca.*
>
> *When he saw the pocket watch, Luca was shocked. He instantly recognized it as the exact pocket watch he found at the base of the castle's tower about two years earlier. He didn't exactly know why it was in Venice but suspected his ex-fiancée had sold it there.*
>
> *After he told me he this story, I was stunned, too. It was as though the timepiece had a mystical power and wanted to return to its home in Tuscany.*
>
> *Most importantly, the pocket watch would play a pivotal role in bringing us together. But not for another year.*

Mary closed her eyes and thoughts drifted to those first sizzling encounters with Luca – enjoying the views from the tower, sharing lunch in Florence, riding on his motorcycle, making love in the castle's courtyard.

The attraction she felt on the day she met him was still the same, if not stronger.

She missed having him at home and lost the mood to write. So she closed the laptop and checked the time. It was 5 p.m., which meant it was 11 p.m. in New Jersey. She always did time calculations when Luca traveled to keep track of his day. They were good about keeping in touch with short email messages while he was gone. It was considerably less expensive than talking on the phone.

She went back to the kitchen and arranged a colorful antipasto platter of meats, cheeses and marinated vegetables.

As she was putting it in the refrigerator the phone rang. It was the new German renters calling from the apartment at Cielo.

"Hello, this is Herr Proske in Unit 2, and we have a problem. We cannot shut off the water in the kitchen."

Mary grimaced but kept calm.

"Okay, thank you for calling. I will have our manager Giovanni there in a few minutes."

She hung up, wanting to curse out loud, but refrained knowing Enzo was nearby. They had to make so many repairs at Cielo.

She dialed Giovanni's number and after she told him the problem, he did enough swearing for both of them. Curse words were some of the first Italian words she learned, mostly so she could understand Luca's gruff brother.

"*Merda!* Shit! I told you not to buy that old fucking place," squawked Giovanni. "It is cursed and always has been. I tell you, THE SARDI WON'T LEAVE."

Mary bit her tongue and asked if he could go right away.

He grumbled but then agreed because they paid him to do repairs at both rental properties.

She recorded the repair in a log, and as she looked at the long list of work orders, she wondered if the myth was true. She couldn't understand why so many things had gone wrong at Cielo.

Learning more about the property's history from Giovanni or Rossana wasn't likely. All Giovanni did was complain, and it was impossible to get Rossana to talk. She was somewhat introverted and never cared much for Mary. In fact, Mary knew as little about her sister-in-law as she did when they met twelve years earlier. And by now, Mary had given up trying to have a relationship with her.

Moving to Tuscany, marrying Luca and opening an art gallery still felt like a dream, and she loved it, but living in Italy wasn't as easy as she expected.

Mannerisms and customs from the U.S. didn't always mesh with the Italian way. And paperwork was virtually impossible for her to do, so she tried to leave the bureaucratic tasks to Luca. He could better navigate the Italian politics and procedures.

Her life was wonderful, but without him she doubted she could have overcome all the challenges.

But she knew she couldn't be too dependent on him either.

She'd observed the American mother of one of Enzo's friends do this. Julia didn't learn to speak Italian and relied on her husband for everything. She smothered him, which made him become distant. He started coming home late – or not at all. Eventually, she moved back to Atlanta and took their son. Whether or not they legally divorced, Mary hadn't heard.

So she learned from watching others' mistakes and intentionally created some independence from Luca. She socialized with other Italian ladies by volunteering at Enzo's school and with a local clothing exchange program.

While Luca was gone, she took care of all the business matters so he could focus on selling and marketing. She wanted to be a strong partner.

She didn't plan to tell him about any problems at Cielo until he was home. She could handle it.

CHAPTER 9

⋇⋇⋇⋇⋇

Siena, Tuscany

CHARLES WAS STANDING outside the CyberCafé pacing, so Jessie hurried from Alex's car to greet him.

"Are you okay?" he asked. "Where's our car? And why didn't you answer your phone? What happened?"

Discovering the gallery was one of the most exciting experiences of her life, and she needed to convince Charles of the same - quickly. She answered him as fast as he had asked the questions.

"I'm okay, and sorry I'm late. The car is still at the art gallery, and there are no problems. I met the owners, and they are the coolest family. Guess what? They live in a castle and they make their own Chianti and I, um, well, I drank too much. It's why I didn't drive. And I must have turned off my phone to keep from getting roaming charges."

Alex stepped out of the car.

"This is Alex," Jessie said. "His family owns the gallery and winery. It was his stepmom, Mary, who I was drinking with. She's the artist."

Charles shook Alex's hand. Southern politeness wasn't optional in his formal New Orleans family.

"I'm Charles Durbridge. It's a pleasure, thank you for driving my fiancé here."

"You're welcome. I enjoyed talking to her."

Then Charles gave Jessie a private look, and she knew exactly what it meant - "You have some explaining to do because I was worried about you, and who is this goddam good-looking guy?"

"Mary asked us to have dinner at the castle," Jessie said. "It's a beautiful historic place. Won't it be fun?"

"Sure," he said.

It didn't sound like he meant it.

Alex flashed a smile at Jessie, supporting her during the obvious power struggle.

She seemed favored to win because it was easy for anyone on the outside to see Charles was completely enamored with her. Most men were. She was striking. Her eyes twinkled when she laughed, but only Jessie knew all the turmoil lurking inside.

They hopped into Alex's car, and Jessie sat in the back to give Charles plenty of legroom up front. He was slightly under six-feet-four with a broad, athletic frame.

This car was better sized for him than their small, standard-shift Fiat coupe – the only size available at the Florence rental agency. Neither Jessie nor Charles could believe how little most cars were in Italy, but it made sense with all the narrow roads and limited parking.

"Your vacation was interrupted by work?" Alex asked Charles.

His tour guide skills had kicked into gear, engaging a new rider in conversation.

"Yes, unfortunately," Charles said. "Our day started great in Florence. We got up early and the line at the Duomo was short, so we were able to climb to the top."

"Believe it or not, I haven't climbed it. I keep thinking I'll go, but have managed to put it off for years."

"Well, before we came here, I read an interesting book called 'Brunelleschi's Dome' by Ross King. It gave the history of how the dome was built. It's a dome inside a dome, and there are places where you can see the interior dome's construction."

"I need to go in the winter when there aren't many tourists."

"You should. And Florence was fascinating, but a mob. Venice, too. Now we're staying in Castellina in Chianti. It's been good to get out of the crowds."

"Gorgeous area," Alex said. "It's rich in Etruscan history."

"We're visiting my uncle there. He owns a big villa, but his Wi-Fi wasn't working today. After I rushed to get some documents ready, I couldn't email them. My uncle's assistant suggested the CyberCafé because we wanted to visit Siena afterward and have Jessie's birthday dinner there."

Charles turned toward Jessie with his eyebrows raised.

She was listening, but didn't react. She was glad to make Charles slow down and bypass touring Siena for the day. She had visited more museums and churches in the last five days than most people do in a lifetime. She loved the breath-taking art and notable histories of Venice and Florence, but the crowds were overbearing. And she knew Rome would be worse, especially on Charles' tightly packed schedule.

"Maybe we can tour Siena tomorrow morning," Jessie said. "You're going to love where we're going, I promise."

Charles conceded.

"It is your birthday, and I told you we'd go any place you want. I'm the one who fucked up our plans by having to work."

"I think it worked out to our benefit," Jessie said. "Wait and see."

She had a view of Alex in his rearview mirror. He was smiling at her again, cheering her on.

She liked Alex. He was so laidback, unlike Charles who was a bit feisty and matter-of-fact. And Alex never stopped smiling, while Charles was serious most of the time. Like now.

Those weren't the only differences, and she couldn't stop comparing. Wedding jitters were putting Charles under the microscope.

Alex had a mop of wavy blond hair and a sun-kissed olive complexion. Charles' dark hair was starting to get some wisps of gray at his temple and was thinning on top. He'd probably go bald like his father. And he had no tan because he spent countless hours in his office and always would.

"Does Mary know it's your birthday?" Alex asked Jessie.

"Nope. I didn't mention it, but it will be fun to celebrate with her."

"No doubt. She's a great cook."

"I'm sure we'll enjoy it more than any restaurant," Jessie said.

"How long are you staying in Tuscany?" Alex asked.

"Only a couple of days," Charles said.

"Too bad. You could spend weeks here. Like I told Jessie, it's a living history book. But it requires driving, unlike the cities where it's more compact and walkable. I can give you a list of my favorite places, or at least the ones you shouldn't miss on your first trip here. Then, if you want, I can give you a list for your next trip, because I'm sure you'll come back. Everyone does."

Alex smiled at Jessie again through the rearview mirror.

"I'd come back to Tuscany in a heartbeat," Jessie said.

"I can also give you two a list of some romantic spots," Alex said.

Charles sat up straighter. He was already several inches taller than Alex, and now it looked like he was trying to tower over him.

"How private are they?" Charles asked.

"Private enough," Alex said.

Listening to their banter, Jessie blushed and imagined the visuals surely occupying everyone's thoughts.

"Thanks," Charles said. "But we only have tonight and tomorrow. We have to leave early on Friday to get to Pompeii at a decent hour."

"Next time I suggest you two plan to stay longer around here. You'll be glad you did."

Alex changed the subject.

"So I hear New Orleans is home for you."

"Yep, I've spent my whole life there, except for my years in college and law school. I doubt I'll ever leave."

Jessie stared off to the horizon and blinked hard. This was a huge concern of hers. She knew Charles never intended to leave New Orleans, but she didn't know if she could stay there for the rest of her life. The city stimulated her creative soul, but she hadn't grown up with the same privileged life he had. She knew its gritty side well.

Jessie half listened as the guys talked about Tuscany, Italian soccer and local history. She was drowning in her own thoughts.

Within minutes of meeting Mary, she admitted to her that she wasn't sure about marrying Charles. It was unlike her to share something so personal, but she was instantly comfortable with Mary. And she was getting frustrated with Charles and their tightly packed agenda during the trip. He had been a taskmaster, rushing from museum to museum, eating lunch while waiting in long lines and waking up at the crack of dawn. She had never seen him this intense, and she wasn't enjoying herself as much as she thought she would. It made her think of all the other little things that bothered her, like his unwillingness to change the toilet paper roll and or put the lid on the toothpaste.

She closed her eyes for a moment and focused on her breathing to stay calm. She had done this often on the trip.

"Are you okay?" Alex asked.

"Me?" Jessie opened her eyelids. "Yes, just relaxing."

BECAUSE OF TUSCANY 41

"She always does that," Charles said. "She drifts off to another world. I'm not sure where she goes."

Charles laughed, but Alex looked concerned.

She smiled and tried to lighten the situation.

"I'm being a silly tourist who doesn't look out the window."

She gazed at the dreamy scenery again and tuned out Charles and Alex until she saw the tower.

"Look at the tower on the hilltop, Charles. It's where we're headed."

"Very cool," he said.

Alex headed up the rugged dirt road with the tower going in and out of sight. They passed towering cypress trees, vineyards, cattle and dense woods. At a rustic hand-painted sign – *Galleria di Ribelli - Arte di Chianti* – Alex turned and parked in the gravel lot.

CHAPTER 10

༺ৡৢৡৢ৶৶ৣ

Terzano, Tuscany

"HERE WE ARE," Alex said.

"Wow," Charles said. "This is impressive."

"The gallery used to be a chapel," Jessie said. "This is where Alex's stepmom sells her artwork, along with the wine and olive oil they make."

Charles immediately walked to its uneven fieldstone walls and rubbed his hand over the thick, rugged mortar and stones. He shook his head, clearly fascinated.

Alex offered more information.

"The last time it served as a chapel was for the wedding of my dad and Mary. The main building is a fourteenth-century fortified villa, but looks like a castle because of its tower. Everyone around here calls it 'the castle' or in Italian, '*il castello*.'"

He winked at Jessie.

"Can we climb the tower?" Charles asked.

"We sure can, and we will. Ready to head in?"

Charles nodded and followed Alex and Jessie through the gallery's charming recessed entrance lined with lavender and potted plants, including a lemon tree.

Inside, Charles admired the small chapel and approached a faded fresco of the Madonna. He appreciated the historical aspects of the building more than the art. Jessie knew it was his preference and not a criticism of Mary's talent.

Alex went to the tasting table and filled two wine glasses with Ribelli Chianti, giving one to Charles first.

"You need to drink and catch up with the ladies."

Alex handed the other glass to Jessie.

"Where's your glass?" Charles asked Alex.

"I'm going out with my girlfriend later, so I'll wait."

Jessie wasn't surprised he had a girlfriend. He was so attractive and likeable. She surmised being an American helped, too.

Charles took a sip of his wine.

"Tasty, very tasty. Second only to Marker's Mark."

He laughed and continued to survey the building's terra cotta floors and beamed ceiling. Then he took a few minutes and observed the artwork on the stucco-covered walls.

One side was devoted to Mary's photography and paintings of the property – the vineyard, castle and farmers. On the other she featured scenic images of Siena, Florence and Venice.

"These were all done by Mary," Jessie said. "My favorites are the pieces depicting real life in the vineyards. I love the one of this farmer's calloused hands as he's pruning the vines."

"That's Giuseppe," Alex said. "He's been a farmer his whole life and lives at the bottom of the hill. He walks here every morning."

"He looks like he has good stories to tell," Jessie said.

"Would you believe he loves to write poetry? If you find him in the field, you'll hear him reciting Dante or practicing his own rhymes and meters."

"Does he have a family?"

"Oh yeah, a wife, five children and scads of grandchildren."

"Wow, a big family."

Jessie had always dreamed of sharing her room with a sister and having a big brother to chase off the boys who wanted to date her.

"I could tell you lots of stories about the people who live around here. They're a passionate bunch, and a few are quite odd."

"We wouldn't learn about this kind of stuff in a museum," Jessie said to Charles. "Isn't it interesting?"

"Yes, more so than I thought."

"Let's head to the house and find Mary," Alex said.

Alex guided them to the rear of the chapel and they exited through double wooden doors to a cozy patio and garden.

This was Jessie's first time seeing this area. It was accented with overflowing terra cotta pots full of geraniums and potted lemon trees. A border of cypress trees lined the courtyard, making it private and romantic like so many gardens in the French Quarter of New Orleans that were hidden in courtyards behind gates and fences. Jessie always loved finding them.

Mary sat at the wrought iron table dressed in white, making her skin look really tan. She wore a long, flowing cotton top with loose cotton pants. A pocket watch hanging from a long silver chain was the only jewelry she wore, except for a simple white gold wedding band and silver hoop earrings.

To Jessie, everything about Mary eluded calmness and beauty. In white, she seemed angelic.

Mary stood up and extended her hand to Charles.

"Hello, I'm Mary Rusconi. Pleased to meet you."

"Hi, I'm Charles Durbridge. Good to meet you. This is a beautiful home. Thank you for opening it up to us."

"You're welcome. I'm glad you could come back this evening because my sons are deserting me."

"Where is Enzo?" Alex asked.

"In his room. He has to read a chapter of "Harry Potter" in English before going to his cousin's."

"She's a tough mom," Alex said and winked at Mary.

"I think he likes that I make him do it, but he won't admit it."

"Is he going to play with Carlo today?" Alex asked.

Giovanni and Rossana had only one child, Marco, who was about ten years older than Luca. And Marco's son Carlo was close in age to Enzo.

The young second cousins played together as often as they could, which was nearly every day in the summer.

"Yes, Giovanni is going to pick him up in a few minutes," Mary said. "After he finishes a repair at Cielo."

"Another problem?" Alex asked.

"Yes, plumbing, this time."

Mary shook her head before telling Charles about the properties.

"I'm not sure if these two told you, but we own two rental properties. Cielo is the villa with the problem, and the other one is the Ribelli *agriturismo* - the namesake of the wine you're drinking."

"Do those names have translations?" Charles asked.

"They do," Mary said. "Cielo means sky, and Ribelli means the rebels."

"Interesting, you certainly have a lot going on," Charles said.

"We do and we keep getting busier. Recently we began distributing wine in the U.S. and that's where my husband Luca is now. He's promoting our wine to distributors. He usually gives the tours of this wonderful home he inherited from his father, and he likes to talk about all the restoration he did. But since he's gone, you're stuck with me. Want to take a look?"

"Absolutely," Charles said.

The phone rang.

"I hope it's not another problem," Mary said. "Please excuse me."

Mary picked up the cordless phone.

"*Pronto.* Oh, Stella, it's you!"

Mary covered the mouthpiece.

"It's my friend from Philadelphia. Give me a minute or two."

Alex stepped in and offered to begin the house tour.

CHAPTER 11

❧❧❦❦❧❧

"MY GRANDFATHER RUSCONI bought this place as a summer home when my dad was young. The family lived in Florence, and my grandmother wanted to return to the Chianti region in the summers as she had done when she was a child. But unfortunately my grandmother became very ill soon after the purchase. She died a few months later and was never able to see it. The family never ended up living here either. My grandfather was heartbroken and refused to sell it but also refused to visit it."

Jessie nodded because she had heard most of this story earlier from Mary.

"Eventually my dad restored it, and he and Mary made it their year-round home."

They started the tour in the foyer of the rectangular-shaped building and moved to the living room. It was open with a view of the courtyard. Old and contemporary furniture filled the area and Mary's paintings accented the walls.

Mary caught up with them.

"Sorry again. That was my best friend, Stella. She drank wine all night and has a horrible hangover. Crazy Stella! She's flying here this weekend and had some questions."

She didn't mention that Stella was bemoaning a one-night stand, too.

"When does she get here?" Alex asked.

"Saturday."

From the living room, they moved down the hallway into the kitchen. It had an old-world look but was furnished with modern appliances. There was also a small wood-burning fireplace.

"How great to have an open flame here!" Jessie said.

"We use it all the time. You sound as though you might like to cook."

"She does, and she's good at it," Charles said, patting his stomach.

"Yes, I love to cook, but all my recipes are for southern food. You know, red beans and rice, gumbo, jambalaya..."

"My mouth is watering at the thought!" Mary said. "It's been an incredibly long time since I've eaten Cajun food. I'm not sure if you've noticed, but there isn't a lot of diversity in regional Italian cuisine and there are few non-Italian restaurants. There's one Chinese restaurant in Siena we go to every now and then, but it's not so good."

"You're right," Jessie said. "We've eaten beef, ham, cheese, bread, pasta and pizza almost everywhere, except in Venice. We had seafood there."

"And polenta," Mary said.

"Of course," Jessie said. "Sounds as though you're desperately in need of some red beans and rice."

"Or gumbo," Mary said.

"I make the dishes from scratch. They're my Aunt Norma's family recipes."

Some of Jessie's fondest memories were in Norma's kitchen.

Charles nudged Jessie.

"Oh, Aunt Norma isn't really my aunt. I lived with her growing up, so she's really a surrogate mom. She's a black woman who took care of me while my mom worked as a live-in maid, and I always called her my aunt. An angel is what I should call her."

"She sounds wonderful, and you're lucky she taught you to cook," Mary said. "I'd love to have you make some of her recipes."

"I'd like that," Jessie said.

She wondered if she could find Cajun ingredients in Italy. She highly doubted the stores sold Zatarain's mixes or Tony Chachere's seasonings – staples in Norma's kitchen.

They left the kitchen and passed a small bathroom before entering an open dining room with a large, aged wood table. From here it was easy to look outside to the brick courtyard and across to the living room.

"Some of this furniture is well over two hundred years old," Mary said. "I love it. I wish it could talk. Can you imagine the stories?"

"Could be amazing," Jessie said. "Can I take a photo of this room for a backdrop of one of my paintings?"

"Take pictures of anything you'd like."

Jessie removed her camera from her messenger bag and framed the shot.

"She's a talented artist," Charles said.

"I'd love to see your work," Mary said.

"If we can get online, I'll show you," Jessie said.

The phone rang again and Mary excused herself to answer it.

"*Va bene, va bene.* Okay, okay. Alex can take him. *Ciao.*"

After hanging up she told Alex that Giovanni needed more time to fix the plumbing than he expected. So he would be late picking up Enzo.

"Do you mind taking Enzo to their house?" Mary asked Alex.

"It's no problem. I can go now," Alex said. "After I drop him off I'll head to Elena's."

"Thanks."

She called for Enzo who took his time coming downstairs.

While Alex waited for him he suggested Charles and Jessie adjust their schedule to stay in Siena and see the Palio.

"The what?" Charles asked.

"The Palio. The famous Sienese bareback horse race. It's a historic rivalry between the seventeen neighborhoods of the city, and it happens twice each year. The next one is in five days on August 16th."

"I think we'll have to stick to our original schedule," Charles said. "It's too bad I didn't know about it. I don't think our tour book mentioned it, or we would have planned for it."

"Well, if you change your mind, I'll have you join the small group of Americans I'm taking. It's a really unique experience and well worth the effort to go. The event is a big deal to the Sienese, and it's impossible to describe the importance because nothing compares to it in the U.S."

"Is it like winning a Super Bowl?" Charles asked.

"Bigger. It defines their identity and has so for nearly five hundred years. As a spectator you feel as though you've stepped back in time."

"Luca's family is from Florence," Mary said. "So our family is not immersed in it like the Sienese are. But Alex's girlfriend is Sienese."

"It's been fun getting the inside scoop from her," Alex said.

Enzo bounded down the steps carrying his blue and white soccer ball, excited to be going to his cousin's house.

"I'm on page 51 now," Enzo told his mom.

"Good job," she said. "Looks like you're ready to go. Bye, sweetie."

She kissed the top of his head.

"I'll pick you up in the morning," she said.

"Please excuse me," Alex said to Jessie and Charles. "I probably won't be back, so have a good time tonight and hopefully you can come back for the Palio sometime. It's the experience of a lifetime."

After her sons left, Mary said, "I'm lucky to have Alex here. He helps me take care of Enzo who completely idolizes him."

She wished Enzo had little brothers or sisters, but after Enzo's difficult delivery the doctor had advised her not to have more children.

"Alex seems like a highly responsible young man," Charles said.

"He is. With three younger half-brothers in New Jersey he learned to be a good 'big brother.' And he's so even-tempered. In spite of not living with Luca during his childhood, he's practically a clone of him - in looks and mannerisms."

Mary said this with a big swell of pride.

"Elena is his latest romantic interest. He's been fighting off the girls since he arrived in Italy."

Jessie wasn't surprised. She thought about how much more she would have flirted with him if she weren't engaged. There was just something about him.

"Since you're so into history, it sounds like the Palio is something you'd love," Jessie said to Charles.

"We definitely can't add time to our schedule. Today my father asked if we could cut the trip short a couple of days. He may need me back in the office."

Jessie didn't say a word and showed no reaction. She'd practiced hiding her emotions her entire life, but she was disappointed with the thought of leaving early. And she thought Charles' dad was too tough on him.

"We need to talk about it later," Charles said.

"So where were we?" Mary asked, changing the subject.

In reality, Mary was thinking she couldn't believe what she was hearing. She was getting a strong sense of déjà vu remembering her trip to Italy with Garrett. She knew exactly how it felt, and she also knew this might not be good for Charles and Jessie's relationship.

"Oh yes," Mary said. "The old wood table. We take meals here in the winter, but as soon as it's warm, we eat on the patio."

"I need to snap a couple more shots to get the lighting right," Jessie said, going back to taking photos of the room.

"Take your time."

CHAPTER 12

❦❦❦

Terzano, Tuscany

ONCE THEY HAD made a full loop of the ground floor, they were back at the foyer where they climbed a well-worn terra cotta staircase.

When they reached the second floor they could see the open-air courtyard below.

"Take a look if you want," Mary said inviting them to step outside onto one of four balconies.

Jessie went first and Charles followed. They had a full view of the courtyard where they could see several pots of green shrubs and Enzo's scooter propped up against a column.

"This is such a warm home," Jessie said. "It feels so safe."

"I believe we have guardian angels watching over us," Mary said.

She clasped the pocket watch hanging from her neck.

Jessie winked because she knew about Mary's lucky discovery of the piece in Venice and its special meaning to Luca and Mary.

"We have five bedrooms and two bathrooms up here," Mary said, once they were back inside. "Follow me and I'll show you."

They walked along the hallway and Mary stopped at one of the bedrooms.

"Take a look at this guest room. You'll see the bit of New Orleans I told Jessie about earlier."

"Look, Charles! Jazz Fest posters!"

"Now this feels like home." Charles said, laughing. "You know Rodrigue's Louis Armstrong poster is now worth well over $1,000, and that's unsigned, like this one. What did you pay? $50?"

"Exactly," Mary chuckled. "I had no idea how popular these posters were until I went the first time."

"They're a big deal at home," Charles said.

"What do you think of the Dr. John poster," Mary asked.

"I like it," Charles said. "That painter's art has become quite valuable too. Michalopoulous opened a gallery in the French Quarter on Bienville Street. He sells his original oils, and we'd love to buy one."

"You sound like an art connoisseur," Mary said.

"Only New Orleans art!" Charles said. "I only know the local stuff."

"Well, you're making me want to go back soon," Mary said. "Luca has never been to New Orleans, and I'd love to take him. I hope it's on our itinerary when we make our winter trip to see distributors."

Jessie hoped it was, too.

"You would have such a good time," Jessie said. "And we could take you to our favorite places."

"I forgot to mention another up-and-coming artist in New Orleans you should check out," Charles said.

"Who?" Mary asked.

"Jessie Morrow, soon to be Jessie Durbridge. She sells her work in a coffee shop on Magazine Street called Java. Keep an eye on her. She's going to be another famous one."

He smiled and put his arm around Jessie who was blushing.

"Thanks, Charles. I can dream."

"Dreams can come true," Mary said. "Now this is perfect timing to visit the everyone's favorite place in the house - the tower. *Andiamo!* Let's go."

CHAPTER 13

໖ஐ໖൬໖

THEY CLIMBED A STEEP set of old but solid wooden stairs to reach the tower's sturdy platform. From here they peered out the north, south, east and west lookouts.

"This is incredible," Jessie said as she moved from one opening to another, taking photos.

"Absolutely incredible," Charles said.

"Luca proposed to me here at the southern lookout."

Mary thought about her fateful first visit to the tower twelve years ago. It was permanently etched in her memory and she loved reminiscing about it. She had been exploring the Ribelli property alone because Garrett was working at an Internet café. She was taking photos and making sketches when she discovered an overgrown path to the *castello*. Curious for an up-close view, she climbed a short hill to see it.

Much to her surprise, Luca was there doing renovations. It didn't make sense to her because she had seen him a couple of times before at the Ribelli farmhouse and thought he was a farmer.

After a friendly introduction – and sizzling but unspoken attraction – he offered to show her the castle tower so she could take photos. That's when she learned his family owned the castle and Ribelli farmhouse – and that Giovanni was his brother and Rossana his sister-in-law.

Standing by his side at these same lookouts on that first day, she was consumed with him as much as she was with the spectacular vista.

"You must have felt like Cinderella," Jessie said.

It was as if she was reading Mary's mind.

"I did and still do," Mary said.

"Every single one of you ladies dream of being a princess," Charles said.

"Why not?" the ladies asked in unison, as if they'd practiced.

"We men don't stand a chance," he said.

They all laughed.

After Jessie took plenty of photos of the early evening view, they went back to the kitchen.

Mary served more Chianti, then she grabbed the antipasto plate and they moved to the patio. It was the beginning of a long and sumptuous dinner.

CHAPTER 14

ജ൏ലൃ

Terzano, Tuscany

"I NEVER DREAMED we'd have the opportunity to have dinner in an Italian home," Jessie told Mary. "I didn't tell you, but today is my birthday, and I can't imagine a better way to celebrate. This is a great gift."

Mary raised her glass to toast Jessie.

"Happy birthday! *Buon Compleanno!*"

They all drank the Ribelli Chianti.

"I wish I had known," Mary said. "I could have asked my friend Dorotea to make a cake for you."

"Just being here is enough," Jessie said.

She loved being on the quaint patio. It was a picture-perfect setting.

"I couldn't agree more," Charles said.

Charles and Jessie asked Mary a lot of questions about living in Italy and she gladly answered them. Then she finally revealed she was writing a memoir about her Tuscan experience.

"I'm sure it will be interesting and romantic, like your life," Jessie said. "The story of how you and Luca met melts my heart."

"That will be the biggest part of the book, but I'm also thinking of adding other things like the history of these properties. But it's been difficult getting people to talk. Most people are very private."

Even Dorotea wouldn't say much, which surprised Mary since she liked to gossip so much.

"It's been like trying to build a relationship with my father's ancestors in a small town south of Rome," Mary said. "The older culture can be protective of their identity and possessions. Many are suspicious an American like me might try to steal the family fortune, no matter the size."

"You have Italian relatives?" Jessie asked.

"Yes, but I have no relationship with them because of a historical division. The Italians here no longer know why they didn't like my dad's half of the family who moved to the U.S., but they still don't like them. And they've passed along the sentiments to their children and grandchildren. I don't want to give up, but Luca and I are out of ideas for how to improve the situation. It's too bad."

"I'm surprised they're like that. Are you going to put it in the book?"

"Yes, I'll put it all in – the good, the bad and the ugly."

"What about ghosts? I'm sure you have them with all these old places."

Jessie laughed after she asked this question, but she was serious. New Orleans was full of ghosts and she often felt their presence.

"Funny you should mention it. Luca's brother swears the Cielo villa is hexed. He keeps saying some Sardinians who occupied it after World War II cast a spell on it. At that time, many farms in Tuscany were vacant because people had migrated to the cities for jobs. Gypsies and vagrants would move into the empty homes and stay until they were kicked out. Sardinians, or Sardi, did this often because they came to the area looking for work in the fields. Many of them were shepherds."

Mary stopped and took a sip of wine before continuing.

"Giovanni gave me the basic story. He said the Sardi occupied the empty Cielo villa until a new owner kicked them out with only minutes to collect their possessions. The head of the clan reportedly did a crazy incantation and hexed it as they were pushed out."

"Do you believe it?" Jessie asked.

"I'm starting to because of all the problems we're having. But who knows? The building is hundreds of years old so it's no surprise it needs so many repairs.

"I will say, though, nearly everyone in Tuscany has at least one ghost story. And most have more. Lots of people died in this region during the many battles between Siena and Florence, and the region is reported to be haunted. But I haven't had any personal encounters."

Jessie didn't comment, but she wondered if she'd sense any spirits. Her psychic ability was random, but it seemed to happen when the spirits chose to talk to her and not the other way around.

She knew how to read tarot cards, too. She'd been exposed to them her whole life by Aunt Norma who read cards for a living at a small café on Esplanade Avenue near their apartment.

But the kids in grade school had teased Jessie and called her a witch the day she brought in the cards for show-and-tell. So she had learned to keep it private.

Now she embedded their icons in her paintings, but they only had meaning to viewers who understood tarot.

She had never mentioned any of this to Charles because he had once called card readers on Jackson Square a bunch of con artists. So he didn't take notice of the symbols in the paintings as anything other than decorations.

"How hungry are you?" Mary asked.

Before Jessie or Charles could answer she teased them.

"We can eat right away if I make Barilla boxed pasta, but if you're willing to wait, we can make homemade gnocchi."

"Ooh, homemade gnocchi, please," Jessie said.

"Same," Charles said.

Mary laughed.

"All right. That's what I thought you would say. And it's what I wanted to prepare. I keep the boxed pasta on hand for days when I don't have time to make fresh pasta. But the gnocchi comes with one condition. You'll have to be my sous chefs since Alex and Enzo aren't here."

"I'm ready," Jessie said.

"Then let's head to the kitchen," Mary said.

As they walked in, Charles grabbed Jessie's hand and kissed the back of it, and Mary saw him do it.

If Jessie is Doretea's lady, Mary thought, then he sure doesn't seem like her devil.

CHAPTER 15

‫ଛ୮ଊଓଔ‬

"I'M NOT A COOK, but I'll do whatever you need," Charles said as he looked around the kitchen.

Jessie laughed.

"He's burnt ramen noodles, so you may not want him to touch anything."

"I'm embarrassed to say that's true," Charles said.

"How about grilling?" Mary asked.

"Of course!" Charles said. "What guy can't grill?"

"Then you have a job."

Mary pointed to the fireplace.

"It's ready to light. Matches are on the mantel."

While Charles checked out the fireplace, Mary started teaching Jessie how to make gnocchi.

"Gnocchi is one of the easiest and most basic recipes. After I've boiled these potatoes in salted water for about fifteen minutes, we'll peel off the skins. It's undoubtedly the hardest part, because they will be piping hot. Then we'll mash them and add a couple of eggs and about two cups of flour or enough until the dough is just beyond sticky. We'll knead it until it forms a ball. Then comes Enzo's favorite part. We'll take portions of the dough and roll them into long 'snakes' until they're about a half-inch thick."

"The recipe sounds easier than I imagined," Jessie said. "Charles, are you paying attention? Even you could make this at home."

"Sure, sure," he said.

He rolled his eyes, making fun of himself.

Mary continued with the directions.

"Once we have the 'snakes' ready we'll cut them into pieces about an inch long and press indents into them with a fork. Then we'll drop them into the boiling water in batches. They're done when they rise to the top."

"Sounds easy," Charles said.

"How many minutes do they usually boil before they're ready?" he asked.

"Only a few. You pull them out as soon as they rise to the top."

Mary gave him a hearty smile.

"While the potatoes are boiling, I'll go ahead and start the pecorino sauce. This one is easy, too. Pay attention, Charles."

She winked at him.

"Yes, ma'am," he said and saluted.

"How did you learn these recipes?" Jessie asked.

"They were taught to me by my friend who lives down the hill in the hamlet of Terzano. It's the Dorotea I mentioned before. She's 92-years-old and has become one of my dearest friends."

"Is she homebound?" Jessie asked.

"Are you kidding? She walks downhill to the cemetery every day to place flowers on the graves of her husband and son. It's a half-mile downhill, and then she climbs the half-mile back up. I'm amazed by her."

"What happened to her son?"

"He died after a stroke when he was in his sixties, and his wife died soon after from cancer. The grandchildren are near Florence, but they don't visit as often as she'd like. She's such a sweetheart, and I wish they would spend more time with her.

"I pick up groceries when she needs them, but she mostly eats what comes from the garden behind her house. I think it's why she's lived such long, healthy life, along with her steady supply of Chianti and grappa.

"It's her recipe for pecorino sauce we'll make now. After boiling the water, we'll add the grated cheese with a small amount of milk, and someone will have to stir it non-stop."

After Mary put all the cheese sauce ingredients into the pot, Jessie started stirring while Mary went back to preparing the gnocchi dough.

"I want to take a photo of Mary. Do you mind stirring Charles?"

"Are you sure I'm allowed to touch it?" he asked.

"We'll supervise closely," Mary said and winked.

Dorotea's gnocchi recipe was as easy as Mary had described and after taking photos, Jessie jumped back into the action with Mary. She left Charles stirring while she cut the "snakes" and pressed the small dumplings with a fork.

Jessie thought sharing the kitchen with Mary was as much fun as it was with Aunt Norma. The only difference was that Mary drank Chianti while she cooked and Norma's beverage of choice was rum and Coke.

While the dumplings boiled, Jessie moved back to stirring so Charles could start grilling the sausage links over low flames.

Mary told him to sprinkle the meat with Chianti for flavor. They would let the sausage cook slowly while they ate their *primo piatto*, or the first course – gnocchi in pecorino sauce.

Seated at the patio table, Mary toasted to her two new friends.

"*Salute* and *benvenuto! Buon appetito.*"

With each bite of food, Jessie and Charles "oohed" and "aahed." Mary was delighted with their reactions.

She explained pecorino cheese was made from sheep's milk and was exceptionally fresh, from the nearby town of Pienza.

"If you have time to go to there, you must," Mary said. "It's prettier than a fairytale village. I think it's the most beautiful of all the Tuscan hill towns, and that's saying a lot because they're all gorgeous."

"I don't think we'll make it on this trip," Charles said. "But it gives us another good reason to come back to Italy."

"Oh yeah, I've been meaning to tell you I don't plan to go back to New Orleans – I'm staying here," Jessie said, laughing.

She wished she wasn't joking. She wanted to extend her time in Tuscany.

When they finished the gnocchi, Mary asked Charles if he would turn the sausage, but she said there wasn't a big hurry to move to the next course.

"One of my favorite Italian traditions is slow meals," Mary said. "Eating is about the conversation and time together as much as it is about the food."

Jessie loved this tradition, too. She seemed to be loving everything about Tuscany.

CHAPTER 16

ಹೊಞಾಿಞಾ

"TELL ME HOW you met," Mary said after Charles returned from turning the sausages.

"I fell for Jessie the first time I saw her in Java."

"That's where I work," Jessie said. "It's next door to his family's law firm."

"Before we met, I used to go to Starbucks for coffee. One day it was raining and I was running late for work. I ran into Java and Jessie was standing behind the counter wearing a cowboy hat and funky earrings. I was hooked. I started going to Java every morning for coffee. I added a midday cup and an afternoon one, too."

"Double shot of espresso early in the morning," Jessie said. "Americano midmorning and decaf in the afternoon."

"I did this every day for about three months before she finally agreed to go out with me."

"I didn't think we were each other's type. Charles is really conservative and –"

"And she's a spitfire," Charles interrupted. "I heard someone once say if you date a bronco, you gotta be ready for a bumpy ride."

His eyes sparkled when he looked at Jessie.

"Are you saying it's easy for me?" she asked him.

"Good point," he said.

Mary laughed. She liked their banter, and she thought Charles seemed crazy about Jessie.

"Two years later I asked Jessie to marry me. Thank God she said yes."

"Cheers," Mary said.

She lifted her wine glass.

"I'd love to hear how you proposed."

Charles nudged Jessie to tell the story.

"It was the perfect combination of romantic and surprising. I thought Charles was simply taking me out for dinner at our favorite French Quarter restaurant called Irene's. It's where we had our first date.

"We usually have late dinners, but this night was different. Charles said we needed to eat early so he could work later that night. I was disappointed we weren't going to be able to make a big night of it, but I know his job is important.

"Well, it turned out he had something else up his sleeve I didn't know about."

"I love surprises," Mary said.

"Me, too. We got to the restaurant as soon as Irene's opened. The host sat us in the back room while he sat everyone else in the front room. I was surprised we were alone and our room didn't fill up right away. The restaurant is always packed from open to close.

"Charles ordered champagne, and then the pianist walked in and began warming up. I was a little confused because the piano isn't usually in the back room. Anyway, a few minutes later the pianist asked if I had a favorite song."

"She does have a favorite song, and I knew what it would be," Charles said.

"I requested Elton John's 'Your Song.'"

"Oh, that's one of my all-time favorites," Mary said.

"When the music started, Charles stood up and asked me to dance. I didn't hesitate since the room was empty. Then at the end of the song, he grabbed my hands and said, 'It's a little bit funny, this feeling inside, and I hope you don't mind that I want to spend the rest of my life with you. Will you marry me?'"

"Aww," Mary cooed.

Charles beamed and said, "She didn't hesitate. Her answer was 'yes!'"

"How romantic!" Mary exclaimed.

"It was amazing," Jessie said.

She was now wracked with guilt for having second thoughts about marrying him.

"*Salute*," Mary said. "Great proposal. Did you get to keep the room all to yourself?"

"Nope," Charles said. "It was all I could do to get the manager to delay seating for the fifteen minutes I needed to propose.

"Now all we need to do is to walk down that aisle on December 31. I'm willing to simply go to the Justice of the Peace the day we're back home if she would agree."

Charles was always saying this. He was ready to start a family.

"It's your parents who are making all the wedding decisions," Jessie said. "They would be furious if we went to the Justice of the Peace, but you know I wouldn't mind."

She thought about how this would eliminate her worries about not having any family on her side of the church.

"We have a beautiful chapel for weddings right here."

Mary pointed toward the gallery.

"It's where Luca and I got married. But I doubt you could get your paperwork together fast enough for a wedding tomorrow. I'm sure you've heard about the horribly inefficient Italian bureaucracy. Maybe you could plan another trip for a wedding?"

"What a dream that would be," Jessie said.

"I think Tuscany is the most romantic place in the world," Mary said.

"I agree," Jessie said. "It's incredible, but this is my first trip outside the U.S., so I can't compare it to much."

"Tuscany is growing on me," Charles said. "That's one of the reasons why I love Jessie. She's good at making me do things I might not try on my own."

He leaned in to kiss her cheek.

She was surprised by his comment. She felt always somewhat beholden to him – and his family – because she had needed them more than they needed her. At least that's what she thought.

But now she realized she might be able to influence him more than she knew. Maybe it was still possible to have quiet dinners in romantic settings, stroll old city streets and watch golden sunsets before they left Italy.

Mary stood up.

"Please give me a few minutes. I'm going to check on the sausage, which should be ready any minute now. While I'm in the kitchen, I'm going to put zucchini on the grill and some pears in the oven. Stay out here and relax. Pour more Chianti if you'd like. There's water, but you might not want to drink it. As the Tuscans say, 'it rusts your pipes, ruins bridges and the fish pee in it.'"

They laughed as Mary headed to the kitchen.

As Mary headed in she found many reasons to dismiss Charles as Jessie's devil. He seemed to love her very much. She reasoned that there must be more going on in Jessie's life. But it would be hard to get her to talk with Charles around.

While they waited at the table, Charles grabbed Jessie's hand and asked if she thought they'd truly be ready for their New Year's Eve wedding.

"Probably," Jessie said.

But the wedding made her nervous for so many reasons.

"I hoped this vacation would help you get refreshed and ready to finish the plans."

She didn't say anything.

"You know that marrying you and starting a family are the two most important things in the world to me."

Jessie cringed inside. She wanted a family, too, but she was nervous. Robbed of the family experience, she wasn't sure if she could be a good wife or mother. She often thought she needed to meet her own family before she started one.

"We'll figure things out soon," Jessie said. "I promise."

She said this to soothe Charles, but in reality she had no idea what to do about the wedding. She was still getting over her mother's untimely death along with the lies her mother had told her. Her emotions bounced between angry and sad. And there was some guilt, too. Jessie couldn't help but blame herself for most of her mom's difficulties in life. If her mother had never gotten pregnant, her mother's life might have been better.

And these were only some of the reasons Jessie hurt deep inside. She was keeping some other secrets from Charles, and she didn't know if or when she would be able to tell him.

Jessie was also seeing a side of Charles she didn't like, but she knew it might only be her own wedding jitters.

The only thing she knew for sure was that she needed to delay the wedding. But she wasn't ready to suggest that yet.

CHAPTER 17

MARY RETURNED SOON with the *secondo piatto*, the second course - roasted sausage. She said a local butcher prepared the meat and it was nicely seasoned with fennel.

She also served the *contorno*, the vegetable dish - long, thin ribbons of grilled zucchini.

More "oohs" and "aahs" came from the two Americans.

"I didn't know I liked zucchini," Charles said. "But this is great. What's different?"

"I picked it from the garden tonight, so it's exceptionally fresh. All I do is thinly slice it lengthwise and brush it with our olive oil. Then I lightly grill it over the open fire. Quite simple."

"Maybe that's the reason it's so good," he said. "There's not much else done to it."

"Most Tuscan cooking is simple and prepared with fresh, seasonal ingredients," Mary said. "I love it, and I feel healthier eating like this."

She smiled warmly.

"I don't know if this is too healthy for you, but guess what else we do with zucchini? We deep-fry the flowers."

"Flowers?" Jessie said.

"Yes, zucchini have yellow blossoms, but they are thrown out in the U.S. Here they are often dipped in light batter and fried. They're wonderful. You'll have to try them. Look for them on menus. They are called *fiori di zucca*."

"Well," Charles said. "We eat fried okra, fried dough, fried shrimp and fried everything else in New Orleans, so

I'm surprised I've never eaten a fried zucchini blossom. But why not?"

They all laughed.

"I already told Jessie about how I loved visiting New Orleans," Mary said. "I had friends who lived in Uptown. We went to Jazz Fest a few times and once to Mardi Gras. We had so much fun!"

"We live and work in Uptown, too," Charles said. "I'm glad to call it home."

After they polished off the sausage and zucchini, Charles and Jessie took the dishes to the kitchen while Mary went to the gallery to get her computer.

Back at the patio table, they went online and Jessie pulled up her artwork.

"I call this series 'Recherche,'" Jessie said. "It's French for 'searching.'"

She showed Mary bold and colorful New Orleans street scenes featuring a beautiful lady in the foreground dressed in sultry clothing.

"I like how New Orleans seems to bring out the sensuality in people," Jessie said. "I'm always watching tourists – mostly women – carry a swagger I don't think they have at home. And I'm not talking about them being drunk. I feel like the women I see are looking for something – or someone – to soothe their souls. When I watch them, I make up stories about the holes in their lives, and I paint them.

"So all these ladies in my paintings are searching for something – true love, families of their own or maybe just some excitement away from their ordinary lives."

Mary was astounded at the emotion in the painting. Now she knew where Jessie let out her true feelings.

"Where do you sell them?"

"In the coffee shop where I work on Magazine Street. I might do better if I moved them to the French Quarter where there's more foot traffic. But the owner of the coffee shop has been so nice to me, and I hate to leave him. His name is Jeremy and he was the first person to agree to sell my work. He hasn't said I can't take my work elsewhere, but he acts like he doesn't want me to."

"Well," Mary said. "He's found a talented artist and doesn't want to lose you, but you need to get this work some more exposure. Has he helped you coordinate any special events or openings to get more people in?"

"Not yet. We've talked about it, but haven't organized anything yet. I need a bigger portfolio."

"Maybe you should plan one during Jazz Fest when there are a lot of visitors," Mary said. "That crowd seems to be older with money to spend."

"Good idea," Charles said. "And I think she needs to be in more galleries, too. Jeremy can't keep her from selling in other places. There's no binding agreement between them."

"I should be able to build my portfolio after we get back from Italy, because I have a lot of ideas brewing."

"Pursue them," Mary said. "You have a true gift, and you could make a living doing this."

"Thank you," Jessie said.

"You're welcome," Mary said. "Let me get our *dolce*. You're ready for something sweet, aren't you?"

"All the time," Charles said.

CHAPTER 18

For dessert Mary served baked pear halves. They were peeled and had their centers removed. Amaretto cookies filled their hollow cores.

"This is incredible," Jessie said. "I've never eaten a baked pear."

"The first time I had one I was in Venice with Luca. I fell in love with the recipe, and now I make them all the time when pears are in season. Dorotea makes the amaretto cookies. And Enzo always wants extra cookies."

"Smart kid," Charles said.

After they finished dessert, Mary served espresso and they kept chatting.

"Do you have siblings?" Mary asked Charles.

"I do," he said. "I have twin sisters who are four years younger than me. Rebecca is married and her husband, James, works in our office. He's an attorney, too. My other sister Diane lives in Chicago and is an attorney for the SEC. She works more hours than anyone I know."

"They adore Charles," Jessie said. "He's a good big brother and is very protective."

"You sound like Alex," Mary said. "That's sweet."

"Before you two say anything else to make me blush, I think we need to call it a night," Charles said. "It's getting late and we should hit the road."

"You should stay here and sleep off the wine," Mary said. "We have the empty New Orleans bedroom where you'd feel at home. You can leave early tomorrow morning."

Charles watched Jessie nod her head in agreement with Mary.

"Driving on the dark country roads would be challenging enough without having any alcohol," Jessie said.

"Okay," Charles said. "We'll take you up on the offer. Thank you so much for your hospitality. But we'll have to 'sleep and run.' We need to leave early tomorrow to get to Pompeii for an afternoon tour."

"That's a full day," Mary said.

Jessie thought the same, but didn't say it.

"We want to see everything possible," Charles said. "Who knows when we'll be back?"

"Hopefully our next visit with each other will be in New Orleans," Mary said.

Jessie smiled at the possibility.

"I'd have you stay with us, but it's not a castle, and we don't have too much room," Charles said.

It was a historic shotgun house he rented from his parents. Jessie loved it because it was the first house she'd ever lived in.

"No worries," Mary said. "Let's head upstairs, and I'll show you your room."

"Thanks," Charles said. "One more thing, if I may. All the traveling and car riding has made my back tight. I was hoping to take a hot shower before going to bed. Would you mind?"

"I don't mind at all."

Charles went in the bathroom and turned on the water.

"How about you, Jessie?" Mary asked. "Are you going to bed now or want to stay up with me a little longer? I'm just going to be out on the patio."

Mary hoped Jessie would come back.

"Sure, I'll come down after Charles gets out of the shower."

Jessie waited in the bedroom. She wanted to find out what time Charles wanted to get up.

When he finally walked in, he had a towel wrapped around his waist and his dark hair hung down in his face. He dropped the towel on the floor, crawled in bed and leaned against the headboard.

Jessie sat on the edge of the bed.

"You know what?" Charles said. "We've never done *it* in a castle. Ready to crawl under the covers with me?"

He ran his fingers through his hair slicking it back, the same way he styled it for work.

"I love the idea of castle sex, but Mary's waiting for me downstairs. I want to talk to her some more. What time do you want to leave in the morning?"

"No later than seven," he said.

"Okay."

She kissed his muscular shoulders built from years of playing lacrosse.

"Don't you just love it here?" Jessie asked and started to stand up.

"I do."

"I feel like I belong here. I'm attracted to this place in a way I can't really explain."

"You're such a romantic. Of course you think there's something magical about it."

As she took one step away from him, he moved his hand under her dress and cradled her waist. Then he inched his fingers inside the delicate lace edge of her panties. He adjusted his body angle so he could slide his hand farther down.

"Because there is magic here," she said. "It's an enchanting place."

She let out a heavy breath as soon as his fingers reached all the way between her legs. His touch always aroused her instantly, like lighting a match.

"We have to get up early tomorrow," he said. "We'll get our bags at my uncle's villa and then we'll head south."

His fingers explored the already slippery spot between her legs.

Jessie gave him a pouty look.

"Don't do that to me," he said. "It kills me."

His fingers kept working his own personal magic.

She tried to resist him, but couldn't and quietly fell back on the bed next to him.

"I wish we could spend more than two days in Tuscany," she said.

Her breath grew heavier between each word.

"I'd like to explore the area," she said.

"I'm enjoying the exploring that I'm doing right now."

She let out a big breath.

"Pompeii, the Amalfi Coast and Rome are waiting for us," Charles said. "I want to tour the Coliseum, the Vatican, the Sistine Chapel, the Trevi Fountain, the Pantheon."

"Rome. Can. Wait," Jessie barely said.

She grabbed a pillow and buried her face to keep from letting out any loud screams as Charles made her climax.

She finally caught her breath and moved the pillow away.

"How do you make me do that so fast?" she asked.

"I got your number," he said. "Hurry up and come back to bed. I want some more of your lovin'. We need to celebrate your birthday right here in this bed."

She kissed him, straightened her dress and headed downstairs. Her body was still shuddering inside.

Charles had an amazing ability to know what she liked and how to drive her to screaming with that hand. Or with his other hand. Or with his mouth. Or with his penis. It was the glue in their relationship. But in Italy, even sex was more intense and she had become exhausted.

His sexual stamina on the trip had been boundless. The late night soft porn on public television had amped him up in a way she'd never seen, and they stayed up late every night having wild sex, almost like they were stars in their own porn movie. Then he would wake after a few hours of sleep ready to go again.

At home they had sex often but she'd never seen him like this. She guessed it was because he was away from the daily pressure of work.

CHAPTER 19

❧❧❦❦

Jessie returned to the candlelit table and was glad it was dark so her glowing red cheeks weren't so obvious.

Mary looked tranquil in the pretty setting. Jessie admired everything she knew about her. She was beautiful, talented and so in love with her husband and family.

"I bet Charles is already asleep," Jessie said. "He looked comfortable in bed."

"I've always slept well in this house. It feels so safe."

"Everything about your home feels 'right.' I keep thinking about how you said you even feel like Luca is your soul mate. I've read about people who meet and think they known each other from another lifetime, but you're the first person I've met who has actually experienced it."

"It's true, but I don't know how often it happens."

"Not as often as people would like," Jessie laughed and continued. "I have to admit I don't have that kind of connection with Charles."

"You're analyzing every detail about whether or not you should marry him, aren't you? From what I've seen, I think he's crazy about you."

"I feel like he loves me, too. And truthfully, I haven't worried about whether or not we're soul mates. I've been more interested in finding a stable and secure relationship, along with the love."

"That's important," Mary said.

Jessie took a big gulp from her wine glass and thought about the reasons she was attracted to Charles. Unlike him, she wasn't one of the privileged kids of New Orleans who went to a private school knowing she would go to college. For her it was a fight to simply move from Tremé to the French Quarter.

"But I don't want to marry him for the wrong reasons. I feel more security and support than I ever have in my life. And that's what I want since I don't have a family."

"You're an only child?"

Jessie glanced up at the night sky and her toes curled inside her boots. She wanted to tell the truth. And she hoped Mary wouldn't judge her. She knew it wasn't her fault, but it was embarrassing to say she had no family. Mary was easy to talk to, and it was entirely possible she'd never see her again after the following morning.

"Yes, but it's more like my family is non-existent. I've never met my dad and my mom died nine months ago."

"Oh, I'm sorry. I had no idea."

Mary knew the heartbreak of losing a parent because her dad died while she was in college. And she was surrounded with stories of unknown fathers – Alex learned about Luca when he was eighteen, and Luca had never met his own biological father.

"What about aunts, uncles and cousins?"

Jessie shook her head.

"None. My mother was an only child, too."

Mary lightly shook her head in disbelief and could tell there was more to Jessie's story.

"Did something tragic happen?"

"Yes. She –"

Jessie automatically stopped herself. She wasn't used to sharing personal information. But she really wanted to tell someone about the things she'd learned when her mom died only months earlier.

"Talk only if you want," Mary said. "It's up to you."

Jessie had an unusual level of comfort with Mary. In fact, she'd never connected so well with anyone.

"Thanks," Jessie said. "It's hard to talk about. I haven't even told Charles. He has the perfect family, and I don't think there's any way he could understand what I've been through."

She fidgeted in her seat and played with the ruffled hem of her dress.

Mary's brow furrowed before she spoke.

"Jessie, don't kid yourself. I'm going to say something now I never want you to forget. Perfect families do not exist, so don't let appearances fool you. If Charles cares as much as I sense he does, he loves you because of the person you are. Your family situation doesn't matter. And if he does judge you because of that, then you may want to reevaluate your relationship. But I doubt that will be necessary."

"I'm sure you're right."

Jessie wiped away a few tears trickling down her face.

"This is so hard," Jessie said. "The day after my mom died, Aunt Norma told me some things about my mom I never knew. It turns out my mother lied to me my entire life."

She stopped and took a deep breath before continuing.

"Mama had always told me she was an only child of parents who were only children, too. She claimed her mom and dad died in a car accident, and they were cremated. That's why we never visited a cemetery.

"It was a lie, but the worst lie I'm dealing with is about my dad. Mom had always told me I was the result of an accidental pregnancy with a married man who already had a family."

Jessie ran her fingers through her hair.

"Basically she told me he didn't want me."

Mary's eyebrows drew in, her lips tightened and she lightly shook her head while thinking Jessie was definitely the one who Dorotea predicted was coming.

"Everything was a freakin' lie," Jessie said, her eyes filling with tears.

It was easier to continue, now that Jessie had admitted this out loud.

"The real story is that Aunt Norma met my mom on a Greyhound bus in Nashville in 1979. Mama was alone, only seventeen and pregnant."

Jessie wiped away tears.

"She was scared and had nowhere to go. She was so lucky to meet Norma because she has the biggest heart of anyone I know. Norma let mama live with her."

"Norma truly sounds like an angel."

"She raised me in her little two-bedroom apartment on the second floor of a house, and my mom was a live-in housekeeper for a wealthy doctor in the Garden District."

Jessie tried to smile, but it was hard to do.

"My mom isolated herself from everyone, including me."

"I'm sorry," Mary said. "This must be so hard to talk about."

"It's okay. It feels kind of good to let it out. You're the only person I've told."

Jessie didn't have any close friends. She wished she did. She mostly talked to customers in the coffee shop, and she didn't know any of them nearly well enough to talk about such personal things. She was getter closer to a customer named Papi, and they sometimes talked about doing something together, but it never seemed to work out.

She paused and then continued.

"At my wedding, I will be the only Morrow in the chapel. Charles keeps telling me not to worry about it because his parents' friends and business associates will fill the church, but I don't want all those people I barely know at my wedding."

She paused. She hadn't admitted this to anyone yet either.

"I've been thinking I'd like to find my dad before I get married, but I doubt he knows I'm alive. I don't think my mom ever told him she was pregnant."

Mary's heart ached. Even though she didn't get along well with her own mother or sister, she loved them and was happy to have family. She especially loved her niece and nephew. But they were all in Philadelphia. She knew what it was like without their frequent company, but she did have the security of knowing they were always there.

"I can understand why," Mary said. "It's a very special day in your life and I know how you feel. I've been married three times now and my dad wasn't at any of my weddings."

Jessie looked surprised.

"You only told me about Garrett."

"He was my second husband. I got married right after college but I was way too young. It only lasted a couple of years. Then I married Garrett and it didn't even last two weeks. Bad decisions. Enough about me. Let's get back to your dad. How much do know about him?"

"I only know his first name and where he worked with my mom when they were teenagers. Talking to Alex today I realized I might be as lucky as he is and turn out to have a cool dad like Luca."

Mary patted Jessie's shoulder like a mother would do to her child. Then she put her hand back on the table.

"I tell Luca the same thing about finding his biological father."

"What do you know about his dad?"

"We know his name is Luke Davis, and he was in the U.S. Army during Vietnam in the mid-sixties. I think this is enough information to find him, but Luca refuses to try. And his dad probably doesn't know Luca exists. From the diary I found written by Luca's mother, Anna, she became pregnant the first time they ever made love, which was most likely the last time they ever saw each other. She had the baby in a

convent and left him with the nuns. She married a man she
hardly knew soon after and was able to adopt Luca, but it
was a secret her whole life."

Jessie was startled.

"That is hard to believe."

"It is, and I tell you because family stories are often
complicated. I can only imagine how much you want to
meet your dad. I had a great relationship with my dad and
miss him more than words can say. He died when I was in
college, way too young."

"I'm sorry to hear that."

Jessie suddenly wondered what she would do if she found
out her father had already died. She decided to refuse to
consider this possibility.

"Speaking from a totally objective standpoint, you may
need to find your dad before you're able to marry Charles,"
Mary said. "When you didn't know anything about him, you
could tuck away that desire. But now you have some facts
about him, and I'm sure it's hard to ignore, isn't it? That's
probably why you can't talk to Charles about it."

Jessie nodded.

"How can I find my dad with such limited information
and not let Charles know about it? I've tried crazy searches
on the Internet but nothing comes up."

"It sounds like you would need to hire a detective."

Jessie nodded her head. She had thought about this, but
in reality, she was afraid.

Mary thought of Patrick Sullivan, a guest at the Ribelli.

"We have one staying here now. Do you remember me
telling you about the detective earlier this afternoon?"

"The one who tried to make you not get involved with
Luca?"

"Yes, that's him – Patrick Sullivan."

"That's a good idea, but we're leaving early in the
morning."

Mary wished Jessie could stay longer, especially if she was Dorotea's lady. But there were phones and computers for communication.

"I can ask him where to start and send you an email."

"Okay, that sounds good. Thank you."

Jessie took a drink of Chianti and smiled for the first time since she started telling Mary her story.

"I can't believe I told you all this," Jessie said. "You know more about my life than anyone else."

"I'm glad it was me," Mary said. "*In vino veritas!* In wine there is truth. So maybe the wine made it easier! It's often a truth serum for me."

Jessie agreed but knew it was really Mary who made it easier.

"It was good to get it off my chest," Jessie said.

"Well, it sure is nice for me to sit here and talk to you. I don't have opportunities like this often. I've never gotten as close to people here as I did in Philadelphia. Maybe it's the language barrier? I'm not sure."

"I don't have anyone at home to talk to either, except Norma."

"I have an idea. There's something you might really enjoy, and it doesn't require any talking."

"Sounds right up my alley," Jessie said.

"You might like a walk in the vineyards in the early morning. It's where I connect with nature and do my best thinking. I stroll up and down the rows with the vines as my company. People have lived and worked on this land for hundreds and hundreds of years, and the land is saturated with their wisdom. You might hear their messages. I do. And so does my friend Stella. She says it's the best place to clear her head, and she needs it because she's usually trying to get over some guy. She has the worst luck with men, but a terrific sense of humor about it. I'm sure she'll be out there after she arrives in a couple of days."

"I love being outdoors, so I'm sure I'd enjoy the walk."

"The roosters crow before sunrise, which means I'm up before daybreak every day whether I want to be or not. So get up early and I'll take you before Charles wants to get on the road."

"Okay, I'd like that. I wish we had a couple more days here so I could meet Stella, but we'll be on the Amalfi coast then."

"You're covering a lot of ground in a short time."

"Tell me about it," Jessie said. "But we're getting to see so many interesting sites. I do appreciate the chance to see them all."

Mary smiled at Jessie's positive twist, but she knew Jessie really wanted to slow down.

"We better go to bed or we'll never wake up," Mary said.

"I'm ready," Jessie said.

They took the glasses and linens to the kitchen and before going up to bed, Jessie hugged Mary.

"What a wonderful, unexpected birthday gift. I can't thank you enough."

"It was a gift for me, too. I enjoyed your company. Do me a favor. Take these to put in your pillowcase."

Mary handed her some dried lavender blooms from a basket in the kitchen.

"Their scent will help you relax and fall asleep easily. Luca said his mother always did this."

"Okay, thank you. I'll be glad to. It's my favorite flower. I grow it in pots at Charles' house and at Norma's apartment."

CHAPTER 20

꽃꽃꽃꽃

JESSIE QUIETLY STUFFED the lavender into her pillowcase and took off her dress. She sat gently on the edge of the bed trying not to make any noise, because she was ready to crawl in and go to sleep. But a creak in the mattress woke Charles.

"There you are," he said.

He rolled on his side to face her. Then he slipped his hand under her hair and slithered it from her neck down her spine.

She always loved how he touched her body, and this moment was no different. There was enough pressure to keep from tickling, but it was light enough to be sensual and arousing. She knew she wouldn't be going to sleep soon.

His fingers traveled slowly and dipped between the swells of her butt. It sent a chill up her spine and on its way back down, it turned into a flame centered between her legs. His touch. He aroused her every time he made contact with her, and this lust always softened her mood and clouded any negative emotions.

Back up her spine and along the curve of her waist his hand traveled.

"Mm," he moaned.

She knew he loved touching her as much as she loved feeling it.

His hand glided up to a breast and he rolled her nipple between his fingers. More heat and currents of sizzling fire surged through her body. Nerves sizzled and muscles contracted involuntarily in that small hot space at the base of her torso.

She arched her back, rested on her elbows and let her hair fall on his body. She wanted more of him.

His hand slid down the midline of her body over her belly button and slowly went down farther. And farther. But he wouldn't go *there* yet. He liked to get her totally aroused.

He inched his strong body closer to hers and shifted to kiss her side, just below her ribcage near the fleur-de-lis tattoo on her hip. With his tongue, he traced the outline of the ink.

Her torso trembled, and her breathing kept getting heavier.

He gasped when his hand went down her thigh.

"You're still wearing your boots. That's so hot."

He inserted his hand inside the leather shaft and kneaded her calf. When he pulled his hand out, he delicately traced the back of her knee, never taking his lips away from her torso.

"I'm glad you left those on," he said.

He slipped his hand inside her thigh, heading north.

She wanted him to touch her. Now. But he wouldn't yet. She knew him too well.

He sat up and gently moved so he could wrap his smooth naked body around her backside with his long legs enveloping her. His erection pressed into her back, and her head rolled onto his shoulder as she angled her chin toward him so their cheeks touched.

"Spread your legs," he whispered.

His hand slipped between her thighs ready to arouse her to the very edge of climaxing.

He slipped a finger deep inside the full and wet cleft of her most private and sensual area. Then he barely traced toward her belly along the natural groove he'd told her so many times he loved.

He moved slowly, very slowly. He traveled the full length of her fleshy, female anatomy, driving her mad with desire. Once he crossed that most sensitive spot he completely pulled away his hand. This wildly stimulated her and made her want more.

Following the same slippery pathway, he slowly retraced the folds of her swollen skin and drew his hand away again.

This time a shiver traveled up her spine, and her entire body shuddered.

"Oh," she sighed and exhaled heavily. "You're incredible."

"One more time," he whispered close to her ear.

With a slower touch, more delicate than before, he did the same thing. He tormented her by lifting his hand away again.

Her body shook and primal desire overpowered any ability to think. Passion, heat and nerves possessed her. Now a puppet of his magical hands, she did whatever she asked.

He whispered.

"I'm going to move back, and then I want you to get on your hands and knees."

In slow controlled motions, they shifted their bodies until she was on all fours with her knees fully bent and her ankles flexed.

Charles grabbed her ankles, and as soon as he had a firm hold and stable position, he slid inside. After a couple of long, slow thrusts he pulled out and slid a hand between her legs. His touch made her explode with pleasure and her body writhed while she stifled any noises. He quickly slipped back inside, grabbed her hips and with only a few hard strokes he experienced the same intense pleasure as she had only seconds earlier.

Having to sneak and be quiet intensified their pleasure, and they needed more time than usual to catch their breath and cool down.

Once they were curled up under the sheets, he nearly apologized for how quickly he had climaxed.

"I knew we had to be quiet and fast," he said. "So I didn't take too long."

She never thought he was selfish in bed.

"You took care of me first," she said. "Then I didn't care what happened."

Charles rubbed her arm.

"Sex with you makes me crazy," Charles said. "You're like a drug. And I can't wait until we're married. I love you."

He kissed her shoulder, and she snuggled in closer before quickly falling asleep to his rhythmic breathing and the soothing scent of lavender.

CHAPTER 21

ᔕᔎᘉᘓ

MARY WOKE BEFORE the roosters and hurried to dress. Then she went to the kitchen and checked for an email from Luca as she waited for her espresso. There was one.

Subject: Good morning, *bella*!

I am in a new hotel in New Jersey and just went to the buffet breakfast. Americans eat a lot! Eggs, potatoes, bacon, sausage, bread, muffins, fruit, yogurt!

I cannot find a good cup of espresso. Everyone tells me to go to Starbucks, but they do not make real espresso. I settled for American coffee and a piece of toast with honey.

The meeting yesterday was good, like the one in New York. The distributor here in New Jersey will carry our wine. We are meeting again today to negotiate quantities and prices. It is our second victory.

Tonight, I go to Chicago.

Tell the boys I miss them. I love you.
Luca

Mary was thrilled. In two appointments, he had secured two contracts. She hoped the same would happen in Chicago, and she was optimistic that it would, especially with Dorotea's prediction. She laughed at his comments about American food and coffee.

When she first moved to Italy, she often talked about the differences between the two countries. Finally Luca asked her why she complained so much about her new home.

But she didn't think of it as faultfinding, she was just noticing differences and remarking on them. In time, she learned to be more conscientious of expressing her opinions to the Italians about their country. They naturally became defensive, the same as she did when they made remarks about the U.S.

Today, she knew he was harmlessly making observations about the food and coffee. He loved the U.S., and had spent many childhood summers on the Jersey Shore with his cousins.

She closed the laptop and drank her first cup of espresso, her thoughts turning to Jessie's family, or lack of one. She needed to help Jessie and truly wished she could introduce her to Patrick Sullivan.

CHAPTER 22

❧❧❦❦

JESSIE WOKE TO the sound of distant rooster crows, as Mary said she might. But Charles didn't stir, which was unusual since he was a light sleeper who woke easily.

Jessie carefully slipped out of bed and stepped to the bedroom window.

The sky was barely lit, and she had a sweeping view of the valley. In one direction below them was a small town or a hamlet – probably Terzano – but she wasn't sure. In the other direction, orderly vineyards and bushy olive trees surrounded a sprawling farm, and she wondered if it was one of the properties Mary and Luca owned.

She quietly cleaned up and dressed before waking Charles.

"What time is it?" he asked, stretching his arms and yawning.

"About six."

He immediately zeroed in on his job responsibilities.

"It's midnight at home, so I need to get online to see if dad sent anything late last night."

Charles and his brother-in-law James LeBeau were on the same track for a partnership in the family firm. His dad had alluded to deciding at the end of the year, and if both men were selected the practice would renamed to "Durbridge, Durbridge and LeBeau." But this would only happen if the two proved they were worthy, and his father didn't cut Charles any slack because he was his son.

"Okay," Jessie said. "I'll meet you downstairs in the kitchen."

"Not so fast," he said.

He slipped his hand under her dress and all he found was her naked legs and hips. He knew she wouldn't wear the same panties two consecutive days, and it wasn't uncommon for her not to wear them at all.

"You're going to make me crazy imagining what's under your dress, or what's not under it."

She flashed her naked ass at him, winked and grabbed her messenger bag.

Then she headed downstairs in her rumpled cotton dress and vintage cowboy boots.

Mary was sitting at the patio table in a casual black sleeveless dress adorned with the pocket watch necklace. Her long hair was pulled into a ponytail, and an empty espresso cup and a breakfast plate were in front of her.

"*Buongiorno!* Want some espresso?"

"Definitely, thank you," Jessie said.

She needed it to clear the cobwebs from all the Chianti she'd had the previous afternoon and evening.

"I'll run inside and make a cup for you."

"Let me go with you," Jessie said.

She dropped her bag in a chair.

"I want to see if your machine is like the one we use in the coffeehouse."

Mary laughed.

"You're going to be surprised. It's very simple and very easy."

In the kitchen, Mary showed Jessie the stovetop coffee-maker. It was a teapot-looking device that boiled water in its lower half creating steam to pass over the grounds.

"I love it," Jessie said. "I assumed every Italian kitchen had a sophisticated double espresso and cappuccino maker."

"The coffee shops and bars have them but most of us use these at home."

They returned to the patio just as Charles got there, too.

"*Buongiorno!*" Mary said.

"Good morning," he said. "I just had my best night of sleep since we've been in Italy."

"Good," Mary said. "Did you sleep well too, Jessie? You look rested."

"I am, but I woke up when I heard Alex come in. Did he bring his girlfriend back here?"

Mary looked confused.

"No, he's not here. He stayed in Siena with a friend."

"But I thought I heard them," Jessie said, shaking her head.

She distinctly heard people talking and laughing in the middle of the night.

"Maybe it was just some creaks coming from this old place."

"I guess so," Jessie said.

She doubted it. She had definitely heard giggling.

"Mind if I use your Wi-Fi to check my email?" Charles asked.

"No problem," Mary answered. "You can work here or move to the gallery. But do you want coffee first?"

"Absolutely, thank you."

When Mary went to the kitchen, Jessie asked Charles if he heard any people laughing during the night.

"Nope, after we made love I was out. I haven't slept that well in a long time."

Jessie grimaced and decided not to talk about the giggling any longer. After drinking all the wine, she might have dreamed it, and she thought it was best to not mention any possibility of ghosts.

"Mary and I are going to take a walk while you're checking email."

"Sounds good," he said. "Let's try to leave in about thirty minutes."

Charles drank a double espresso and ate one brioche then moved to the gallery to work. Mary quickly helped him get set up on Wi-Fi.

"Come on! Let's head to the Ribelli farmhouse," Mary said to Jessie as soon as she returned to the patio.

CHAPTER 23

࿓࿓࿓

THE LADIES WALKED down a path that trailed off the patio and along the building's perimeter. It led them to a shortcut down a hillside and through a beautiful garden.

"This area was overgrown when I moved in, but Luca and I spent a lot of time cleaning it up."

Mary was pleased to see Jessie break off a few sprigs of lavender to carry with her on their walk.

"We have a lot of lavender, and we always will because it was a favorite of Luca's mother, too. He was exceptionally close to her. She must have been really sweet and exceptionally bright. She spoke Italian, French and English, and she was a painter. She had all of these darling little sayings Luca remembers, and now he says them to Enzo."

"How old was Luca when she died?"

"Seven."

"Oh, my. That had to be hard."

"Some days it still is."

Jessie nodded. There were days when she missed her mother so much she didn't want to get out of bed, but on other days she was more robotic and pushed through life's routines.

At the bottom of a hill, they passed a large field altar – a monument for daily prayer and offerings by the farm workers. Then they walked along a dusty road for several minutes before cutting through an olive grove and arriving at the Ribelli farmhouse.

The rustic house was like many others Jessie had seen driving around. There was a large main building of brick and stucco with many smaller buildings surrounding it.

Mary led them toward the swimming pool on the far side of the house, telling Jessie the vineyards lined the hillside below it.

Before they got to the pool, Mary stopped.

"I stayed here on my first trip to Italy, and it's where I met Luca. He was standing right there with his brother and a group of workers. I thought he was one of the farmers."

She pointed to the exact place she first met him.

"I'll never forget the moment. I was enchanted as soon as our eyes met. It was like we already knew each other. But I didn't know what to do about it since I'd come on the trip with Garrett. All I said to Luca was 'hello,' but our eyes said much more."

"I love that story," Jessie said. "I can't wait to read about it in your book."

"Thanks, if I ever finish it."

"How many pages have you written?"

"About seventy-five. It hasn't been easy, but I keep plugging away trying to remember everything that happened and find interesting ways to tell the story."

"What about making it a steamy romance? Those novels sell really well."

Mary laughed.

"I should think about that. The memoir seems too methodical in its current version. This happened, then that happened and on and on. Maybe it does need some sizzle."

"You could also write it as if Luca's mother is telling the story. It seems like she was the matchmaker, even from her grave. That version would have a supernatural feel."

"You're right. The coincidence of finding the pocket watch is still hard to believe. And there were other signs with the lavender. I'm still organizing all my facts, but that's a good idea."

Mary noticed Jessie was still holding the lavender in her hand. Maybe Luca's mother was watching over them right now, just as she had since Mary met Luca.

At the vineyard, Mary told Jessie she would give her some time alone to think.

"Are you comfortable retracing the path?

"It shouldn't be a problem. I'll be back soon."

"Okay, enjoy yourself."

CHAPTER 24

JESSIE DID EXACTLY as Mary suggested and strolled slowly up and down the rows. The thick and tangled vines were slightly taller than she was, and they were full of grapes. Beyond the vineyards were forest-covered hills.

She tuned her senses to the sights and sounds of nature and tried to hear its message.

All she could think as she stood in the vast rolling landscape was how she had been living a small, fearful life, hesitant to grow. And she was stuck. Stuck in her thoughts and stuck in New Orleans.

Standing in the middle of ancient Italy, she acknowledge-edged her desire to experience more of the world.

It could happen with Charles because he said travel was important to him. And he wanted them to travel together. She just wished he didn't want to travel so fast with such a carefully constructed schedule.

She had a more adventurous nature and wanted to explore by intuition. But Charles had paid for this vacation, so she didn't want to criticize his agenda.

Jessie savored the quiet moment. She didn't want to forget being here, so she pulled out her camera and took several photos of the vineyards, the farmhouse and the castle tower. These homes were five or six hundred years old, older than anything in New Orleans.

As she took more photos, she wondered how many people had lived in these farmhouses and tried to imagine their lives.

They were undoubtedly difficult and short lives like her mama's, she thought.

Her mom's life wasn't too difficult physically, but it was emotionally. Her pain was deep, but it never came to the surface because she wouldn't let it.

Jessie suddenly realized she was behaving like her mother, stuffing her emotions.

Charles accepted her and was ready to marry her. He hadn't ever tried to change her, but she knew she needed to resolve her own issues before she got married. Mary was right about that. She wouldn't be ready for a wedding until she had met her dad.

But that meant she would have to delay the wedding. Jessie's heart skipped a couple beats because the thought of asking Charles made her nervous. But it also excited her to imagine having her dad be part of the wedding.

She knew she couldn't ignore her feelings any longer. She decided she needed to listen to herself, and she hoped Charles would understand.

The trip to Italy was giving Jessie a taste of the bigger world she was missing, and it was helping her see her own self-destructive behavior. She was ready for change.

She picked a grape and held it up to the sky to see its color in the early morning sunlight. She felt something tingle in her chest - like a seed sprouting. But it wasn't a seed. It was her own heart bursting. She had never felt more honest with herself.

As she walked between two long rows of grapevines toward the edge of the vineyard, she imagined it was a wedding aisle. She held the lavender and the Wedding March played in her head. She walked to the sound of the music to see if it felt right.

An image of a simple wedding came to mind. A strong man walked her down the aisle as she carried a bouquet of fresh lavender. Her groom waited at the altar in a casual tan suit. But she couldn't see any faces.

Jessie smiled at her silliness. She knew a wedding was in her future, she just didn't know when and told herself to be patient and let her heart guide her.

With renewed energy she headed to the gallery only to find Charles pacing the floor. He didn't do this very often, but when he did, work was typically the trigger.

"What's wrong?"

"Dad's putting pressure on me to prepare more documents today. I can't say no. You know how he is."

"That's not good."

"It means I can't spend the next five or six hours in the car, because I need that time to edit these contracts and letters. They need to be emailed by 8 p.m. Then I'll have to get on the phone with my dad in the middle of the night to go over them."

He didn't stop pacing.

Jessie grimaced. She knew Charles was a planner, and he would carefully decide how to manage the situation. It was best to wait for him to work through the logistics.

"We need to cancel our plans to drive south today," he said after a few minutes. "And I'm not sure about tomorrow."

"Stay in Tuscany?"

She was beginning to see a bright outcome to this dilemma.

"Yes. We might need to stay here two nights, which means cancelling our plans to going to Pompeii and the Amalfi coast. We'll have to head straight to Rome on Monday and take our originally scheduled flight home on Wednesday."

Jessie's heart rate picked up, and she barely refrained from jumping in his arms for a big hug because this was the best news she could have imagined, even if it was for the wrong reason.

"You'd be okay with that, wouldn't you?" he asked.

"Of course, I would. You know I was wishing we could stay in Tuscany longer."

One of her vineyard wishes was already coming true.

"Let me cancel our hotel rooms and tours online. Then we can check with my uncle about staying a couple more days at the villa."

"What if we rent an apartment here? I just visited the Ribelli farmhouse, and it's really beautiful. It's not quite as formal as your uncle's villa but it's in better condition. You'd like it, and I'm sure it has good Wi-Fi."

"I tell you what, you make the decision since I need to get back to work."

He confirmed what she had been thinking in the vineyard – it wasn't other people who didn't trust and respect her opinion. She was the one limiting herself.

"Okay. I'll talk to Mary."

"After I do the cancellations, I'll stay in here working unless Mary needs me to move."

Mary was excited about their change of plans and suggested they stay at Ribelli because of the problems at Cielo. She cut the rate in half to 40 Euros per night.

"Thank you," Jessie said. "We'll move here tonight."

"Wonderful! Did you enjoy your walk in the vineyard?"

"Yes. It was spiritual, and it was better than any church experience I've ever had."

"I've never walked a labyrinth for meditation, but I imagine it's a similar experience. It's easy to tune out the rest of the world and listen to your soul."

"It is."

Mary smiled, knowing Jessie was a kindred spirit. Now she was certain Jessie was the lady who Dorotea predicted would come into her life. She was ready to help, but Mary didn't know the extent of Jessie's secrets yet.

CHAPTER 25

❧❧❧❧❧

Castellina in Chianti, Tuscany

AFTER JESSIE AND CHARLES left for his uncle's villa, Mary prepared her gallery for a group of American visitors. They were arriving at 11 a.m. to meet Alex for a tour of Etruscan remains.

This tour was one of his most popular since he knew about artifacts not well marked on maps. These sites delighted his customers because they got to look at history few people could see. It was one of the ways he distinguished himself in the competitive tour business.

Meeting at the gallery for the tours was also part of the family's business strategy. They could sell prints, wine or olive oil to customers who might not have come to the gallery on their own.

❧❧

Around 10:30 a.m., Jessie and Charles arrived at the villa to pick up their bags, shower and change clothes. Gregory and his business partner, Jacopo, were about to run off to Florence for a shopping day, so they said a quick farewell.

Charles didn't mention their revised travel plans to stay an additional two nights in Tuscany because he didn't want to offend his uncle by not staying at his villa. Even though it was clean, it needed a lot of updates and maintenance, and it wasn't comfortable.

Jacopo had been given responsibility of the property's management. But it seemed Jacopo was more interested in being the best-dressed and manicured vine master in Tuscany. Both Jessie and Charles noticed Jacopo didn't have a single callous on his hands.

Charles' family had worried that Gregory's idea of operating a Tuscan estate was more romantic than realistic. It seemed they were right.

They were trying to pack quickly, but the room where they had stayed was uncomfortably warm, so Jessie ran downstairs to get a couple of water bottles from Gregory's assistant, Maria Rosario. She was also the housekeeper and cook.

"Hello, Jessie. I wanted to come upstairs to see you. A courier delivered a package for you."

"What?"

Jessie's face went blank with shock before it reddened. A flush of heat rushed through her body, and she thought she was going to drop to the floor.

No way, she thought.

She eyed the envelope as Maria pointed to it.

"It is there, on the table," Maria said.

With her stare fully directed at the ugly yellow envelope, Jessie's knees actually trembled.

"Okay, thanks," she said with a small voice.

This was the third consecutive arrival of a letter on her birthday but the eighth letter in total. Its cursive salutation in black ink was identical to previous ones – "To Jessie."

The letters came from a mysterious stalker, but whoever it was had found her in Italy when so few people knew she was coming with Charles and even fewer knew the location of Gregory's villa.

Each time an envelope had arrived, Jessie's mind would race to figure out the stalker's identity. Today, she zipped from one person to another, knowing it had to be someone who knew she was in Tuscany.

The only positive aspect of this delivery, she thought, was that her suspects were narrowed to those who knew her specific vacation plans with Charles. The list was short.

It included Charles, his family, their office staff, Jeremy and Aunt Norma. And none of them seemed like a stalker.

"The courier apologized for being a day late," Maria said. "He said the envelope slipped under his seat, and he forgot to deliver it. I do not know if I believe him because our couriers are not reliable. Yesterday he may have taken a long lunch instead of working."

Maria shook her head and pursed her lips.

Consistent with past deliveries, the letter was supposed to arrive on her birthday.

"Thank you, I'll take it with me."

Jessie grimaced and picked it up gently as if it were a bomb ready to explode.

"Did he leave a receipt?"

"No."

She held the envelope close to her body wondering how she could hide it from Charles.

"It's okay," Jessie said. "I think I know what it is. A birthday card from my dad."

She lied. It was a little white lie she told to protect herself. Unfortunately she did this more than she wanted to. She was honest at heart but sometimes when she was desperate or threatened, she disguised the facts. She learned this bad habit from her mom and knew she needed to stop doing it. She wondered why she didn't simply say "thanks." And she wondered why she mentioned her unknown dad.

"May I get some water and wine to take with us?" Jessie asked.

"Of course. How much?"

"Several bottles of water and two bottles of Chianti."

Maria would have to put this many bottles in a bag or a box. Then Jessie could hide the envelope with the bottles.

"Wait here, please," Maria said.

Jessie didn't open the envelope and wasn't sure when she would be able to. She didn't want to risk anyone else seeing its contents, which she knew would be embarrassing.

Maria returned with a shipping box full of even more than Jessie requested.

"Gregory would want you have all this. He enjoyed your visit."

There were four bottles of water and four bottles of Chianti.

"*Grazie*," Jessie said. "This is generous."

Jessie stuffed the envelope along the inside wall of the box and took the box to their car. She grabbed two bottles of water and hurried upstairs.

"Where did you have to go for water?" Charles asked. "Back to Siena?"

"Gregory gave us a box of wine and water, and I went ahead and put it in the car."

"Oh, okay. I'm ready whenever you are."

"Give me a few minutes."

She grabbed her toiletries from the bathroom and in the vanity mirror she noticed how bright her cheeks were. She was still shocked and angered by the delivery.

She put on an ivory cotton dress that looked like a long tank top and pulled on a brown crocheted sheath dress over it and belted it She had made the dress in high school with Norma's help.

A few minutes later they were headed to the Ribelli farmhouse with the envelope still in the box. For once, she was thankful Charles was preoccupied with work. It kept him from noticing her stress.

CHAPTER 26

✦✦✦✦

Terzano, Tuscany

THE TWO-BEDROOM apartment at the Ribelli farmhouse was considerably nicer than the ones at Gregory's villa. This one was larger with a small kitchen and living room. And there was no frayed furniture or sunken mattress.

Jessie offered to empty the car so Charles could set up his computer right away, and so she could burn off her anxious feelings.

On her first trip back to the car, she ran into an older man. He had a white goatee and a large furry stomach exposed by his unbuttoned Hawaiian shirt.

"Hello," he said in American English.

"Hi!"

"First time here?"

"Yes, we'll be here for a couple of days."

"Most people stay longer," he said. "My guess is you'll be back next summer for at least a week. This corner of the world grows on everyone."

"I wish," Jessie said.

He extended his hand.

"I'm Patrick Sullivan, and I come for at least a month every year."

"I'm Jessie Morrow. Mary Rusconi has told me about you."

"I hope she said nice things."

Jessie laughed.

"I've heard *everything*."

"Well, fuck. Then you know the good, the bad and the unimaginable."

Jessie laughed. Mary had told her Patrick was a retired detective who came every year to visit the Florence-American Cemetery and honor his father, a casualty of World War II.

He was notorious for eavesdropping and getting in the middle of everyone's business or at least making up gossip about it. So Jessie knew it was better to be his friend than his enemy.

"Sounds like you and Mary have made up," she said.

"Yes, Mary's a sweetheart, and she made an honest man of lady-killer Luca."

Jessie giggled again at Patrick's exaggeration.

"You traveling alone?" he asked.

"No, I'm here with my boyfriend, I mean, my fiancé."

"You don't plan to get rid of him and take up with one of these Italian men do you? Luca's got a handsome son about your age."

Jessie chuckled more.

"I've met Alex, and he is a cute one, but I've heard his hands are already full with the Italian ladies."

"You're not kidding. I can't count the number of ladies I've seen with him. Well, I hope you enjoy your stay here and maybe I'll see you again."

He lit a Lucky Strike cigarette and scuffed away in his slip-on sandals.

Jessie carried the box upstairs. Charles was already on his computer, engrossed with edits. This gave her the opportunity to discreetly transfer the envelope from the box to her messenger bag. What she really wanted to do was rip it up and throw it away, but she knew she needed to open it and confront her villain. Hopefully this letter would contain a message that would help her identify the sender.

Charles said he needed more time to work but suggested they go to San Gimignano in the late afternoon to sightsee and have dinner.

"Sounds good, I really want to see it," she said. "I'm going to explore. Be back soon."

She headed to the castle via the shortcut she learned earlier that morning. She found Mary at her desk in the gallery.

"Hi, Mary."

"Are you settled in? You look like you're worn out."

"Oh, I just did the unloading while Charles worked. We love the place. And guess what? I met Patrick Sullivan."

"Of course you met him. Somehow he knows when everyone comes and goes. It must be in his blood after being a detective for so long. Did you mention you might need his help?"

Jessie's face reddened.

"Nope, I didn't want to take a chance of Charles hearing the conversation."

She didn't give Mary time to comment.

"Is it okay if I take a look at the Cielo property?"

"Sure. The first floor is a common area for our guests with comfy chairs and lots of books about Italy. Make yourself at home."

Mary gave Jessie directions for walking there and said it would take about ten minutes on foot.

CHAPTER 27

JESSIE FOLLOWED THE path easily and found the villa. This property had a more formal look than Ribelli.

It was a two-story stucco-covered building with a belvedere embellishing its roof. The view of the valley from its lookout had to be beautiful, but Mary said they blocked off rooftop access because it needed repairs. When Giovanni had fallen down the stairs on his first trip up to the belvedere, he blamed it on the Sardi ghosts, but Mary said the real problem was rotted timber.

There was lavender planted near the entrance of the villa, and Jessie assumed Mary and Luca planted it. As she walked along it, she ran her fingers over the blossoms and breathed in its cleansing fragrance.

When she was only a few feet from the villa's entrance, a chill ran through her body. It was the same sensation she often felt in New Orleans in places that were reportedly haunted, including the neighborhood where she and Charles lived.

She slowed her pace and gripped the strap of her bag, knowing there were restless spirits inside. Giovanni's theory about the Sardi might be right, she thought.

Inside the building, the foyer was decorated with a few pieces of antique furniture and a couple of inviting overstuffed chairs. She cozied up in one, and the envelope beckoned her to be opened with that same negative persistence of a freeway accident attracting gawkers. But it would remain sealed in her bag until she was ready. Or until she forced herself to open it.

She picked up a pictorial book on Tuscan farms. The images conveyed the laborious and rustic lifestyle and gave her ideas for a new painting series called "Tuscan Women."

When she finished rifling through the book, she warily lifted the flap of her messenger bag and looked around to make sure she was alone. The coast was clear, so she pulled out the envelope.

She carefully slid her finger under the seal, but closed her eyes before removing its contents. It was always hard to accept what was inside.

When she opened her eyes, she saw a black and white photograph of herself. She was on her back and only the top edge of her naked body was illuminated, showing off its soft contours. Her love for this photo – and all the others taken by her ex-boyfriend Frankie – was tainted since now it was being used as ammunition.

In the same style as all the other previous deliveries, there was a message written with a black marker in block printing across the top and bottom borders of the photo:

> You can't get away from me in Italy. Marry Charles and I'll send all your photos to him.

This further narrowed the list of suspects to someone who not only knew she was in Italy, but also knew she was engaged to Charles.

This ruled out Frankie, who was the obvious suspect since he took the photos. But he knew nothing about Charles and her trip to Italy, and he already told her once he wasn't sending them. After she received the first letter, she tracked Frankie down to ask him about it. She remembered the dialogue of their call:

"Why would I send those photos to you? You have copies of all the digital files on the computer." Frankie said.

"I don't have them anymore. My computer was stolen right after you left," Jessie said. "Remember?"

"Oh, that's right. Somebody is really fucked up if they're doing that to you."

"No kidding."

Today's message, like the others, didn't indicate whether it was a man or woman. Jessie shook her head and stuffed the photo back into the envelope. As her eyes started to fill with tears, she chided herself for crying.

She reminded herself she'd been getting the letters for two years, and so far the sender was all talk and no action. She didn't want to let it ruin her vacation, so she put down the bag and distracted herself by looking through more books.

She picked up one by Henry James called "Italian Hours." It was a collection of his essays about Italy, published in 1909. She found a chapter called "Siena Early and Late" and thought it might be interesting, but it was very verbose and dry.

The only line she liked was Henry James' description about the houses under the moonlight of Siena's large piazza, the Campo – "We are haunted houses in every creaking timber and aching stone."

She closed the book and then her eyes. The stress of the day must have finally caught up with her because she dozed off quickly.

Fifteen minutes later she awoke from a vivid dream:

As she sat in the same chair at Cielo, a man tapped her knee and spoke a language she didn't understand. His hair was long, stringy and tangled, and he had tears smudging his dirty face. He smelled like the earth, and she knew he needed help, but she couldn't communicate with him. He pointed outside and from her seat, she peeked through the window. There were sheep running everywhere and children crying. Two older men in fitted suits yelled and pushed everyone away. She watched the commotion for several minutes until all the dark-eyed, long-haired people walked away from the house carrying only a few possessions and herding their sheep.

The front door of the villa opened, and Jessie jumped a little in her chair.

A guest with reusable grocery bags walked in the foyer. He had blonde hair and was tall and muscular.

"*Buongiorno*, hello," he said with a distinctive German accent.

"Hello," Jessie said.

The man quickly passed through the foyer to the staircase that led to an apartment.

With the dream fresh on her mind, she walked to the window to see if any of the long-haired people were outside. She didn't really expect to see them, but she knew her dream had significance especially since she had sensed a presence when she got near the villa.

It must have been the Sardi ghosts, she thought.

She hurried back to the gallery and told Mary about the dream.

"I think it was a vision," Jessie said. "It happens to me every now and then. This was one of the strongest I've ever had though."

"You're psychic?"

"I think so, but it happens at unpredictable times. If you'll loan me a sketchpad, I'll draw some images while they're still fresh in my mind."

Intrigued, Mary watched Jessie sketch the man who tapped her knee.

"Yes, the dark hair and dark close-set eyes are typical features of the Sardinians. Most in Tuscany were shepherds, which explains the sheep."

"Is it too early for a glass of wine?" Jessie asked.

She wanted to drink for several reasons, including the vision.

Mary laughed.

"Help yourself, but I'm going to wait because Enzo will be home any minute. He ended up playing all day with Carlo, but he's ready to come home and Marco is bringing him."

Jessie sipped the Chianti she'd become so fond of during her short time in Tuscany.

"I'm still so shocked," Jessie said. "That was much more vivid than usual."

"I believe in restless spirits and psychic abilities," Mary said, "But I've discounted Giovanni's opinions about the hex because he's fairly dramatic and is known for stirring up trouble."

"It might be time to believe him," Jessie said.

"You sure make me think I should. Your vision verifies some of the stories we've heard."

Jessie took a few more sips of Chianti, which was helping her calm down.

"I'm probably going to get your heart rate up again," Mary said. "And I'm going to sound like a mother."

Jessie spun the stem of the wine glass between her thumb and first two fingers.

"Okay..." Jessie stretched out the word to three syllables.

"I can't stop thinking about you and how hard it must be to not have a family. I know life isn't fair, and it seems like it's been less fair to you, but that's taught you be tough. And by tough, I mean emotionally impenetrable. I can tell you work hard to keep people from getting to know you, but I can see through it. You truly want - and need - help with your family issues, but I don't think you know where to begin. I want you to talk to Patrick Sullivan and get his professional opinion on how to find your dad."

"But - "

Jessie didn't know what to say after "but." It was her natural reaction to disagree to offers for help.

"You need to do this," Mary said. "It's not going to be easy to open up, but if you don't do anything, then nothing will change. And I truly believe you're ready."

Jessie let out a deep breath.

"Talking to you about my dad last night was the first time I told anyone about it. I have to admit I felt better afterward."

"I promise each time you tell someone, it will get easier. You'll find people you can trust who want to help you."

Mary smiled while Jessie fidgeted. But Mary didn't give Jessie a chance to say no.

"We'll go to the pool at 4 p.m. Patrick is always there."

They heard a car pull up. It was Marco dropping off Enzo and Carlo.

Mary told the boys to put on swimming trunks because they were going to the Ribelli pool. They ran upstairs to get ready.

She closed up the gallery, and they headed down the hill.

"If we run into Charles I'll have to do this at another time," Jessie said as they approached the farmhouse.

Fortunately, they never saw him.

CHAPTER 28

PATRICK WAS A PREDICTABLE MAN. He was in a chaise lounge by the pool with three farm dogs keeping him company. They were waiting for treats because he always had some in his pockets.

"Hello, ladies," said. "Here for a swim?"

"Only the boys are going in. Jessie's heading to San Gimignano soon, but we're hoping to get a few minutes of your time."

"Anything for two pretty ladies. What's going on?"

Mary started.

"I'll get to the point right away. I'm wondering if you can help my friend Jessie. She's from New Orleans and – "

Patrick interrupted.

"That's home of my best friend Vic Trudeau. He used to work with me in Boston, but after a nasty divorce, he headed back home to The Big Easy. Said he hated Boston, especially his ex-wife's prissy family."

Though Patrick's stories were usually interesting, Mary didn't have time for them today. They needed to stay on topic, so she picked up where she left off.

"Jessie is an only child, and she needs help finding her dad who she's never met. All Jessie knows is his first name and where he lived and worked as a teenager. She only learned these things nine months ago after her mother died, and she doesn't have any aunts, uncles, cousins or grandparents."

Mary's mouth tightened as she said this. She couldn't understand how Jessie could be so alone in the world.

"How can she find him?"

"Well, how did you learn the recent info?" Patrick asked Jessie.

She took a deep breath and swallowed hard, remembering Mary's advice that she had to do something different or things would never change.

"My childhood babysitter, Norma White, told me. She's the lady who practically raised me, but she promised my mama she wouldn't tell any of the family secrets.

"After mama died, I think Norma was feeling guilty because her death meant I had no family at all anymore.

"We sat in her kitchen the day after mama died and she told me the truth about how she met my mom and why we lived in New Orleans. It was the first time I'd ever heard the story."

Jessie told Patrick and Mary an abridged version, but she vividly recalled every minute of the conversation in Norma's kitchen.

CHAPTER 29

୫୭ଌ୰୪ଈ

New Orleans, Louisiana

NORMA SAT AT HER old Formica kitchen table, the familiarity of the kitchen soothing Jessie. She had grown up in this kitchen, right here at this table. Stringing and breaking green beans. Shucking summer corn. Sorting rocks from dry red beans. Talking about school. Dreaming about life outside of Tremé. Learning to crochet and macramé.

"Open that cabinet and pour some dark rum over ice," Norma said. "And add some Coca-Cola. Make one for yourself, too."

Jessie did as ordered and opened the white aluminum cabinet door next to the kitchen sink. Ever since Jessie was a toddler, Norma kept her rum in a high cabinet so Jessie wouldn't accidentally find it. But the location also gave Norma quick and easy access.

After Jessie made the drinks, she sat down in the turquoise vinyl seat of the dinette set and stared at the random pattern of silver flecks on the table's white background. Her eyes were swollen from crying.

"Child, it's time we talk, even though your mama made me promise never to tell you any of what I'm about to say. She asked, but honestly I never officially agreed. So I'm not betraying her. I thought she would tell you this someday. You're her flesh and blood, so she really needed to tell you all this.

"But now you're gonna hear this from me 'cause it sure isn't gonna be her. God rest her soul.

"They were your mom's secrets. Not mine. Poor Loretta, she lived like she was treading in water, about to drown, not knowing if her feet could touch bottom if she relaxed. She began life in a painful way, and she was always afraid of the next bad thing that was gonna happen. She thought if she didn't talk about the bad stuff, it would make it go away, but all she did was carry pain like a ball and chain."

Tears ran down Jessie's cheeks. It had been less than 24 hours since her mama had died.

"Jessie, I met your mama in Nashville when she was 17 years old."

"Nashville?"

"Yes, it was 1979, and I had visited my brother Maurice. He was a mighty fine musician and played with all the famous singers, even Elvis Presley. Maurice was a funny man, you know?"

Jessie nodded. She already knew everything about him even though she had never met him. Norma was so proud of him and always boasted about his music career. It started in New Orleans and took him to Memphis. Then he went to Nashville, where he stayed.

"He never spent a dime of his money. It's like he was waitin' for the end of the world. Every time he got a pain, he thought it was cancer. Well, he never had cancer, but he had enough savings to pay for all the treatments. I always thought he was kind of crazy, you know?

"But he loved music more than life. It's all he ever wanted to do. He performed from sunset to sunrise, and then he practiced from sunrise to sunset. He only took little naps throughout the day in his one-room apartment. And he never drank alcohol. Said his talent was a gift from God, and he respected it.

"I can't believe he died of a stroke so young. Maybe it was from all the unfiltered smoke in those bars where he played every night. I'll never know."

Norma's gravelly voice soothed Jessie. Just as Maurice could play music non-stop, Norma could tell stories non-stop. And she didn't spare any details.

"I got sidetracked, didn't I?

"It's okay," Jessie said. "Maurice meant a lot to you."

"Yes, he did. So it was 1979 when I visited Nashville – the only time I've been there in my life. I was so nervous to travel alone, but I got up the courage to buy a bus ticket and go. That's where I met your mama, on a bus."

Jessie's eyes widened.

"My mama was on a bus?"

Jessie thought she had never left New Orleans.

"Yes, honey. When I was comin' home from Nashville, the seat next to me was the only one open, and the last person to get on was your mama. She was a young little thing like you and still in high school."

"Why was she in Nashville?"

"That's what I'm about to tell you," she said.

Norma took a big swig of her rum and Coke.

"Your mama took the seat next to me. I could tell that poor young girl had troubles, you know. Her hands kinda shook, and she fidgeted with everything she touched including a sparkling diamond ring on her left hand."

"A ring?"

Norma chuckled and played with the buttons on her dress. She gathered the fabric to keep it from gaping across her bosom.

"I knew she had troubles, and I didn't want to scare her by comin' on too strong, you know. So I left her alone for a while. Once she seemed settled, I finally talked to her. I asked her where she was goin' and she said, 'home.' Then I asked 'where's home?' She hesitated for a moment said,

'New Orleans.' I told her I lived there, too, and I asked where her house was. She said, 'in the city.' Right then and there I knew she was making it up, because anyone from New Orleans would have said home was the Quarter, Uptown, the Warehouse District, or somethin' like that. Nobody calls it 'the city.' Your mama didn't know New Orleans.'"

Jessie clasped her hands to keep from tapping her fingers on the table. She wanted Norma to tell her story faster today. Most times it didn't matter, but this was the biggest news she'd ever heard in her life.

"I didn't let on I was suspicious. I just nodded my head and knew I had work to do, you know. I needed to get this young lady to talk 'cause I was sure she needed help. So I opened a bag of salted peanuts and offered some to her, but she declined. I ate them and didn't say a word so I wouldn't scare her. After a short time she fell asleep, so I read a worn copy of the Reader's Digest someone left in the seat. I always liked the page where they taught you new big words."

Norma played with her blouse again.

"When your mama woke up, I offered her the magazine and she took it. I told her the article about the Bermuda Triangle was interesting and she read it. I got her to talk about the story and it helped her relax. Then I asked her why she was in Nashville, and she said she had gone to her Aunt Priscilla's house in Cincinnati, Ohio, for Thanksgiving and stayed longer to spend time with her big family."

"Aunt Priscilla in Cincinnati? She told me her mom and dad were only children. Priscilla sounds like a phony name. Isn't that Elvis Presley's wife?"

"Yes, it is Mrs. Presley's name. I'll caution you, a lot of your mama's story was peppered with lies, but let me keep going."

Jessie didn't know if she was confused, frustrated, sad or angry.

"After that, I made a comment that got her real upset. I mean real upset. I told her she was lucky to have family, because I had lost my parents in Hurricane Betsy in 1965. It was horrible. Flood waters came, buildings collapsed, and they drowned. Maurice and I lived 'cause we weren't home when it happened. Then your mama started sobbing. Her body shook, and she cried like it had been her own parents. Everybody on the bus kept looking her way and my heart ached for her, you know."

"Why did she do that?"

"Well, I told her to calm down and that I wouldn't let anything happen, but no words would console her. She had troubles deep inside she was holding onto tight. Real tight. You know, I call those people 'stuffers.' They're ones who don't talk about their feelings and then one day they blow up. That was your mama."

"Did you get the story out of her?"

"Well, I gave her time to relax and I finally spoke. I said, 'I been on this earth a lot longer than you, and pain has come and gone in my life. It isn't easy, and it doesn't get better until you let go of it, you know. You can't hold it in, and people want to help you. Then I told her I may or may not be the right person to help but I had big ears like my daddy. You know, big ears mean you're a kind person, not to mention a good listener? Look at these things."

Norma lifted her gray hair and showed off her long ears with droopy lobes, and Jessie giggled.

"These are good listenin' ears," Norma said. "And I told your mama I would listen all night long. We had hours left to ride. I said, 'Talk if you want and when you want. Don't be scared.' As soon as I told her that, she finally said her first words, 'I am scared.' Her voice was small, like a child. But I knew she would talk. I told her the secrets would stay on the bus."

"What did she say?"

Jessie was ready to cry again.

"Well, all she said at first was, 'I don't know where to begin.' So I helped her and asked simple questions she could answer and that worked. I asked her where her real home was because I didn't believe it was New Orleans. And she said to me, 'It's complicated.' So I asked her where she was living before she got on the bus, and she said it was Ashland, Kentucky."

"Kentucky? She told me she lived in New Orleans her whole life."

"I'm just telling you what she told me. Then I asked her if she lived with her mommy and daddy and she cried again. Between sobs, she finally told me they were dead, and then she rattled out even more. She told me they died exactly like my parents had. They were in a flood in West Virginia and her two sisters and brother were killed. Everyone died in the flood except her."

"Oh, my God," Jessie said. "That explains why Mama hated rain. I mean hated it. It upset her when the roads would flood during heavy rain. I remember her always saying 'Sometimes I hate this city because of those levies. If they ever break, we're in big trouble.' Then she would complain about not having enough money to move away."

"A lot of people are stuck here whether they want to be or not," Norma said, nodding.

"When Katrina happened mama went crazy. Remember? She kept repeating to herself, 'We better get outta here before people die. I don't like floods. I don't want to see people die. We gotta go. I can't stand floods.' She was so panicked, and we couldn't get her to calm down until we got to Houston."

"Your mama went through more than you can imagine. Where was I? Oh yeah, we were on the bus. My heart ached for her. I told her she was awfully young to hurt so much. You know, it's the kind of pain that hurts like you never want to get outta bed again. Like there isn't a tomorrow. She cried and cried and finally rested her head on my shoulder. You know these shoulders, Jess. They're big and soft and good for holding crying girls."

Jessie smiled because she'd cried on those shoulders her whole life.

"When your mama calmed down, I asked her who she was livin' with and she said her Aunt Beverly and Uncle Joseph, but they had six kids - two boys and four girls. She said it was a crowded house, and she slept in the room with the girls who were only four and seven. She said the family was kind to her, and she worked at the new McDonald's to help pay bills."

"McDonald's?"

"Yes, I asked her if she made those hamburgers and fries, and she said she made milkshakes and her boyfriend was a cook. As soon as she said this, she stopped abruptly, like she didn't mean to tell me she had a boyfriend, you know. But I wasn't going to let her stop talking. 'Boyfriend?' I asked. 'Where's he right now?' Well, this made her cry again and she told me she left him in Cincinnati."

"Cincinnati?" Jessie asked. "I thought she lived in Kentucky."

"This is where the story gets more interesting," Norma said. "I don't know my geography real well, but she told me Ohio and Kentucky are only separated by the Ohio River, and Cincinnati is about a hundred miles away from Ashland on the other side of the river."

"So why was she in Cincinnati?"

"Good question. She wouldn't talk after giving me the geography lesson, so I pulled my tarot cards outta my purse and told her to shuffle them and select one."

"She must have thought you were a witch!"

"I don't think she had ever seen tarot cards, but she did what I told her, and the first card was the Ten of Swords."

"Makes sense, she felt hopeless."

"Yes, and then her next card was the Knight of Pentacles. I asked her if her boyfriend was rich and she nodded her head. So I had her pull another card and it was the Fool. I told her she was gettin' ready to start a whole new life. And do you know what? Her whole new life began in New Orleans with me, and seven months later you were born."

Jessie shook her head.

"Mama told me my dad was someone she met in a bar one night. She said he ran back to his wife and kids when he found out she was pregnant."

"She didn't want you know about her past, I suppose."

"She knew who my dad was, and I have a right to meet him."

"I'm so sorry I'm the one telling you all this. I tried to get your mama to tell you so many times, but I tell you, when she got off the bus here in New Orleans it was like she erased her memory. She didn't want any part of the life she left behind, and I couldn't make her say another word, you know."

"What else did you find out?"

Jessie was almost as angry with her mother as she was sad.

"Well, it took the whole trip and a bus transfer in Jackson, Mississippi, but she finally told me. Her daddy was a coal miner in West Virginia and on one horrible Saturday morning a dam broke and wiped out nearly the entire coal town. I think it was called Buffalo Creek or Buffalo River. I remember being surprised there might have been buffalo in West Virginia. Anyway, she had stayed the night with a rich friend whose house wasn't damaged by the water. She said all the rich people lived high up on the hills and not in the hollers."

"What's a holler?"

"I had to ask her the same question. It's a valley in the mountain. Your mama's family lived in the holler and died

that horrible morning in a matter of minutes. It was an
awful tragedy, and she lost everything except the clothes she
was wearing. Her only family left alive were her aunt and
uncle in Ashland, and they took her in to live with them
and all their kids. She didn't want to talk about them and
never gave me their names. And I agree with you, I think
Priscilla was a fake name.

"But she did seem to like workin' at McDonald's while
she was goin' to high school. That's where she met her
boyfriend. His name was Will, but she never told me his last
name."

"Will," Jessie said. "Will is my father! It's probably short
for William. I like it. And I like the name Will better than
Bill."

Norma smiled at her.

"It's a fine name for a daddy. You know, I think she left
him because she loved him so much."

"What do you mean?"

"She said Will's daddy was a doctor, but they made Will
work so he understood what it took to earn money. Once he
graduated from high school, he was going to a big fancy
school in the Northeast."

"You know so much," Jessie said.

"I know some. Your mama loved Will, and when she
found out she was going to have his baby, she knew it would
ruin his life and his plans. She figured out how to run away,
and fate helped her in a tragic way. She and Will went to see
a big rock concert in Cincinnati by The Who. They don't
play music I like, but it became another misfortune for your
mama. People were trampled to death trying to get in the
building for the concert. She was already inside and didn't
realize it had happened until they got out of the concert, but
eleven people were killed and it was national news. She said
she had a big black cloud over her head."

"I can't imagine."

"Well, she and Will were supposed to stay at his cousin's house for the night and drive back to Ashland the next day. But as soon as Will fell asleep, she snuck out. She went to the nearest bus station and took the first route out of town. It happened to be going to Nashville. When she got there, she had to decide where to go next, and she picked New Orleans because she didn't think anyone would look for her there."

"Wow," Jessie said, shaking her head. "But that doesn't explain the diamond ring. Are you sure they weren't engaged?"

"I don't think so. You know, I never saw it again. She might have sold it because she had so little money."

Jessie kept shaking her head.

"I can only imagine how upset you are right now, but your mama did the best she could. She felt so much pain and heartbreak when she was young. On the bus, I told her she could come and live with me until she could get a job and take care of herself. When you were two, she got the live-in maid job with the doctor, but he wouldn't let you live there, so I told her you could stay with me."

Jessie scooted her chair back and stood up so she could hug Norma and bury her teary face in Norma's big soft shoulders.

All Jessie could think about now was the fact that her dad probably had no idea she existed. Meeting him was her top priority.

"I'm going to find my dad," Jessie said.

"I understand, but try not to be too angry with your mama. You meant the world to her even if she wasn't the best role model."

"I don't understand why she couldn't move on and let go of the past."

"Honey, I keep hearing about all these soldiers who return from war traumatized. They call it post-traumatic stress disorder on those TV talk shows I watch. I think your mama had the same problem.

"She lost her family so young and never had any help with her emotions. She carried on in the best way she knew."

"You're probably right," Jessie said. "But I still don't know why she wouldn't tell me about my dad. He surely doesn't know I'm alive. Don't you think he wants to meet me?"

"He may and he may not. I see movies like that all the time on those cable channels. Some long-lost relatives are welcoming and some aren't. You could get more heartbroken if he doesn't want you in his life."

CHAPTER 30

❧❦❦❧❧

Terzano, Tuscany

MARY PATTED Jessie's shoulder as she finished telling the story.

"Your poor mother," Mary said. "What a tragic life."

"The very last time I saw my mama, I realized how little I knew about her. She spent her entire life alone."

Jessie thought about how she didn't want to repeat her mom's mistakes.

Patrick cleared his throat before speaking.

"I'm sorry, Jessie. There is something we can do about this. We might be able to find employment records from McDonald's. I emphasize 'might' since it was 1979 and records were on paper then. Their retention policies probably required them to be destroyed. But it's possible there's someone who's worked there all these years or knows someone who once did. Do you have money to hire a private detective who can do some snooping in Kentucky? Or could your fiancé help? He looks like he might be wealthy from the way he dresses in those preppy clothes."

"I wouldn't ask Charles for money, and I'd rather not tell him about all this."

Mary tightened her lips. She believed Charles would want to help Jessie if he knew she was struggling. But she didn't comment.

"My mother's employer gave me some money after she died. I think it's enough."

Jessie thought about those days following her mother's death when she marched through life's everyday events. She had never been so numb, and she and Charles continued to argue about her mom's employer, Dr. Winn.

From the time Charles met Jessie's mother, he hadn't liked the fact that Dr. Winn paid Loretta cash and didn't give her any benefits. He thought Dr. Winn had used Loretta and underpaid her. And he thought the final reconciliation of paying the medical bills and giving Jessie $10,000 wasn't enough.

Jessie disagreed because she knew her uneducated mama had always been thankful for the opportunity, and Jessie surmised that she was glad the government – or anyone – didn't know she existed.

Dr. Winn had always been nice to Jessie and even remarked that he was sure it was tough as a young child to not have a mother at home. Your mama was lucky to have such a good sister to take care of you, Dr. Winn had said the day he gave her the money.

Jessie realized he must not have known the whole truth all those years about "Aunt Norma."

Her mother was a master of the protective technique of never telling more than she had to. And Jessie had become an expert apprentice.

"Yes, I have some money," Jessie said.

"It will probably take about two to four weeks to get any information," Patrick said.

"Really? That soon?"

"I figured you wanted it to be like those TV show detectives who solve everything within five minutes by opening a computer. You know that's not the real world, don't you?"

Jessie laughed for the first time in a while.

"I've waited a lifetime, so what's another month or two?"

She thought about how this could impact her wedding plans and still felt nervous about having a conversation with Charles about delaying the date.

Patrick looked toward Mary and said, "I like your new friend."

Jessie opened her bag and found a business card for Patrick.

"Here you go," Jessie said. "Thank you!"

"I'm glad to help any friend of Mary's."

"He's still paying off his debt after trying to break up Luca and me," Mary said.

"You'll never stop reminding me, will you?"

"Nope, never. You almost ruined one of the best gifts of my life."

Mary had forgiven Patrick and he knew it, but they still joked about his attempt to portray Luca as a womanizer.

"Thank you again," Jessie said. "Oh, and if you could do me a favor, don't bring this up in front of Charles. I don't plan to tell him about this."

"Confidentiality is part of my job," Patrick said.

Mary bit her tongue, knowing she had already done enough meddling for one day. But she still wished Jessie would ask Charles for help.

CHAPTER 31

𝕭𝕺𝕺𝕮𝕽𝕺𝕾

San Gimignano, Tuscany

JESSIE AND CHARLES made the winding, picturesque drive to San Gimignano, a beautiful hilltop town with fourteen of its original 72 towers intact - often called the Manhattan of Italy.

Visiting in the evening was highly recommended because the busloads of day-trippers would be gone. The only negative for Charles was that the museums were closed.

The lack of a schedule allowed Jessie and Charles to aimlessly wander the walled city's maze of cobblestone streets. There were enchanting archways, narrow alleys and towering old homes.

To Jessie, it was an artist's dream. The low sun created strong shadows, and she loved the rustic elegance. Old buildings were brought to life with overflowing flowers in window boxes and laundry hanging out to dry. Noises from televisions blaring and dishes clanking flowed into the street. She loved these sounds of "home."

As soon as she and Charles happened upon a quaint *trattoria*, they agreed it was the perfect place to have dinner. There were only six tables - two inside and four outside. They took the last available table outside.

The menu was in Italian, and they recognized some words like spaghetti, *salumi*, *formaggio* and *insalata*. Jessie flipped through her English-Italian dictionary attempting to translate the unfamiliar dishes.

They ordered a half-liter of the local white wine, Vernaccia, and had cantaloupe wrapped with prosciutto as their appetizer. It was a dish they ate at home, but they agreed this cantaloupe seemed sweeter and the ham more savory.

They switched to drinking Chianti with their pasta dishes, and Jessie knew she would love the dish she ordered mainly because of its name – *Pappardelle alla Papà*. It was homemade wide flat noodles in a sauce of wild boar and onions. There was an option of *Pappardelle alla Mamma*, but she chose "*Papà*" hoping it was an omen she would find her father. "Dad" seemed to be the word of the day.

Charles ordered *Lasagna al Forno* – baked lasagna with meat sauce. His noodles were homemade, too.

They devoured the meals.

"I could probably eat a second serving," Jessie said. "But I'm saving room for gelato."

Their server checked on them often and spoke simple English words like "good" and "more." Jessie spoke simple Italian words like "*grazie*" and "*prego*." It was enough to understand each other.

After they polished off the last bit of Chianti, they drank espresso and asked for the check, *il conto*.

"*Il conto* later," the server said when he returned to the table. Instead he brought them two bottles of *digestivi*, compliments of the house, with two small glasses so they could pour their own after-dinner shots.

They poured one shot of each and Jessie tried both. One was anise flavored and the other was grappa.

Jessie told Charles to smile, and she snapped a photo of him sitting at the small table with his shot glass of grappa.

After dinner, they strolled the streets and stopped for gelato on Piazza della Cisterna. They sat on a bench and Jessie ate *cioccolata* while Charles had *nocciola* or hazelnut.

Since most of the tourists were gone, they were able to watch the local residents.

There were grandparents, parents, children and grandchildren. Young couples in love walked arm-in-arm, while older couples helped each other stay upright.

Jessie loved seeing the big families spending time together. She dreamed of coming back to earth as another person, living on a farm in Italy with a large family and eating gelato every evening.

Relaxed and inspired by the families surrounding her, Jessie wanted to tell Charles about what happened earlier that day – not about the letter, but her conversation with Patrick.

But she was worried about how he would react and still afraid to talk about it. She knew she should, it was just so hard to open up. Suddenly, she burst out in tears, not able to help herself.

She stood up and walked a few steps away from Charles to try to hide them.

But of course, he followed her.

CHAPTER 32

"JESSIE, WHAT'S WRONG?"

"I don't think I can talk about it."

"Jessie, it's me. You can tell me anything. I love you."

She blurted it out.

"Who's going to walk me down the aisle?"

Charles wiped away her tears with his thumbs and wrapped his arms around her.

"We'll figure it out, Jess."

"I don't want to pick anyone. I want to find my dad. I have to find my dad. Soon."

He leaned back so he could look directly in her eyes.

"I didn't think you could. I mean, I didn't think you had enough information to find him because your mother never told you anything. But if you've changed your mind, we'll figure out a way to find him. We won't have much information to help us, but we'll try."

"Norma told me some things recently. Mama lied about everything. When she was teenager she got pregnant and ran away from home."

Opening up like this made her heart race and she got a sour taste in her mouth, but she had to tell him the truth about this if she was going to spend the rest of her life with him. Mary's nudging was exactly what she had needed.

"What?" Charles asked.

"I know some new stuff."

"Like what?"

"His first name and where he lived when he was a teenager."

Charles rubbed his brow.

"No last name?"

"No, but we might know where he worked when my mom got pregnant, and we know his dad was a doctor."

"Jessie, how long have you known this?"

"Since the day after mama died."

"Why didn't you tell me? You know I can help you. We do investigative work for our clients all the time. I can get a paralegal on this right away."

"I'm embarrassed, and I don't want your family to find out about this."

"Why?"

"My dad might be a deadbeat or in jail."

"Would that change who you are?"

She started crying harder and he held her tightly.

"Jessie, there's nothing we can find out that will make me leave you. And no one in my family can keep us apart. I love you. I always will. We can have a simple ceremony with a Justice of the Peace. It would take off the pressure of the wedding."

Jessie knew this was a reasonable suggestion, but she wanted more time.

"I want a wedding," she said. "And I want him to walk me down the aisle. Could we find him quickly?"

"I don't know."

He looked off in the distance over Jessie's shoulder and clenched his jaw. Anyone within eyeshot of him would've seen a tense and frustrated face, but Jessie didn't.

She had no idea it would be so liberating to share this information with Charles. She was scared, relieved and surprisingly joyful, all at once.

She wished she had the courage to continue confessing and tell him about the stalker, but that would have to stay locked up inside for now. She wasn't nearly ready.

"I'm such a mess," she said.

"Yes, but you're my mess! And you're a beautiful mess."

He smiled and rubbed her tears away again.

"Let's walk," he said and took her hand.

They meandered quietly along the narrow cobblestone streets and after nearly an hour, they ended up at the walled gate where they could exit for their car. Next to the gate was a small pastry and souvenir shop that sold wine. Charles asked her to wait while he went in. When he came out, he flashed a bottle of prosecco.

"I think you need something to smile about, and we didn't have any of the bubbly stuff for your birthday. So let's drink this tonight at our apartment."

"Okay, good idea."

She appreciated his lighthearted mood and that he hadn't pressed her to talk more.

Back at the Ribelli farmhouse, they went outside to enjoy the rest of the evening. At the pool, Charles sat down in a lounge chair and Jessie nestled her body inside his. With her back to his chest, she rested her head on his shoulder and they stargazed. There was a romantic crescent moon, and she loved being in his arms.

"We should have brought the prosecco," Charles said. "Be right back."

Jessie leaned forward so he could get out of the chair. He jumped up and in minutes he returned with the bottle, two glasses and a blanket.

"Let's see if we can find a quiet hideaway in the vineyards."

They walked to a desolate spot on the hillside near the vines and put down the blanket. They began drinking the prosecco, then undressed each other and savored each other's bodies. They were sleeping naked in each other's arms when a bug bit Jessie's ankle. This prompted them to dress quickly and go back to the apartment, but not before Charles took her in his arms.

"Happy Birthday, Jessie, I love you. I want us to be together on your birthday for the rest of our lives, no matter what happens to the world around us. Nothing can eclipse the love I have for you. Nothing. Always remember life isn't perfect, and we all have faults and skeletons. But I love you just the way you are."

"Thank you."

She kissed him.

"You're the best birthday gift I've ever gotten," she said. "And I'm sorry if I've been so difficult lately. Losing mom, worrying about the wedding and finding my dad have been more than I can handle."

"It's because you were trying to do it alone. But I can help you. We'll find your dad together."

"So you think we can delay the wedding date?"

"It's my parents I'm worried about," he said after thinking about it. "They're counting on the big celebration on New Year's Eve."

"It's our wedding, not theirs," Jessie sighed.

"You and I know that, but it's impossible to say the same thing to them. Let me do some digging when we get home. I might be able to find your father quickly. Let's not make any decisions yet. We'll work on it, okay?"

A tear trickled down her face. She wondered why she would have ever considered not marrying him. She loved him, and she knew she hadn't been fair to him. He had parental pressures she'd never experienced, so she couldn't truly relate to his world.

Back in the apartment, Charles made one last call before going to bed. He had to discuss the latest documents with his dad.

At the end of the call, Jessie heard him say, "We'd prefer to stay until Wednesday, but I understand if we can't."

She didn't ask him for details and hoped they wouldn't have to leave early.

CHAPTER 33

✥✥✥✥✥

Terzano, Tuscany

THE SAME EVENING while Jessie and Charles were in San Gimignano, Mary stayed home and had dinner with Enzo and Carlo.

After dinner she told Enzo he needed to stay home alone for a night. She wanted some one-on-one time with her precious son. So she took Carlo home, and she and Enzo spent some time playing checkers. He won four of five games.

When she put him to bed, she stayed with him while he read several more pages of "Harry Potter and the Chamber of Secrets" out loud.

Then it was her turn to do the reading. She read him two short books and told him some nighttime stories about the games she played as a kid in America. They were stories he'd heard over and over, and she loved telling them. She never wanted the tradition of him falling asleep to her stories to end.

Once Enzo was sleeping soundly, she moved to the living room. After reading a few chapters of her book and drinking a couple glasses of wine, she went to her bedroom. She took her laptop so she could write to Luca.

Subject: Hi

Tonight, I polished off half a bottle of Chianti and wish you were here to share the other half. I miss your company, especially at the end of the day when it's quiet. Enzo went to bed easily. He read his book, and then I read to him and told him stories until he fell asleep. He looks like such an angel when he's sleeping. He keeps asking when you'll be home.

I haven't mentioned it, but the American couple who had dinner with me last night is now staying at Ribelli. They're from New Orleans. You and I need to visit that wild city someday soon while our bodies are young enough to handle it. Maybe on our next trip to the U.S.

Last night, the Americans (Jessie and Charles) had dinner with me, and I learned the young lady has spent her whole life not knowing who her father is. She desperately wants to meet him. All she knows is his first name and possibly the state where he lives, so I had her talk to Patrick Sullivan about hiring a detective.

I can't help but be fascinated by all the stories of "lost dads" in my world. You and your biological father have never met. You and Alex didn't have a relationship until he was 18 years old. And now I'm helping Jessie. It seems I'm a catalyst for linking each of you to your fathers or at least helping you figure out who they are.

Hope you had another successful day. Business is running like normal here.

I love you,
Mary

While there were problems at Cielo she didn't mention them. She didn't want him to worry.

After she finished the email, she opened her manuscript. She thought about Jessie's suggestions, especially about making it a steamy romance. She had never written sex scenes and wondered where she should start.

She closed her eyes and dreamt of sizzling romantic encounters with Luca. She didn't want to write about something they'd already done, but a new fantasy. She imagined an escapade under the big, old oak tree near the vineyard.

She put her hands back on the keyboard and wrote a "love letter" to Luca. The little erotica scene was surprisingly easy to write, and the descriptions she wrote made her miss Luca and his tantalizing body even more.

She hit "send" and wondered how he would react when he read it.

CHAPTER 34

࿓࿓࿓࿓࿓

Siena, Tuscany

ON FRIDAY MORNING, Charles rose with the roosters and took a long, hot shower to wake up. He needed to finish working before he and Jessie met Mary at 10:15 a.m.

Mary was taking them to Siena to attend their first Palio event at the Campo, the city's large shell-shaped piazza. This is where the race would occur, and today was the important lottery for the horse assignment.

No one wanted to miss this exciting event except Enzo. He was more interested in playing with Carlo. So Mary took Enzo to his cousin's house and closed the gallery for the day since most everyone would be in Siena anyway.

Jessie sat in the backseat of Mary's car where she gazed at the picture-perfect scenery of the countryside. She never tired of looking at the rolling vineyards, shimmering olive groves, old stone walls, majestic cypress trees and ancient farmhouses.

When they reached the highway, the view wasn't as charming, especially after they took an exit through a commercial district of stores, business offices and gas stations. But they drove through it quickly and then headed up a steep hill on a one-way road, making tight curves with big, old homes closely hugging the roadside.

They reached a massive arched gate called San Marco where they entered the walled city of Siena. Mary told them the city had strict restrictions for car use as she made an immediate left onto a narrow one-way street to park just inside the city's wall. Fortunately she knew where she was going.

Mary acted as their tour guide and had them walk up a steep hill toward the Campo.

They passed coffee shops, tourist gift shops, churches, fountains and small squares. Jessie fell in love with Siena and its medieval charm. All the cities she'd visited in Italy were old, but Siena was old in a different way, as if time stood still from long, long ago.

"Siena, with its 17 neighborhoods, has a distinctive appearance for the Palio," Mary said. "Each neighborhood, or *contrada*, has a name and its own colors and insignia. During the Palio, you'll notice most people wearing a colorful scarf called a *fazzoletto* to show their neighborhood loyalty."

She recited some names of neighborhoods in English and Italian – "There is Caterpillar, or *Bruco* in Italian, Tower – *Torre*, Goose – *Oca*...you get the idea."

"Those are unusual names for neighborhoods," Charles said.

"In most cases they represent the historical role of the neighborhood. For example, *Bruco*, the Caterpillar *contrada*, is where the silk workers lived."

"Interesting," Charles said. "I'll have to read more about it. Our tour book doesn't have much information on Siena."

"But a lot was written about Florence, I bet."

"Yes, and that's why we spent two days there. We could have easily planned time here, too."

"Most visitors do the same thing you've done. They devote their time to Florence and either skip Siena or make a daytrip and just see the major attractions. And the reason is deeply rooted in history. There were many battles fought between Siena and Florence, and Florence ultimately won in the sixteenth century. The Florentines intentionally isolated

Siena by not developing major roads into the city. So the town became a preserved medieval gem. When visitors arrive, they're usually surprised by all of Siena's treasures.

"Of course, the local businesses appreciate all the day-trippers, but Siena is best enjoyed on an overnight trip. Once the crowds clear in the late afternoon, you can truly experience it."

"Like San Gimignano last night," Jessie said.

Mary nodded her head.

"Exactly. Now I'll take you through some neighborhoods before we reach the Campo. You'll see the insignia change as we walk. Take a look at the lamps on the buildings. They're painted in the colors of the *contrada* and are only installed for the Palio events."

For the first time Jessie noticed yellow and red ornately painted lamps mounted high on the buildings at city street corners. And there were large, vibrant flags in the same colors hanging from most homes' windows.

"Each neighborhood has a distinctive flag. For example, this red and yellow flag is of the *Chiocciola*, or Snail, neighborhood. Do you see how most of the street's windows display Snail flags? It's because we're walking through the *Chiocciola* neighborhood. But notice the window over there with two different flags – a Snail and a Panther. A 'mixed' couple lives there."

Charles laughed.

"I've never seen anything like this," he said.

"It's so festive," Jessie said. "It reminds me of Mardi Gras parade days."

They continued walking uphill.

"I think all three of us are in good shape and could make it to the Campo without stopping," Mary said. "But it's time for a drink."

They entered a bar that served coffee, *panini* and *liquori*. Mary ordered three glasses of prosecco.

"Here's to enjoying your first Palio event!"

Before they left the bar, she called Alex and agreed on a location where they would meet him on the Campo.

When they started walking again, Mary's phone rang. She assumed it was Alex calling again, but it was Luca. She gestured to Charles and Jessie to wait for a moment as she talked to him.

"What were you trying to do to me with that email?" Luca asked.

"Make you understand how much I miss you."

"It is driving me mad. I want to get on a plane right now and come home and jump your bones."

Mary laughed.

"Do you want me to stop writing messages like that?"

"Are you kidding? No! I had no idea you could write that stuff."

"I didn't either. Maybe I should write a different book than I planned. I could call it 'Love Letters to Luca."

He laughed.

"I like that idea, but if you write it, I only want my eyes to read it."

"No worries, they're only for you."

"What are you doing now?"

She explained their plans, and he told Mary his plans.

He was in his hotel room and would soon meet the Chicago distributor.

"Tonight, we are going to dinner, too. I hear they have good steaks in this city."

"Some of the best."

"As good as *Bistecca Fiorentina*?"

"Of course not."

She knew he wouldn't want her to give any other answer.

"I guess they're going to make me eat *insalata* before the steak?"

"Yes, but you'll survive."

"I will. But I would rather be home with you taking a walk in the vineyard to the big oak tree."

He laughed.

"That's where I'd rather be, too!" she said. "I miss you."

"I miss you, too. And did I tell you I want you? I mean really want you."

"Same here!"

"Ciao, my little love kitten!"

She laughed.

"Ciao, *amore mio!*"

CHAPTER 35

As MARY, CHARLES AND JESSIE closed in on the Campo, the crowds got heavier and there were many more retail businesses.

Jessie liked the clothing and shoes displayed in the shop windows, because they were trendier and different from what she saw at home.

They reached an entry to the Campo and walked down a sloped sidewalk to some steep steps. Then they went under temporary bleachers to access the large piazza.

Jessie and Charles were amazed at the size of it.

Tall buildings that looked like apartments and offices lined the perimeter of the piazza, and there were thousands of people waiting for the horse lottery.

"See the dirt path along the border of the piazza?" Mary asked. "It's where the horses will race three laps. It was temporarily installed for this event."

"Here?" Jessie and Charles asked simultaneously.

The Campo was large, but Jessie thought it seemed small and dangerous for a horse race, especially with its sloped ground and tight turns.

"Yes, right here. It's quite dramatic. Oh, there's Alex."

He was with two American couples who were busy taking pictures of the large crowd gathering for the horse lottery.

After quick introductions, Alex took the group closer to the action and explained what was happening.

"Of the seventeen neighborhoods in Siena, there's room for only ten to compete in the race," Alex said. "The drawing today is for their random horse assignment. Every neighborhood is hopeful for the fastest horse."

As they waited for the lottery to begin, Jesse pulled out her camera and snapped photos of the large tower, Torre Mangia, at the base of the Campo where the lottery was staged.

Then large groups from each of the racing neighborhoods entered the Campo, singing, waving their flags and wearing the *fazzoletto* of their neighborhood.

Finally, the drawing began and everyone became quiet – eerily quiet for such a large crowd.

The first neighborhood was announced and the *contrada* residents screamed and rushed to retrieve their horse and move it to their neighborhood stable for care. This continued until all the horses were assigned.

Jessie and Charles were astounded by the event, as were Alex's customers.

Mary promised they would continue to be enthralled with the Palio. Then she took Jessie and Charles to a busy *trattoria* behind Torre Mangia where they drank Chianti and ate the local pasta, *pici*, a thick spaghetti-like noodle.

Charles excused himself from the table to go to the restroom, and in the time he was gone, Jessie quickly explained to Mary she had told Charles about wanting to find her dad.

"Telling him was one of the hardest things I've ever done."

"What did he say?"

Jessie responded with the largest and brightest smile Mary had ever seen from her.

"He told me he wanted to help!"

"He really loves you," Mary said.

"He said their legal office often does investigations like this, and he never offered because he thought I didn't have any information to use to find him."

That confirms it, Mary thought. Charles is definitely not her devil. But she still wondered who it could be.

"He's a sweetheart," Mary said.

"I'm beginning to see and appreciate that more since we've been in Tuscany. I think it's because he was forced to slow down with the adjustments to our trip. And because I've opened up."

Jessie blushed a bit.

"It will keep getting better for the two of you."

"I hope so," Jessie said as she twirled some *pici* on her fork.

After lunch, they went to a gelato shop. Mary ordered lemon, Jessie chose strawberry and Charles had mocha.

"Do you have a favorite *gelateria*?" Jessie asked Mary.

"Believe it or not, no. All the shops are good. The competition is stiff, so bad ones don't survive for long."

"I could eat it every day."

"Me, too," Charles said. "Jeremy should sell it at Java. Think of all the hot New Orleans afternoons when customers want something cold and refreshing."

"I'd eat it all and he'd never make any money," Jessie said.

Walking out of the *gelateria*, Mary guided them through the maze of narrow streets to see Siena's major sites, including the Duomo and St. Catherine's Church. Then she left them alone to shop and explore.

They had until 11 p.m. when they would meet Alex in the same garage where Mary parked. Alex was giving them a ride back to the house. So Jessie and Charles had time see a 7:15 p.m. trial run at the Campo. This was for the horses and jockeys to become familiar with the tricky shell-shaped course.

After the trial, they walked along old cobblestone roads, ducked into dark archways, stole kisses and stopped in small bars for wine.

Around 9 p.m., they found a small *trattoria* near the garage where the car was parked. It was during their *al fresco* dinner that Charles brought up Jessie's father. He said he'd given it more thought and would do the research himself.

"Since the topic is delicate and personal, we'll keep it between us. If it works out the way you hope, we'll tell the good news to everyone. If not, only you and I share it."

"I like your idea," she said and her heart melted.

But Jessie didn't know Charles was doing this for more than one reason. He had to control the situation because he didn't want to give his parents a reason to suspect the wedding might be delayed. He was under a lot of pressure from them to get his life together or "settle down," as they commonly said.

At 11 p.m., they met Alex. He was with his adorable girlfriend, Elena, who he was also giving a ride home.

Jessie thought they looked happy.

ഇൽരു

Jessie and Charles fell asleep easily that night, but once again Jessie had a vivid dream about the Sardi. This time she was one of them, and was being chased from the Cielo villa. She was distraught and woke up in a panic.

"Are you okay?" Charles asked.

"I think so."

She fell back onto her pillow and wiped perspiration from her brow.

"It was a bad dream," Jessie said.

"I was having a hot dream about you," Charles said. "You were doing a strip tease dance for me and look what happened."

Charles put her hand on his erection. Hard as a rock, he rolled on top to take her, but then he stopped.

"Please roll over," he whispered. "In my dream you were a stripper, and you were on your hands and knees crawling across the dance floor. I loved seeing your ass up in the air. I want you the same way now."

She couldn't believe what he said. Everything in her life seemed to be crashing around her.

She turned over and buried her face so he wouldn't see her tears if she started to cry.

Her year-long stint as a stripper on Bourbon Street was buried in her past, and she planned to keep it that way.

CHAPTER 36

༄༅༄༅

Terzano, Tuscany

MARY HEARD ALEX come in the house around midnight, but she stayed in her bedroom on the phone with Luca. He'd had a rough day and needed to talk about it.

"The distributor never picked me up this morning and he did not answer my calls. So I hired a private car and went to his office. It is in a big industrial park, and I am happy I did not drive. I would have never found the place. And the traffic in this city is worse than the coffee!"

"Be nice," Mary said.

He chuckled.

"I got there at 11:30 a.m. and the receptionist said he was out. I asked if someone could tell me why my appointment was canceled. The receptionist made a couple of calls and found out the owner rescheduled his calendar because our case of wine did not show up."

"But you shipped the wine weeks ago."

"No, it was not me. Alex did it. Will you ask him to look up the record and find out why it was so late? And tell him to look at the shipments for my next meetings in Atlanta and Miami. The wine must be there. Please make sure he knows how important this is."

"Okay, I'll do that in the morning. He's home now."

"It's an expensive trip, and we can't afford mistakes like this. Fortunately I carried two bottles - the most I could get through customs. I wish flying was like the old days. I used to carry cases."

"I'm so glad you remembered to take at least two bottles. Alex is home tonight, so I'll talk to him early tomorrow morning."

"It is a lesson for all of us. It makes me realize I was only one more fucking wine sales guy for this distributor. They see many of us. But I know our wine is not another fucking wine."

Luca didn't cuss like this often, so she knew he was wound up.

"I waited in his office for two hours to prove that to him. When he didn't come back after lunch, I talked the receptionist into calling him and giving me a second chance for the appointment."

"You can charm anyone into doing anything!"

"We'll talk about what I want to charm you into doing for me later."

"Please do."

"The guy said he'd give me fifteen minutes when he returned. So I opened the Chianti and the Riserva to breathe. I was ready with the tasting as soon as he arrived.

"He liked the wine and said mid-range Chianti was selling well in this area and he needed another vintner. He told me he is frustrated with some of the small, specialty wineries that can't supply product consistently, so he needs another source. I assured him we could meet his volume steadily. The price we negotiated made him happy and we got an order. It's the biggest order we have received yet."

"Nice job! Are you still going to get the steak dinner with him?"

"Yes, he'll be here soon to pick me up. He wants to talk about planning a surprise vacation in Tuscany for his wife. That was how I think I finally sealed the deal. I offered two free weeks each year in either of our properties as long as he keeps placing orders."

"I'm glad we do more than make wine. Congrats on negotiating that well."

"Thanks," he said. "I would like to celebrate with you here in this king-size bed."

"Tell me more about that," she said. "I miss you so much."

CHAPTER 37

✸✸✸✸✸✸

Montalcino, Tuscany

CHARLES FINISHED HIS contract edits early in the morning so he and Jessie could take the full day to tour the area south of Siena. Mary and Alex told them it was one of the most scenic parts of Tuscany, not to be missed.

Cocooned in their little Fiat, Jessie and Charles headed south on the highway toward the Crete Senesi, Montalcino and Pienza. The exit they took immediately cast them onto a narrow two-lane road that traveled through rolling hills rippled with golden yellow rows of grain, most of it already harvested.

Villas dotted the landscape with occasional lines of cypress trees along the driveways and olive tree orchards accenting the properties.

Jessie snapped photo after photo, and they stopped a few times so she could get out of the car for better views.

As they were getting close to Montalcino, Charles shared the little he knew about it.

"Alex told me it's the home of Brunello wine. There are big and small producers in the region, and he gave us a tip for trying it."

"We wouldn't want to pass up good wine," she said, laughing. "I've never had so much wine in my life."

"Alex said the Italians call it 'the blood of the earth.'"

Charles had been bombarding Alex with questions about Tuscany and its history.

The hilltop town was small and quaint, and it catered to tourists with several small wine shops and restaurants.

"I hope I followed the directions right for the bar," he said.

He peeked in an open doorway and found the courtyard Alex described.

"Looks like we're here. Alex said they serve a good variety of local wine here, but we won't have to pay the tourist prices of the wine shops."

They went inside and ordered two different glasses of Brunello di Montalcino and a meat and cheese plate. Then they took seats in the courtyard and tried each other's wines while checking out the scenery.

The old building had seen many modifications, and Jessie took photos of the rustic architecture. She also went inside and took photos of the views from the indoor windows. There were postcard-perfect views of the valley below Montalcino.

"I might be able to use these pictures for backdrops. I keep saying that about every place we go, don't I?"

"You're going to be busy when we get home."

"You're not kidding. I'm going to talk to Jeremy about having an opening. I'll need at least two months, but I'd love to have a show focused on Italy."

"I'll help you any way I can," he said. "And so will my parents."

Charles' mother loved Jessie's paintings.

Sitting in the courtyard, they spent most of their time people-watching rather than talking. After that, they strolled hand-in-hand, entering a wine shop to buy a few bottles.

Their last stop before leaving was an old, pentagonal-shaped fortress on the edge of town. Jessie snapped shots of the exterior while Charles went inside and explored it more thoroughly.

Then they hit the road again.

CHAPTER 38

INSTEAD OF GOING directly to Pienza, they took a detour south to a historic abbey called Sant'Antimo. Alex suggested they visit it if they didn't stay in Montalcino too long.

Without much food to accompany the two glasses of wine, they were both lightheaded and giddy.

Charles carefully navigated the hilly, winding country roads and didn't notice Jessie had slid her floral sundress above her naked hips.

After a few minutes, she grabbed his right hand and put it between her legs.

"Oh," he exclaimed. "You're not wearing anything."

"No."

"Shit," he said. "I'm more interested in keeping this hand on you than the stick shift. We're going to have to pull over."

As soon as he found a rural side road, he turned and parked the car in an isolated spot next to a large pasture.

"I can't imagine anyone will come by soon," he said.

Then he gave all his attention to Jessie.

They kissed as his hands worked their magic and had her screaming in delight. The car was too small to do anything too acrobatic so they decided the only option to satisfy Charles' desire was to have him recline his seat so Jessie could give him pleasure with her hands and mouth.

Jessie knew what he liked, and it wasn't long before she noticed him clenching his fists and tightening his hips, so she wasn't surprised at his next words.

"I think I'm about to –"

A loud and unusual noise outside the car interrupted him. Jessie turned her head and Charles looked outside, too.

A huge white Chianina cow stood at the fence curiously viewing their exploits. The cow mooed again and licked her chops at the crazy lovers. She was eyeing their every move.

Jessie and Charles laughed at the "porn-watching cow" until they could hardly breathe.

Eventually, Jessie and Charles got over their shyness and finished what they started. When they were done, they looked out again and now there were two cows at the fence watching them.

"Voyeurs!" Charles said. "Go find a bull and have your own fun!"

Jessie couldn't stop laughing.

"I'll never forget this! Let me grab my camera."

She got out of the car to take photos while Charles zipped up his shorts.

His cell phone rang, but it had fallen under the car seat. Scrambling, he jumped out of the car and moved the seat forward to get it.

It was his father calling. The conversation was brief because the signal was poor and the call kept breaking up. All she heard Charles say was, "Yes. I understand. Okay."

When he hung up, Charles looked at her, and she could see his disappointment.

"Looks like we're going to have to fly home tomorrow. Dad apologized, but he needs me in the office on Monday. I have to call Delta right away."

Jessie was so disheartened, but she was at his mercy. This time she couldn't hide her emotions.

He drew his eyebrows in and slightly tilted his head as he looked at her.

"I'm sorry," he said. "I know I'm letting you down by having to go home early."

"It's okay."

Charles hugged her before dialing Delta.

She knew it wasn't his fault, but she was really upset. She loved Tuscany, had made a fast-friendship with Mary and wasn't ready for the trip to end.

"I'll have to find a better place to do this, the signal is too weak for the call," Charles said.

He wedged himself back in the driver's seat and they rode in silence. The fun of the escapade with the cows had faded.

CHAPTER 39

ഈഈ൰ങ

IN SEVERAL KILOMETERS, they reached a big clearing in a valley. Nestled below the mountains and a hilltop town sat the Abbey of Sant'Antimo, a monastery with origins in the early twelfth century.

They parked in the tranquil, quiet setting. Jessie and Charles walked without speaking, respecting the serenity. Once close enough to the religious edifice, they could hear monks chanting.

Jessie didn't have a strong religious upbringing, but Aunt Norma took her to a Baptist church about once a month. Her mom didn't care if Jessie went to church. Her mother had never said it, but Jessie didn't think she believed in God. She figured her mom had probably given up a long time ago.

They took a seat on a pew inside the Romanesque church, and the scent of incense and rays of sun coming in through the open windows made the scene nearly surreal. It was the twenty-first century and visitors carried cell phones, digital cameras, computers and navigation systems, while the monks were clothed in simple robes with no earthly possessions, following ancient rituals and traditions.

Jessie thought about the stark contrast between modern and ancient lifestyles. This travel experience was another reminder that the world was old and her life was only a brief passing.

The hairs on her arm stood on end and she knew this was a sacred place. These monks had probably experienced frequent conflict over the centuries to fight for their religious beliefs in an evolving world. She felt insignificant and somewhat guilty about the bad choices and lies in her life, but at the same time she had never felt more empowered to make changes.

When they were back in the car on their way to Pienza, Jessie scrolled through the photos stored on her camera and couldn't believe all the places they'd seen. It was a life-altering vacation.

"Thanks for everything we've done on this trip," Jessie said. "It's been the most incredible thing I've ever done."

"You're welcome. Hopefully we can come back someday."

She nodded her head.

CHAPTER 40

ಜಿೂೂಬೊ

Pienza, Tuscany

As THEY GOT CLOSER to Pienza, Charles shared his latest travel tidbit.

"Alex said Pienza is the most fairytale-like town in Italy. It was designed by Pope Pius II. Supposedly, he wanted it to be the ideal city of the Renaissance and had the resources to build it."

"It's also the town where Mary said pecorino cheese is made," Jessie said. "Remember her talking about it during dinner on my birthday? We'll have to take some to her as a small way to thank her for everything."

She couldn't believe the trip was almost over.

They parked in a lot on the north side of Pienza's town wall and entered its gates. Only open to pedestrian traffic, it was quiet and peaceful. Better than a Hollywood movie setting, there were enchanting homes lined up side-by-side, sharing their stone and brick walls. Cozy little restaurants and cheese shops abounded, as well as small shops for leather goods and gifts.

They walked the cobblestones to the Cattedrale dell'Assunta on the main square, Piazza Pio II, and then traversed along the southern town wall where a narrow walkway provided a panoramic view of the Tuscan countryside. Siena's Torre Mangia peaked above a distant mountain and the sun cast shadows on the hills.

They ordered two glasses of Chianti from a small bar and leaned against the thick town wall to savor the "blood of the earth" and the mesmerizing scenery.

"How romantic," Jessie said. "I'm so glad we came."

As she hugged him, she saw a street sign for a narrow alleyway – Via dell'Amore. She could translate this.

"Look, let's get someone to take our photo under the 'street of love.'"

"Okay, then I need to call Delta. I have a decent signal here."

Another tourist gladly took their photo in exchange for a photo with her husband.

Charles pulled his phone from his pocket and started to dial, but Jessie interrupted him.

"Charles."

"Yes."

"How much do you love me?"

He looked up and she could tell he had no idea what she had built up the courage to ask.

"Enough to spend the rest of my life with you. Why? Is there something wrong?"

"Nothing is wrong. Before you call Delta, do you think –"

She stopped. It was hard to ask.

"Think what?"

"That can I keep my flight on Wednesday?"

"Stay here by yourself?"

"Not alone, with Mary and her friend Stella who gets in this afternoon. I want to spend more time with Mary."

She could feel her face on fire. She was so uncomfortable asking this, but now she knew she needed to speak up to make her life become what she wanted it to be.

He walked to the wall and looked west. She couldn't see his face and had no idea what he was thinking, but she moved to his side.

Charles turned around and draped his arms around her neck and shoulders.

"Jessie, I never want to tell you what you can and can't do. I'm the one who's letting you down by going home early, but there's no way I can say no to my father. If it's important for you to stay, that's not a problem. I'll miss you, but it's only three days."

"Really? You're okay with it?"

Her nerves turned to excitement.

"You really seem to get along with Mary. But you have to promise one thing."

"Okay, what?"

Now she had no idea what he was about to say.

"You won't run off with a hot Italian 'Luca' like Mary did."

"Oh, Charles, you don't have to worry. I love you, and these last few days, I feel like we've gotten even closer."

"Ditto."

He kissed her and then made the call to change his flight.

On their way out of the heavenly little village, they stopped in one of the small cheese shops and bought three Pecorino varieties for Mary. Then they made the drive back to the farmhouse via the highways for the shortest route.

Once they were close to the farmhouse, they stopped in a rural trattoria for Charles' final dinner in Italy. As they ate fresh cheese-stuffed ravioli, a couple on a motorcycle pulled up and parked. When they took off their helmets, Jessie and Charles could see it was a biracial couple – a black man and white lady. Charles watched them for a moment and then asked Jessie if she'd ever been in a biracial relationship.

"You know I grew up in Tremé, and as a white kid I was the minority. My first crush was on the kid next door, and he was black, but we never dated. And I never dated anyone seriously in high school. Norma worked so hard to keep me from getting into trouble and constantly told me about the 'dangers of boys.'"

Jessie laughed.

"She always said, 'Men are like trains. A new one arrives at the station every five minutes.' She told me to be choosy."

"I guess I'm a lucky guy."

"You are," she said. "Very lucky as a matter of fact."

She giggled.

"How about you?" she asked. "Ever dated someone who wasn't white?"

"Nope," he said. "Even if I wanted to, it wouldn't be worth it. My family would disown me. They're that old-fashioned."

"They're definitely conservative," she said. "I'm surprised I meet their criteria to be your fiancé."

"Well, they can see what a sweetheart you are, and you know how much my mother loves your paintings. She said it's like looking into your soul."

Jessie nodded.

She thought of one of her favorite quotes by Vincent Van Gogh that she had posted in her studio - "I dream my painting, and then I paint my dream."

She couldn't wait to see what kind of paintings would come after Italy, a place of her dreams.

When they got back to the apartment, they found two bottles of Chianti outside their door with a note from Mary.

"Enjoy the wine! Please come over tomorrow for lunch at 1 p.m. to meet Stella."

Jessie called Mary from the phone in their apartment and explained the latest adjustment to their trip.

Mary was excited and invited Jessie to move into the castle, rather than be alone in the apartment.

CHAPTER 41

෩ඝඁඁ෮

Fayetteville, Ohio

LUKE HADN'T SEEN Caroline for a couple of weeks, so he wasn't surprised when his cell phone rang on a Saturday afternoon in mid-August. He was sure it was a dinner invitation.

"Hello, Caroline."

She could barely talk.

"I need help."

"What happened? I'm on my way."

He grabbed his truck keys, ready to head out the door.

"No, you don't have to come now, but I've gotta leave. It's my mom. She had a stroke."

"I'm so sorry. What can I do?"

"I need to pack up and move to Florida to live with her. She needs help and doesn't have any money. And there's no way I can bring her here."

"I'll head over so we can talk about this."

"Okay. Thanks," she said between sobs.

When he got to her house, Caroline told Luke she wanted to get out of town quickly, and thankfully he was available to help. He put together a plan for her, and three days later, Caroline's apartment was empty. Her personal items were packed, and she had donated her sparse furnishings to the Salvation Army.

Big Blue was ready – the oil was changed and everything was inspected. A neighbor had agreed to take care of his dog Scout.

On Wednesday at 5 a.m., her boxes were loaded in the truck. Luke had packed a small bag of clothes and a tool chest.

They agreed to drive the thousand miles straight through to Florida's Gulf Coast, so Luke packed sandwiches, snacks and drinks.

When they arrived at her mom's trailer in an over-55 community in Bradenton, Florida, Caroline immediately took of her mom while Luke managed everything else.

He unloaded the truck and moved her belongings into the tiny second bedroom. Then he walked around the interior and exterior of the small home and made a list of work that needed to be done. Next, he hit the hardware store.

By Sunday he had painted, caulked, cleaned, lubed and replaced everything needing attention. He told Caroline and her mother goodbye and gave Caroline an envelope full of cash to help her get by until she found a job.

When he got in the truck, he started to head toward the interstate, but then made an impulsive decision to go to the beach. He wasn't the kind of guy to hang out on the beach and work on a tan, but he wanted to breathe some fresh salt air and enjoy the water.

As he walked along the surf at Coquina Beach, he thought about Caroline. They had spent nearly fifteen hours riding south in his truck knowing it was probably the last time they'd ever see each other. But they still didn't talk about their past or their future. Somehow they'd never been emotionally tied to each other.

He didn't know her problems, but he knew his. He had spent his life waiting for Anna, even though the logical part of his mind told him he'd never see her again. But now he felt more alone than he ever had. Caroline's companionship was gone, and he thought at 68, he was too old to meet anyone else.

"It's just Scout and me," he said into the Gulf wind. "And we'll be fine."

CHAPTER 42

೫ಐ಄ೱೞ

Terzano, Tuscany

EARLY ON SUNDAY MORNING, Charles and Jessie loaded the miniature Fiat rental with their baggage and headed to the castle. Driving there was considerably farther than walking because they had to drive to the bottom of the hill to access the road that led back uphill to the castle. But making the drive was easier than carrying the luggage on the shortcut they typically walked.

After unloading Jessie's bags, Charles hugged and kissed her. Then he crammed his long body back into the Fiat.

"See you on Wednesday," he said. "Have a good time and stay away from the Italian men."

"No worries!"

"Especially Alex. I see how he looks at you."

"Don't say that."

"Well, I love you, and you know what I want Jessie Morrow. But I like the sound of Jessie Durbridge better."

He winked.

"I hear you," she said.

She nudged his shoulder like a bashful schoolgirl.

"We'll get the plans worked out," she said. "I promise."

Charles shifted into reverse, and she stole one more kiss before he drove away.

Now Jessie was alone in Italy, the farthest from home she'd ever been. It was one of the boldest things she'd ever done. She had made a new friend, and she was so excited.

She went in the gallery entrance and Mary was waiting for her in her bathrobe, looking ragged. She was glad to see Mary was real – the kind of lady who didn't feel the need to brush her hair or wear make-up to make a greeting.

"Good morning! Come on in! I'm going to have you stay in the same room where you were a few nights ago."

"I loved it, thanks."

"You'll have to forgive me, but Stella and I had one too many shots of tequila last night. I'm going to head back to bed. So is Stella."

Jessie laughed.

"Sounds like a rough hangover."

"It happens every time she's here. She buys a bottle in duty-free, and we try to act like we're still twenty-one!"

When they got to the second floor, they ran into Stella in her pale blue satin, two-piece pajamas, carrying a large bottle of sparkling water.

She looked almost exactly as Jessie pictured – tall, thin, fair-skinned and redheaded.

Stella's brightness and energy lit up the room, even with her hangover.

"At last, we meet! I'm Stella!"

"Hi, you can guess who I am. Jessie."

"I'm looking forward to talking to you after I take Ibuprofen and get a few more hours of sleep. Hopefully this fucking headache is gone by then."

"Good luck," Jessie said. "It's early for me, too. I could use a few more hours of sleep."

"See you later."

Stella shuffled into her bedroom and Jessie and Mary did the same.

CHAPTER 43

༄༅།།

"SO TELL ME about you," Stella said.

She was sipping her first cup of espresso at 11 a.m.

"By the way, I love your embroidered top. It looks like it was made in Mexico."

Jessie laughed.

"I found it at Goodwill."

"A girl after my own heart. I have good finds from there, too, for my boutique and my own wardrobe."

Stella owned a vintage clothing boutique called "Stellar!"

"You know, you sound like 'Mary the Second' staying in Italy alone without your boyfriend."

"It is similar, isn't it? But I have a fiancé."

"Um, so did she. You're lucky ladies. You have men fighting for you, and all I want is to have really good sex one more time before I turn fifty."

"I thought you said you were ready for a husband and not another one-night stand," Mary said.

"Hmm, I might need another really hot one-night stand. That guy last week was awful. Then I'll look for my husband, who needs to be a clone of Luca."

"I hope you brought condoms," Mary said.

"Alex said I could have some of his."

"Stop it!" Mary said

Jessie laughed at the ladies. She loved their banter, and Stella's sarcasm didn't stop.

"Too bad Alex isn't old enough for me."

"He most certainly isn't!" Mary said. "Stay away from him, Stella."

Stella laughed knowing she'd gotten Mary worked up.

"But there is news on that front," Mary said. "He's back on the market. Elena is gone."

"What happened?" Jessie asked. "I thought he really liked her. They were still dating a couple days ago."

"A group of his friends went out last night and Alex was talking to another girl. When Elena saw them, she started crying and refused to believe Alex wasn't interested in the other girl.

"This morning before he left with a tour group, he told me he didn't have time for drama and immaturity. So he broke up with her. I'm sure he'll be dating someone else soon. There's been no shortage of ladies chasing after him."

"No surprise," Stella said. "He's a hunk."

"Well, Italian men have a reputation of being mamas' boys and some live with their mothers until their thirties," Mary said. "They let their moms run their lives. So the American men are well liked for their independence from *mamma*."

"How long did Alex date Elena?" Stella asked.

"About a month."

"Before that?"

"Maria for six weeks."

"He's a heartbreaker," Stella said and then she frowned. "I swear, men have all the damn power. It pisses me off. Where did you put that tequila bottle?"

"You've got to be kidding," Mary said.

"I am."

Stella laughed. But she wasn't shy about looking for love. Since Mary had moved to Tuscany, Stella visited Italy every two or three years to look for her Luca, except for the fourteen months she was married to an older guy named Tye.

"Please tell me Luca has a twin he's been hiding," Stella said to Mary.

"He's one-of-a-kind. And he's mine!"

Stella shook her head and rolled her eyes.

"Some people have all the luck."

Then she laughed at her own silliness.

Jessie hadn't ever met anyone as ballsy as Stella, and she loved her as much as Mary.

"So tell me what you do in New Orleans," Stella said to Jessie.

Jessie told Stella about Charles, their planned wedding, the coffeehouse, her paintings and all the photographs she'd been taking to create paintings. Then she remembered the envelope hidden in her messenger bag where she kept her camera. A funny look must have come across her face, because Mary and Stella asked her if she was okay at nearly the same time.

"I'm fine."

She lied and could tell they didn't believe her, but neither pressed it.

Inside, she berated herself for lying. It wasn't a good way to start new friendships and she knew it.

"I have several clients from New Orleans who buy my formalwear," Stella said. "A few celebrities are ordering now because I'm able to regularly source high-end vintage designer dresses like Gucci and Emilio Pucci. How about you, Jessie? Do you have a wedding dress yet? I can picture you in loose, flowing bohemian style dress from the seventies. You have an earthy vibe about you."

"That sounds beautiful, and yes, I still need to find a dress. But it will probably need to be formal and conservative. My fiancé's parents want to invite their friends and business associates. I'd rather they not come – I'd like to keep the wedding small. Very small."

"Weddings bring out the worst in families," Stella said. "Don't forget it's your wedding. If you decide you want to go vintage, I'm the person to help."

"Thank you."

"If I get my computer, will you show Stella your paintings?" Mary asked.

"Sure," Jessie said.

"We can get on my Facebook page, too," Stella said.

"I should sign up for Facebook," Mary said. "My sister in Philadelphia has been bugging me to get on it so she can look at pictures of Enzo and so I can see her kids, too. But I haven't taken the time to set it up."

"I've met so many customers because of it," Stella said. "I set up a business page and use it to promote my new arrivals. Mary, you could use it to easily promote your art all over the world."

"Let me get my computer," Mary said. "You can show me."

"I bet you don't have a LinkedIn or Twitter account either, do you?" Stella asked.

She obviously loved to harass people.

"Enough from you," Mary said. "Let's tackle one thing at a time and start with Facebook. You can teach me so I can help Luca promote the Ribelli wine."

With Mary's laptop fired up, Jessie showed the ladies her "Recherche" paintings.

Stella's face lit up.

"Wow! I love the colorful backdrop of the New Orleans street scenes. These exotic women look like they have stories to tell. Very soulful and saucy."

Stella pointed to the images in the bottom right corner of each painting.

"What are these?"

Jessie explained it was a tarot card icon giving more insight into the women in the paintings. If someone knew the meanings, as Jessie did, the card would indicate something about the lady, like if she was in love or broken-hearted, scorned or happy, wealthy or poor.

"So you can read cards?" Stella asked.

"A little."

It was an understatement.

"I could use a reading to find out what's going to happen with my love life," Stella said.

"I like getting readings, too," Mary said.

Jessie was relieved she could talk openly.

"I considered bringing my cards, but Charles isn't a fan. So many people are afraid of them. But as my Aunt Norma taught me, they're just a way to read your own subconscious thoughts."

"Well, Jessie, these paintings are fantastic. I'd love to hang them on the walls in my boutique. Don't you think, Mary?"

"Absolutely. Your customers would love them. They seem to say what we all feel – I have something inside me you want, and you won't be disappointed.'"

Jessie loved the way Mary described her work and grabbed a scrap piece of paper from her bag to write it down.

"What about your fiancé?" Stella asked. "Do you have photos of him?"

Mary jumped in.

"Oh, he's adorable. He loves Jessie, and he's very handsome."

Jessie showed Stella a photo from her camera.

"He looks preppy. Is he fun?"

Jessie laughed.

"He's both. He has tight strings to his family, and I think he'd shed the style if his family would tolerate it. But as long as he works for his dad, he'll have a 'uniform' to wear. His whole life has been planned from the day he was born."

"Too bad," Stella said.

"He's okay with it. He's not the rebellious type."

Mary jumped in.

"He's really polite and easy to talk to."

"Is he good in bed?" Stella asked.

"Stella!"

Mary couldn't believe she had asked this.

"It's important, Mary! You know it is! Why can't I talk about it?"

Jessie laughed.

"Yes, he's good! The best. His hands – "

She blushed and stopped herself because she was getting too personal.

"Then he has my approval," Stella said. "Let's look at my store."

Stella had some inventory posted online.

"That looks like a fun business," Jessie said. "I should put your vintage gowns on the women in my paintings."

Stella's face illuminated from bright to brilliant.

"No! You should paint my customers," Stella said. "What a great promotion to sell more gowns and your paintings! So many of my clients are filthy rich. They wear these dresses for special occasions, and I think they'd love to have something to help them remember the time they wore the dress. I wish you lived close to Philly."

"I've often thought I'd love to get out of New Orleans, but Charles never plans to leave."

Stella's eyes brightened.

"Maybe I should come there. I mean open a second store. I've been thinking about doing it somewhere."

"Seriously?" Jessie asked.

"Absolutely. It could be the perfect location for expansion. I'm going to give it some thought."

"If you decide to do it, I'm interested in a job," Jessie said.

"At a minimum, the addition of your portraits in the Philly store and on the website would be great."

"I could use the help," Jessie said.

Her mind spun. She would have to get aggressive with her painting schedule when she got home.

"I'd come to New Orleans for the grand opening," Mary said. "Luca and I have talked about visiting, and that would be a great reason, especially if we can coordinate a distributor visit or wine show."

"I'll keep thinking about it," Stella said. "How about you, Mary? Anything new cooking in your studio?"

"I haven't been painting lately because I started writing a novel."

"No kidding. What's it about?"

"My life in Tuscany."

"Another 'Under the Tuscan Sun'?"

"Well, I want it to be original and not like books already on the market."

"What's it called?" Stella asked.

"I haven't decided."

"Well, when you have a draft, I'll read it."

"Me, too," Jessie said.

"Thanks, but it will be a while. It's not as easy to write as I thought it would be, but I'm enjoying the challenge. And I'm determined to finish it. But we're busy with all the operations we have going on here."

"Are we going to Siena today?" Stella asked.

"Alex is hanging out at the Bruco headquarters with his friends, but he said there won't be much activity since they aren't running in this Palio event."

"We should go if single handsome men will be there."

"Is that all you think about?" Mary asked and laughed. "I need to check on our guests at Cielo and Ribelli, so how about meeting back here on the patio at 2 p.m. In the meantime, nap, walk, read. Make yourself at home."

Stella said she planned to relax at the house, and Jessie said she needed to find Patrick.

Mary winked because she knew Jessie was going to tell Patrick he didn't have to look for her dad anymore. Mary didn't know Jessie had a second motive, though.

Jessie went outside in search of Patrick, but she never found him.

CHAPTER 44

ডওৰওৰ

DURING LUNCH THE TRIO opted to stay home the rest of the day and not go back to Siena. They agreed to take it easy because the next day was the Palio race and they would be in Siena for most of the day.

Enzo was going to be home for the evening, too. He had already asked if Carlo could come over.

As Mary discussed dinner plans, Jessie offered to make Cajun food.

"Great idea!" Mary exclaimed.

Jessie made a grocery list for gumbo, red beans and rice, collard greens and beignets. Mary had all the spices needed – *pepe, sale, origano, paprika* and *timo*, among others. But they still had to make a trip to the Coop for chicken, sausage and collard greens. The menu eventually became a hybrid of Cajun and Italian foods – Italian sausage gumbo, red beans and risotto, Swiss chard greens and beignets.

Stella didn't care for cooking, so she watched as Jessie and Mary chopped the vegetables. Mary gave them Italian lessons by teaching them some vegetable names – *cipolle, aglio, sedano, peperoni verdi* and *pomodori*.

Then Jessie began making a roux for the gumbo.

Stella watched Jessie intensely stirring, unable to step away from the pan for a second.

"What is that?" Stella asked.

"A roux," Jessie said.

"What's a roux?"

"If you don't know by now, you don't need to know," Mary said. "But watch Jessie if you really want to learn how to brown flour and oil for a sauce base. We're taking this one to a chocolate color."

"Chocolate! Now you're talking my language."

"Then get over here and stir."

"Nah," she said. "It looks like too much work. I'll be in charge of cleaning the dishes and emptying the wine bottles."

Jessie and Mary had a great time cooking and listening to Stella's funny commentary. It was no wonder she was so thin. She had no clue how to make anything except boxed brownie mixes and didn't want to learn more. She lived almost entirely on sweets, especially undercooked triple-chocolate brownies.

When dinner was ready, Enzo and Carlo ate in the kitchen and were only interested in the risotto without any sauces or gravies. They waited impatiently for the beignets.

The Cajun dishes were tasty, but the beignets were the hit of the night. Enzo, Carlo and Stella piled theirs high with *zucchero a velo* - powdered sugar - and they all ended up in a food fight blowing sugar in each other's faces.

Jessie laughed as much as Enzo and Carlo, feeling like a kid. Her photos were hysterical.

Before the sun fully set, the three ladies climbed to the top of the tower and toasted to their future successes - Mary's book, Stella's love life and Jessie's art opening.

"In all the years Mary has been my friend we haven't met many other women like us, but I think you fit in perfectly," Stella said. "We're not sorority girls, not biker chicks and definitely not prima donnas. We're Chianti Girls."

"That is so cool!" Jessie said.

"You're the first person who didn't have to ask what it means," Mary said. "So you must be one."

Stella raised her glass.

"To Jessie, another Chianti Girl!"

Jessie blushed and smiled.

"To my new Chianti soul sisters," Jessie said. "You're the sisters I never had."

The three watched Tuscany's evening gift together – a warm and radiant sunset.

Jessie didn't have her camera with her, but she took a mental snapshot of her friends' faces glowing in the oranges and reds of the evening.

She also thought about Mary's account of how Luca's mother stood at this lookout over forty years earlier and watched her lover ride away on a motorcycle. It was the last time Anna ever saw her tall, handsome U.S. Army lover, and nine months later she had his baby – Luca.

Before leaving Tuscany, Jessie planned to ask Mary for a photo of Anna so she could create a painting of her at the lookout tower. It would be a gift for Mary and Luca for their wonderful hospitality.

After more Chianti and hours of talking and laughing, Mary snuggled into bed with her laptop because it was her only connection to Luca at the moment. She didn't like being alone and decided to write another love letter to Luca. Within minutes she came up with a fun idea and called it The Card Game.

In this love letter she told him about how they played cards on a cold, winter night in front of the fireplace. The game was like strip poker, but instead of stripping clothes when they lost, they had to give each other sexual favors. Luca played aggressively and the favors he wanted turned out to be as much pleasure for Mary as they were for him. They only made it through two hands.

CHAPTER 45

ಬ಼ಐಿಐ಼ಃ಼

Siena, Tuscany

MARY WOKE WITH the roosters, and after showering and dressing, she skipped *caffé* and hopped into her car to check on Dorotea who rose before sunrise, too.

"*Ciao, bella artista,*" Dorotea said.

She was holding Vincenzo, her orange tabby cat.

Mary loved when Dorotea called her an *artista*. She kissed Dorotea's wrinkled cheeks and asked how she was doing.

"*Stesso, stesso. Vecchia.*" – "The same. Old."

Mary smiled at her dry humor and they went to the kitchen. Dorotea was excited to share the latest gossip. The Puccis were taking holiday separately this year. Signore Pucci was going with his family and Signora was going with hers. She thought they were arguing again because of their inability to conceive, each blaming the other. And the Moris were buying new kitchen appliances and Dorotea had no idea how Signor Mori had earned the money, but she said she would find out.

Mary nodded. She wasn't a gossiper, but she always let Dorotea share her latest discoveries. When she said all she wanted, Dorotea gave Mary a short grocery list and Euros to cover the cost of the items.

When Mary returned with the groceries, she told Dorotea she was going to Siena for the day with her American friends. Dorotea told her to be careful.

"There are too many people at the Palio for me," she said. "I don't like crowds. I like being at home with my Vincenzo. Be sure to bring Enzo next time, so I can give him some cookies. And take this *crostata* to your friends. Today it is apricot."

Mary went home and while Jessie and Stella ate the apricot tart, she took Enzo and Carlo back to Marco's house.

As soon as she came back, the three ladies hopped into Mary's car and headed toward Siena to meet Alex.

Today their energy level was greatly increased, as was the city's. Emotions were full-throttle for the Sienese who staked their identity on the outcome of the race.

In spite of about a quarter million people in town, Jessie and Stella were surprised about the lack of commercial promotion. The locals wore their regular clothes, and the only sign of loyalty was the *fazzoletto* decorating their necks. There were no sponsors or neon lights, just a centuries-old horse race following the same traditions as it had since the seventeenth century.

Alex's customers had rented a small apartment above the Campo, and they graciously extended an invitation to Mary, Stella and Jessie to join them at 4 p.m. After the trio explored the city, they returned to Mary's car at 3:30 p.m. to pick up wine for their American hosts. They hauled the wine up the steep hill of Siena and then up several narrow flights of stairs to reach the small apartment.

The apartment's best feature was a narrow balcony overlooking the Campo. Thousands of people were already in the center of the Campo and many were already sitting in the bleachers.

"I'm sure glad we're getting to see it live," Jessie said.

"Well, grab a glass of wine because we're in for a long day," Alex said. "The parade should start around 4:50 p.m. and the race at 7 p.m. It'll be fun, but lengthy."

"It's too bad Charles couldn't come," Jessie said. "He's a fanatic about historical events."

"He'd be asking me a million questions," Alex said.

"You're right, he would. Maybe it's better he's not here."

Alex smiled and said, "I like his passion."

"The parade is exactly the same every year for both Palio dates," Alex explained. "The costumes are representative of various segments of Siena's history."

The parade started when Alex said it would, and it was slow. The pace was controlled by drumbeats and periodically it came to a halt when pairs of flag bearers from each *contrada* provided impressive flag throwing techniques.

"I've always had a rule to never date men who wear leotards," Stella said discreetly to Jessie and Mary as they watched the parade. "But some of those guys out there are hot! Those tights show it all! I wonder if I should give men-in-tights a try!"

Mary and Jessie laughed at her.

"Please tell me Luca and Alex don't ever wear one of those medieval get-ups," Stella said.

"No worries," Mary said. "They don't, but you need to know it's a privilege to participate and wear those tights."

"Okay, Miss Serious," Stella said and snarled at Mary.

Jessie smiled as she watched the parade. Oxen carried the actual "Palio" - a hand painted banner - to be given to the winning *contrada*.

Costumes were historically correct, and Jessie realized she would have thought she'd time-traveled hundreds of years back in history if the spectators hadn't been dressed in twenty-first century clothing.

Charles was missing something extraordinary. She knew he would have loved it. She looked at her watch and hoped he still might call today, so she kept her cell phone in her pocket, in case he did.

Like Jessie, Mary brought her camera. She said it was the first time she'd ever watched the Palio from an apartment balcony. It was the Canon AE1 she'd had since her first trip to Italy – the one that used to be her father's. She hadn't up-graded to a digital one in spite of everyone's encouragement. She liked the classic camera.

"Usually we watch it on TV at home," Mary said. "Since we're not Sienese and not involved with a *contrada*, we don't have the emotional tie to the event. But I always enjoy it."

"Everyone does," Alex said. "It's a living history book."

CHAPTER 46

༺༻

ABOUT NINETY MINUTES into the parade, Jessie's phone rang. She hoped it was Charles, but caller ID indicated otherwise. It was an international number. Jessie stepped into the stairwell of the apartment building to answer it.

"Hello."

"Jessie?"

"Yes."

"This is Maria Rosario. I was outside today and found a piece of paper under the bushes with your name on it. I believe it is the receipt from the courier. He must have dropped it outside when he made the delivery. I remember you asked for it. It seemed important to you."

"Thank you, yes. Could you give me the sender's name?"

"It is difficult for me to pronounce. I will try. Dur-breed-je. It is listed two times."

"Durbridge and Durbridge," Jessie said.

She was shocked.

"Does it say anything more?"

"No," Maria said. "That is all. I hope it is helpful."

"More helpful than you can imagine. *Mille grazie.*"

Jessie hung up, wondering who from the office would have sent it.

She thought about the last message – 'You can't get away from me in Italy. Marry Charles and I'll send all your photos to him.' Then she fired through the mental list of every person in the office – James, the paralegals, the administrative assistants, Charles' father and Charles.

The only one who might have motive was James since he was vying for a partnership, Jessie thought, but he really didn't seem like the type to be a stalker. James was a self-described bookworm, and his pale skin and slight physique supported his claim. His wife, Rebecca, had met him when she worked part-time at Tulane University's bookstore.

But she couldn't figure out how James – or anyone in the office – could have had access to the photos.

This new information about the sender's address was more upsetting than having none at all, but Jessie had to get her act together and go back into the apartment.

"Everything okay?" Mary asked, checking on Jessie in the stairwell.

"Oh, yes. It was Charles' cousin. We accidentally left some clothes and his assistant is going to mail them to us."

She couldn't believe she had lied again. She had to stop this bad behavior.

Mary and Jessie went back into the apartment. Soon the parade finale started with local police officials mounted on horses. They were wielding long, shiny swords. On the first lap their horses walked, and on the second they charged. One mishap and it would have been a very bloody scene.

CHAPTER 47

༻ৡ০৫৫৬

IT WAS FINALLY TIME for the race to start.

After nearly ten minutes of nerve-wracking juggling of lineups and re-lineups, the horses took off. At the second turn, there was a horrible collision with four jockeys flying off their horses. Those in the lead were not affected and continued to run the three laps with the Ram *contrada* winning easily.

As soon as the race ended, residents of the Ram *contrada* charged their horse and jockey, smothering and kissing the animal and the athlete. Grown men cried. Women screamed. The jockey became an instant hero, and the horse was worshipped.

Jessie and Stella watched in disbelief.

"We told you you've never seen anything like this," Mary said. "It's astounding."

"I wanted to take pictures during the race," Jessie said. "But I was afraid I'd miss something important if I put the camera up to my face."

"That's what usually happens to me, too," Mary said, laughing. "Days and days of preparation are all over in 90 seconds."

"Sounds like my ex-husband," Stella said. "The 90-second part."

Mary and Jessie were the only ones who laughed, because no one else heard her.

Alex suggested they all walk toward the Duomo where the Sienese would cram into the church for a post-Palio service.

In the streets, some Sienese were jubilant and others were sobbing.

"As I said before, there's an extreme level of pride for the winning neighborhood," Mary explained to Jessie and Stella. "There's only one winner, and coming in second place is worse than last.

"The sociology here is unique. The neighborhood is everyone's extended family, so the community watches out for each other. There's fierce loyalty and respect for one's *contrada* and no one wants to disgrace it. Because of this, the crime rate is exceptionally low. Kids and teenagers can't get away with trouble because they're under the watchful eye of everyone in their neighborhood."

Jessie thought how Siena would have been the perfect world for her, not discounting Norma's successful mothering. If she lived in Siena, her family could have grown to thousands of people.

The group stopped in a bar for prosecco to celebrate their first Palio, and afterward Alex's customers returned to their apartment. Alex went out to find his friends and invited Jessie to join him, but she opted to stay with her Chianti Girls.

CHAPTER 48

❧❧❧❧

Terzano, Tuscany

BACK AT THE CASTLE, Stella decided to go to bed because she still had jet lag.

Jessie and Mary sat on the patio talking late into the night. Jessie had more glasses of wine than she could count throughout the afternoon and evening. She felt happy, but her body language must have been saying something else because Mary asked her what was wrong.

"I'm all right," Jessie said.

"Something happened after you got that phone call earlier. Want to talk?"

Jessie couldn't believe Mary's sensitivity. Her immediate reaction was to say there was nothing. But she wanted to let go of the painful, shaming secret she'd carried for two years. She had tried to work out the problem on her own, but so far, she'd only been successful at keeping it quiet.

And of all people, it was Mary who picked up on it.

"I think you're psychic too," Jessie said.

"Oh, I'm far from it. I'm just like a dog. I watch people's body language and patterns. I sense when something shifts or when people get out of their routines."

"That's not far from being psychic because that's all about trusting your intuition."

"I've finally learned to trust mine," Mary said. "It took a long time. So what happened today?"

Jessie couldn't lie anymore. She had no reason to lie to Mary, and she didn't want to lie.

"You're right. I'm upset, and I've been doing my best not to show it."

Jessie sighed.

"Let's hear it," Mary said.

"I've never spoken about this with anyone."

Jessie's heart was beating fast. She wondered if Mary could see her chest pounding.

"I have a stalker."

"A stalker?"

Mary tilted her head with a quizzical expression. She didn't expect Jessie to say this, but immediately suspected this stalker was probably the devil Dorotea had predicted.

"Do you feel scared?"

"No, not really. I'm more embarrassed by it," Jessie said. "I've tried to make it go away without getting anyone else involved."

"Oh, Jessie. You're so hard on yourself. Let me help. Tell me what's going on."

Jessie nodded and sighed.

"When we went to Gregory's villa for our bags, a letter from the stalker showed up. It's the eighth one in two years, and I am baffled about who sends them, especially this one. Only a handful of people know I'm here."

"What does the letter say?"

Jessie sat quietly for a short time. She had practiced not talking about this for so long it was almost impossible to divulge it now.

"The same type of thing as always."

Jessie paused again not sure if she could do it.

"Does Charles know about this?" Mary asked, even though she thought she already knew the answer to her question.

"No. I can't tell him. I haven't told anyone. Not a single person."

Mary couldn't imagine having a stalker and keeping it secret for two years. She thought Jessie's emotional walls were thicker than the walls of the castle.

"Do you feel like you're in danger?" Mary asked.

"No, not really. They're not threatening in a physical way, but someone surely wants to make me miserable."

Jessie sighed and started to explain.

CHAPTER 49

☙☙☙☙

"I USED TO DATE a really cool photographer named Frankie. It was more than dating, he was my first love. He took hundreds pictures of me, and they were intimate."

She had a hard time looking Mary in the eye as she said this.

"Our agreement was they were only for us. Frankie was perfecting his photography skills, and I was his subject. They were highly sensual, and honestly, it was fun."

Her face blushed and she continued.

"But now someone has all the nude photos of me. On my birthday and at random holidays, one of them is mailed to me along with a degrading message. And since we're here, I really thought I wouldn't get one on my birthday this year."

"That's horrible. Do you think Frankie sends them?"

"No, I don't. He's not the type of guy to do that. And I specifically asked him, and he said he wasn't sending them. I believe him."

"Who else would have his photos?"

"That's what I can't figure out."

Jessie was glad to have someone else give her ideas, so she picked up the pace of her story.

"Frankie was a rambler and made it clear from the day I met him he was a solo traveler. He didn't want to fall in love and be tied down. But he stayed three years. I was surprised it lasted as long as it did, and I think he was, too. It was a wonderful romantic time together. We truly loved each other. But one day he said he had to move on and he didn't invite me. I knew it was coming. I was just glad it lasted as long as it did.

"When he left, he let me keep his computer because I'd been using it for my classes. Nearly all the photos were on the computer.

"About a week after he left, someone broke into my apartment. Drawers and cabinets were emptied and my stuff was thrown everywhere. The robbers took the computer, TV, DVD player, a couple of my gold rings and a leather jacket. I'm sure they stole anything that could be resold for quick drug money."

"Do you have any idea who did it?"

"Not really. There's a lot of crime where I live, so it wasn't a huge surprise. I reported it to the police. They asked if it could have been Frankie, and I'd already called him. He was in Georgia getting ready to hike part of the Appalachian Trail and do some nature photography. He was as upset about it as I was.

"So I think the computer ended up in the wrong hands, but somehow in the hands of someone who knows me."

Jessie didn't say it, but she feared the sender was someone who'd seen her dance at the club. She thought maybe someone wanted to rub her face in the dirt of her past. But she didn't want to tell Mary about the dancing.

"It's so confusing and as you can imagine, my greatest fear is that Charles will find out about the photos and the stalker. And this latest letter has been really upsetting because someone was serious enough to track me down here. I thought the sender was all talk, but now I'm freaked out it's going to get messy."

"The only good thing about getting that letter is that it should help you reduce the number of people you suspect," Mary said.

"I thought the same. But it's still not obvious."

"Have you considered hiring a detective before it gets more serious?"

"Well, I was thinking I might be able to ask Patrick for some direction. I tried to find him yesterday, but couldn't."

Tears started to roll down Jessie's cheeks.

"I want to help you," Mary said. "I know it hasn't been easy to talk about this, so I'm going to suggest you get some rest tonight, and let's talk more over coffee in the morning."

Mary took her off the hook by not asking more questions, which Jessie appreciated.

"Sounds good."

"Stella's had some crazy stuff happen with old boyfriends, but never a stalker. Usually they're deadbeats who take her money, car or furniture and leave her in debt. She's a good one to help you, too, because she's hit bottom more than once. And she can be trusted."

"I don't have any friends at home who I can talk to. It's strange to say this, but I feel like I'm closer to you and Stella than anyone I know."

"Then she and I are the lucky ones," Mary said, and smiled. "Come on, let's head upstairs and get some sleep."

As Jessie undressed in front of the bathroom mirror, she saw the large fleur-de-lis tattoo wrapped around her right hip. The older dancers at the club where she had worked said men liked tattoos and would tip better if she had one. Jessie chose the New Orleans symbol because it was her home, but now it was a constant reminder of those dark months of dancing in the seedy club on Bourbon Street. Now the tattoo's purpose was to keep her humble. And fortunately Charles liked it.

She sighed. Making confessions to Mary felt good. She was always afraid the truth would scare people away. Instead, she realized it could create a closer bond.

After she brushed her teeth, Jessie crawled in bed and fell asleep within minutes to the scent of lavender.

CHAPTER 50

MARY WAS WORRIED about her new friend and couldn't sleep. She was trying to think of who this devil tormenting Jessie could be. She didn't believe Jessie deserved all the challenges life had served up, and she couldn't help but compare her own life to Jessie's and feel thankful.

After thirty minutes of trying to fall asleep, she got up and found her laptop. She slipped back in bed and opened her email account. She had a message from Luca.

> Subject: Re: The card game
>
> How will I negotiate today with your naked body on my mind?
>
> Luca
>
> PS Please do not stop writing these letters!

Mary laughed. She loved his reply, and of course, she would write more for him. It was easy to imagine making love just about anywhere with Luca. But tonight she was feeling highly sentimental.

Even though she had promised more love letters, right now she could only think of his tender affection.

She wanted his warm body tangled with hers. She wanted to hear him breath and to take in the scent of his body. She coveted his love and warmth. He could be so gentle, and that was what she craved most right now.

Subject: Missing you

Hi sweetie,

We went to Siena for the race today and were lucky to watch it from an apartment overlooking the Campo. I think it's the best way to see the race other than on TV. Stella and Jessie really enjoyed experiencing it for the first time.

Ram won easily, and I still can't believe how the event doesn't change from year to year.

Everything else is running like usual, except my body. It's horribly deprived of you. I want you to walk in this bedroom and crawl in bed with me. I want to hold you and kiss you. I want to hear your voice and see your eyes. I want to feel your hands on every square inch of my body. I want to hear your breath and taste your lips. My body is lost without you and so is my heart.

We are so lucky to have each other and to share our love. You are a wonderful husband and father. Thank you for everything you are.

I'm going to close my eyes, and I plan to dream of you.

Mary

CHAPTER 51

❦❦❦❦❦

MARY KNOCKED ON Jessie's door at 9 a.m.

Jessie was already awake and dressed in a vintage printed sheath dress. She had been lying on her bed thinking about a frustrating early morning dream about trying to plan a party, but she kept forgetting to do things and had to keep changing her outfits.

"Good morning, how are you today?" Mary asked.

"Good."

It was a lie.

"No, I'm not good. I'm nervous."

"Remember, you can't do this alone and you don't have to. Your family has grown. You have Stella and me now. We've been around the block a time or two and lived through more crazy situations than you can imagine."

Jessie smiled.

"I know you're right. It's time for me to get my head out of the sand. Thank you for encouraging me."

They met Stella in the dining room and sat down at the well-weathered oak table.

Stella was fawning over Jessie's dress when the phone rang.

Mary jumped up to get it.

"Hello again. I'm sorry. I'll have Giovanni there soon."

Mary called her brother-in-law immediately.

"The Germans in Unit 2 have no electrical power."

She nodded her head as she listened to Giovanni complain and curse before agreeing to take care of the repair. Then Mary returned to the table.

"I'm definitely beginning to believe there's a hex on Cielo. We're having more problems there than we do in this house and Ribelli combined."

"I wouldn't be surprised," Jessie said. "I think you might have friendly spirits here. I heard laughter again last night and went into the hallway to make sure I wasn't dreaming it. I was sure I heard whispers from a man and a woman as I opened the door, but it stopped as soon as I walked a couple steps out of my room."

"Really?" Stella asked. "Ghosts right here?"

"I think so," Jessie said. "Sometimes I sense them. These are friendly, happy ghosts. I almost felt as though they were trying to get me out of my room to have fun."

"It's a good thing I pass out drunk every night when I go to bed!" Stella said. "It would scare the shit out of me!"

Mary laughed at Stella, but told her it was time for Jessie to talk about something serious.

Stella behaved while Jessie reiterated the story she'd told Mary the night before.

"Oh my," Stella said. "Sounds like you need Nancy Drew."

"Nancy who?" Jessie asked.

"Nancy Drew," Stella said. "We read her books when we were kids, but I guess they weren't as popular with your generation. Nancy solved mysteries in a pleated wool skirt, blouse, pearls, penny loafers and a cashmere sweater tied around her neck. People knew how to dress then. My favorite was 'The Ghost of Blackwood Hall' where Nancy, George and Bess go to New Orleans to investigate ghosts in the French Quarter. I'm surprised neither of you have read it.

"There are definitely ghosts in the French Quarter," Jessie said.

"Let's find Patrick," Mary said, standing up. "I'm sure he has a good idea or two, better than Nancy Drew."

She raised an eyebrow toward Stella.

The ladies walked the shortcut to the Ribelli farmhouse.

"I can't believe I'm finally meeting the famous Patrick Sullivan after all these years," Stella said.

"Promise me you'll be on your best behavior," Mary said.

They found Patrick sitting with the farm dogs curled up next to him, drinking coffee at an outdoor table near the office. Like usual, he wore a fishing hat and dark sunglasses.

"Hey, Patrick," Mary said.

"Hi, Mary from Philly and Jessie from New Orleans," he said. "It's a treat to see you today. Who's your lovely redheaded friend?"

"This is Stella, also from Philly."

"Hi, Stella from Philly."

"You moved to the castle without your boyfriend, I saw," Patrick said to Jessie.

"Yes."

"Are you sure you're okay with him being home alone in New Orleans? That's a city where it's easy to get into trouble."

Jessie blushed. No kidding, she thought.

Mary kept the conversation on track with Patrick.

"Are you wearing your detective cap today? We need help."

"What are you girls into this time?" he asked. "Let me guess. One of you is writing a novel and you need an interesting detective character like me for your book to solve a crime of passion?"

Jessie blushed again. She was embarrassed by the whole situation.

"I'm writing a book," Mary said. "But it's not a mystery and that's not why we're here. Jessie has a serious issue, and we're hoping you can give us some direction."

"I'm ready, what's up?"

The ladies sat down on the chairs next him.

Jessie spoke first.

"My family issue is taken care of, so you can forget about that project. I'd rather have your help with this."

"Okay," Patrick said, interested.

"Someone is harassing Jessie," Mary said.

She summarized the situation for Patrick so Jessie didn't have to repeat it.

"I think she needs a private detective," Mary said.

"Well, you've come to the right guy," Patrick said. "Let's get to business."

"You can talk now?" Mary asked.

"Ah, why not? I still have that fucking ten-year old debt to repay."

"You do have a soft side," Mary said teasing him.

"Don't tell anyone," Patrick said. "First let me get some facts from you, Miss Jessie."

Jessie let out a big sigh. She knew she could only make the problem go away if she opened up, but it still wasn't easy. She was irritated the stalker was affecting her new friendships. She wanted easygoing relationships with Mary and Stella, and she didn't want to be so needy.

But she remembered Mary's advice. She couldn't make it go away without doing something about it.

"What do you need to know first?" Jessie asked.

"When did you get the first letter?"

"About two years ago."

"And when did Frankie leave?"

"In 2005, a few months before Katrina."

"That tells me it took time for someone to find the photos and decide what to do with them. Okay, go on."

Jessie sighed again and silently told herself to just let go and open up.

"Seriously, Jessie," Stella said. "We all have a past and sometimes circumstances cause us to behave in ways we didn't think possible. I'm far from perfect, and I like it that way. It means I haven't been afraid to jump in the fire and live. Remember getting kicked out of that dance club for six months, Mary? We deserved it!"

Jessie smiled, curious about Stella's story, but right now she had to confess her own.

Jessie took a deep breath and told them about her upbringing in New Orleans, including her mom and her Aunt Norma.

"Norma tried to teach me right from wrong, and she did a good job. I stayed out of trouble all through school, thanks to her. She never hid anything from me and gave me all the 'adult' talks as soon as I could understand them. She covered drugs, sex, pregnancy and alcohol. She always told me information was power and she wanted me to make good decisions. I did, but I also believed money was power and my ticket to a better life. And I never dreamed I'd go to college."

Her paced slowed. She hadn't planned to go down this path but realized she needed to tell them everything.

"After graduation, I waited tables with a high school friend named Michelle. We wanted to become California girls. But we needed to make money faster to get to L.A. We were desperate."

She rolled her eyes at herself and continued.

"In New Orleans there are many 'easy' options to make big money – being an escort, bartending, waiting on tables at high end restaurants or dancing.

"By escorting we could have made the most money, but we knew it was dangerous. At least we had some sense."

She shook her head.

"Server positions in the high-end restaurants were hard to get, and bartending wasn't a bad option. But we heard dancing was better money. And it was.

"Michelle and I were hired with some other young girls at a Bourbon Street club. The older ladies taught us a few moves, gave us costumes and wigs, and we were in business. My stage name was Jasmine and Michelle's was Moriah. We were paid cash and kept most of our tips.

"For about a year we raked in the dough and got our own apartment in the Quarter, closer to work, but it was still in a rough area.

"One night, Michelle and I got off work in the early morning and were craving pancakes. We went to the Clover Grill and I met Frankie at the counter. He was sitting in the seat next to me. I told him I was a dancer. He was no dummy and came in the club the next night to see me.

"After my shift, he was waiting outside and took me back to the Clover Grill. He told me he had fallen for me when he met me the night before. It was the beginning of my first real relationship. He moved in right away and we truly fell in love. He's the one who made me quit dancing. He said I was too good for it. That's when I started waiting on tables again. I really loved Frankie and it lasted three years, but he had made it clear from the beginning he wasn't the marrying kind."

"He sounds like your old boyfriend Ian," Stella said to Mary. "Those artsy types always seem to be living in muddied waters. They're always trying to find their way."

Mary nodded. She understood. She had loved Ian even though she knew there wasn't ever a possibility of a long-term commitment.

"Frankie was definitely the artistic type," Jessie said. "For several years before we met, he had traveled from city to city living on a shoestring, taking cool pictures.

"He loved New Orleans and took lots of photos of the churches, buildings, roofs and wrought iron balconies. He took photos of the foliage, the river, zoo animals, jazz musicians, nightclubs and bars. He had a real passion for the city and took amazing photos. He was also disheartened by the city's poverty, and he captured troubled people and their situations. He didn't sell those photos, though. He wanted to put together a photo essay."

"Is his website still active for the ones he sold?" Patrick asked.

"No, he didn't have a website. I never saw him sell any photos directly. He was selling them to one of the large photo stock companies."

Patrick nodded.

"He had one more passion for a photography subject. Me." Her face got warm as she explained the nude photos.

Mary watched Patrick purse his lips and rub his beard again.

"Frankie said he wouldn't be happy until he had 365 photos of me, one for every day of the year."

"Did he take that many?"

"Nope, I remember the last one. It was number 222 and he said two's were his lucky number."

"They sure weren't lucky for you," Patrick said. "He could have lied and sold them."

Stella coughed.

Jessie turned a deeper shade of red. This whole experience was so embarrassing.

Everyone knew Patrick had to explore everything, but it was painful.

"I truly doubt he would have sold the photos. How much could they be worth?"

"Well," said Patrick. "You're a pretty girl and those porn rags are always looking for new young models."

"You're right, and I can see why you would suspect him. But I don't."

"Okay, go on," Patrick said.

"Frankie's the person who encouraged me to take art classes and go to college part-time. He helped me understand my 'ticket' to happiness wasn't about having money or moving to L.A - it was about following my talent and passion. Because of his inspiration I finished my Bachelor's degree. It took me six years part-time, but I finally did it. At one point, I was working in a coffeehouse in the early morning, taking classes during the day and waiting tables at night."

"The harder you work for something the more you appreciate it," Mary said.

Patrick stuck to business.

"What happened to Frankie?"

"He kept building his photography portfolio and sometimes he would travel for a day or two for photo shoots. When money was tight, he'd bartend at a place on Esplanade. It was owned by someone he knew from Denver."

"Were drugs in the picture?"

"Um, yeah. He smoked weed and sometimes there were strangers stopping by selling and buying the stuff. I didn't like that part of it. I tried to keep everything valuable locked up, not that I have much. We even had a couple of arguments about it. It was the only issue we ever disagreed about. I told him I didn't want to get involved with drugs because I'd seen people get into big trouble when I was younger.

"After he left, someone broke into my apartment. I assumed it was someone who Frankie had known looking for weed."

"Did your roommate still live there?"

"No, she moved in with another dancer from the club after Frankie moved in."

"Did you report the break-in to the police?" Patrick asked.

"Yes, they questioned me and searched our apartment."

"You had nothing to do with the drugs?" Patrick asked.

His skepticism appeared to be growing.

"Not at all," Jessie said.

Mary defended Jessie.

"I believe her, Patrick. Why would she lie to us? She could walk away right now and never see us again if she so chose. But she needs help."

"Yeah, yeah," he grumbled.

He sounded like the stereotypical retired detective portrayed in TV movies.

"Give it to me straight, Jessie. No lies."

Stella gave Patrick a dirty look.

"I have been and I will," Jessie said.

"Is Charles aware of all this?" Stella asked. "He's a lawyer, so he could access records, I think."

"Who's Charles?" Patrick asked.

"He's my fiancé."

"Oh, the tall one who went home."

"I haven't told him any of this. I'm embarrassed about it. His family has a successful law firm started by his grandfather, and he hopes to be a partner by the end of the year."

"Does he know about your time as a dancer?" Patrick asked.

"No," she said quietly. "And there shouldn't be any record of it, since I was only paid in cash."

"Jessie, if they're a wealthy family, and it sounds like they are, I would think they've already checked you out. Especially since they're in the legal field."

"Well, maybe."

Jessie hadn't really thought about this.

"Would they try to drive Jessie away?" Stella asked. "Could they could be behind all this?"

"Anyone is a candidate," Patrick said. "Tell me about Charles."

CHAPTER 52

JESSIE TOLD THEM about the family law practice and how she met Charles in the coffeehouse.

"We are definitely opposites, but it works. Ten months ago we got engaged."

"Did you get the threats before you met Charles?" Patrick asked.

"The first one was on my birthday two years ago. Let me think. Frankie left in 2005 and I started working in the coffeehouse next to Charles' office in 2007. I met Charles after I'd been there a couple of years, but we didn't go out for months."

"What the hell is up with coffeehouses?" Patrick asked. "Why don't people make their coffee at home? It's better than that over-roasted shit, and it's a helluva lot less expensive."

Mary lightened the subject.

"Patrick used to pack his Mr. Coffee coffeemaker every year when he came to Italy, because he hated Italian coffee and espresso. He likes a big mug, not one shot at a time. Since he's here all the time, we let him leave the coffeemaker."

Patrick resumed his questioning.

"It sounds like the letters started arriving the same year you met Charles. What do they say?"

Jessie sighed. She had them memorized because she was always trying to figure out who was sending them.

"I'll tell you what they say, but I'm not going to describe the photos. Use your imagination."

They all nodded.

"The first one on my birthday two years ago was 'The only way you could attract a rich boy was with your body. He's not with you for your brains.'

"The next one came two months later. It said, 'One year with that asshole?'"

"Yikes," Stella said. "Somebody's got a bad attitude."

"Then there was a Valentine's Day letter – 'Valentine's Day is for idiots and sluts. You're a slut, so I'm sure you'll be celebrating with your idiot boyfriend.'

"The next one was on Mother's Day – 'Your poor mother has a slut for a daughter.'"

Stella and Mary cringed.

"It's awful," Jessie said. "On my next birthday, the message was 'Happy Birthday, skanky piece of Tremé shit!'

"Two months later I got one on our second anniversary – 'Your boyfriend is only dating you for sex. Too bad your present is his pencil dick.' That was the day Charles proposed.

"This year on Valentine's Day I got the first one with a threat about telling Charles. It said, 'You don't get it, do you? You're a slut and Charles needs to know about the 177 photos.' This is the letter that made me decide it definitely wasn't Frankie because I knew the last photo he took was number 222."

"Frankie might be psychotic," Patrick said. "He could change the number to make you believe it wasn't him."

"Right, but I really don't think it's him," Jessie said. "Then the last one I got was for my birthday a few days ago. It said, 'You can't get away from me in Italy. Marry Charles and I'll send all your photos to him.'

"So someone is trying to harass you," Patrick said. "He or she isn't necessarily trying to bribe you. Who wouldn't want you to marry Charles?"

"I have no idea. His parents and sisters seem to like me."

"How do the letters arrive?" Patrick asked.

"In New Orleans, they show up at my apartment mailbox, but I've never seen one delivered. The person is sneaky. Here, in Italy, a courier delivered it. I don't have a copy of the receipt, but I learned the sender was 'Durbridge and Durbridge,' the family law practice."

"Any name could have been written on the receipt," Patrick said. "It could be someone who wants you to think it came from the office."

"Who?" Jessie asked.

Tears began welling in her eyes again.

"Someone who doesn't like you, is envious of you or wants something from you."

"I can imagine someone not liking me, but not someone being envious of me. My life hasn't been something I would imagine anyone wanting. And I have nothing to give."

"Is the packaging the same on all the envelopes?" Patrick asked.

"Yeah. Here's a sample."

She showed the latest one without handing it over.

"Same handwriting every time?"

"Yes."

"You don't recognize the handwriting?"

"No, not at all."

"Do you have any jealous old boyfriends? Or know of any crazy ex-girlfriends of Frankie or Charles? Or how about your roommate, Michelle?"

"Frankie was my first love and my only ex-boyfriend," she said. "Michelle isn't smart enough to do something like this. And neither guy mentioned any serious ex-girlfriends. Charles told me once he intentionally waited to be in a serious relationship until he was close to becoming a partner."

"You believe them?"

"Yes. Both are trustworthy guys."

"Well, let me give all of this more thought," Patrick said. "I'll send my buddy in New Orleans an email and see if I can get him involved. We'll need to track down Frankie since they were his photos. He's a prime suspect although you and the clues might indicate otherwise. How do we contact him?"

"I'm not sure. We lost contact a couple of years ago."

"Do you know the name of the stock photo company that hired him?"

"He never told me."

"Did you two do anything outside of the sack?" he asked, with a raised eyebrow.

She blushed.

"If you see his photos will you recognize them?" Patrick asked.

"I'm sure I would."

"Let me go upstairs and get my laptop. I need to take a piss, too."

He left and the dogs followed him.

Stella laughed at him when he was out of sight, but Mary felt like she needed to defend him.

"He's only gruff on the outside. I think he has a kind heart but doesn't want anyone to see it."

"The hell he does," Stella said. "He did what he could to keep you from getting involved with Luca, and he's been harsh with Jessie."

"It's just his façade," Mary said.

"Bullshit," Stella said. "Think about the consequences of what he did. If he hadn't meddled, you could have saved yourself a marriage and divorce. Luca would have been your second husband instead of Garrett. He fucked things up."

"Maybe. But I can't change the past. And Patrick's willing to help now."

"Let's not give him credit until he delivers," Stella said. "Working with him might be like working with Shaggy and Scooby-Doo. And don't overlook the fact he's talking to us like a chauvinist. He's giving me a headache. By any chance does anyone have alcohol? I'm too sober."

The ladies laughed at Stella. She talked about drinking more than she actually consumed.

Patrick returned, puffing on a cigarette.

"Okay, girls. Let me show you how easy this is going to be since we have his first and last name."

He looked at Jessie and raised his eyebrows.

"Frankie's a nomad so I doubt you'll find anything," Jessie said.

"Then he's not a good businessman."

"He's not worried about that. He's an artist."

Patrick huffed.

Stella pursed her lips.

Patrick entered a search for "stock photos New Orleans" and then asked Jessie if she'd ever done a search like this.

"Nope, because I don't think Frankie is the stalker. I've never thought it was him, and he told me he wasn't."

Patrick shook his head showing his general distrust of people, and he showed her the first website he found.

"Nope, none of that's his," Jessie said.

Patrick continued his search.

"Those are his," Jessie said on the third site he opened.

"No photographer names are assigned to the photos, but let me see what I can find out from this company."

"Isn't his work good?"

Jessie pointed at the photos she recognized.

"Very good," Mary said. "I like the blurred time-elapsed images in black and white. Very mystical."

"I'm going to email the company," Patrick said. "We might be able to find him more easily than you expected."

"What else do you need?" Mary asked Patrick.

"I need a list of information from Jessie – her full name, address, phone number, email and employer, and the same for her boyfriend. I'll send this in an email to Vic when I follow up with the photo company."

"Thanks, Patrick," Jessie said.

Jessie took his computer and typed all the info into a blank email.

"I'll tell Vic to contact you in a week or two after you're back in New Orleans."

"Thanks," Mary and Jessie said at the same time.

"Bye, ladies," he said as he shooed them away.

CHAPTER 53

WHEN THE LADIES arrived at the castle, Giovanni was waiting. He was angry.

"Do you ever carry your phone?" he asked Mary.

"I've only been gone 45 minutes."

"You own a goddam business. It's 24-hour work. You always need to carry the fucking phone."

"I made a mistake," she said. "Why are you so upset?"

"All the electricity is shut down at Cielo. The main breaker of the goddam house needs to be repaired. We need to move the renters out of Cielo."

"What would cause that to happen?"

"The fucking Sardi!"

"All right, all right. We can take care of this. There's an open apartment at Ribelli, and I'll have them move over now."

She called the German renters and Herr Proske answered.

She apologized and offered them a complimentary room at the Ribelli for the rest of their stay. In a matter of minutes, they reached an agreement and she explained the easy directions to the farmhouse and told them she'd meet them there.

"I have the guests taken care of, how long until you have the breaker box working?" she asked Giovanni.

"Depends on when I can get the fucking part. I'll call you, so keep your phone with you."

He huffed and walked away.

"Whoa," Stella said. "For a scrawny, little guy he sure has a loud mouth. What's wrong with him? What did he say?"

"He's just a bitter man," Mary said.

Then she translated the conversation for the ladies.

"I'll need some time to move the guests," Mary said, "But I'll be back soon."

An hour later, Mary's customers were in a new apartment at the Ribelli. She upgraded their rental to the only apartment with a rooftop balcony, and she threw in some bottles of wine.

"The customers liked the Ribelli apartment better," she said.

"What a day," Stella said. "You two are making my life feel like a cake walk."

CHAPTER 54

ཨༀༀ⌘ལ

THAT NIGHT, Alex took the young boys out for dinner so the ladies could have one last dinner together. Then he dropped them off at Marco's house. He planned to go out with friends and said he wouldn't be coming back. He told Jessie goodbye and that he hoped to get to New Orleans one day.

The ladies asked Jessie what she wanted for dinner on her last night and she requested wood-fired pizza. There was nothing like it in New Orleans. Or if there was, she didn't know about it.

So they went to the nearby pizzeria.

They ordered a classic Margherita pizza with buffalo mozzarella, basil and tomatoes. And they ordered a spicy Diavolo pizza with salami, mozzarella and red sauce.

When Jessie took her first bite, she thought she had died and gone to heaven. Busy eating, they all stopped talking and enjoyed the pizza.

Then Mary asked Jessie and Stella what they would eat if they could only eat one food for the rest of their life.

"This!" Jessie said.

"Ditto," Stella said.

"To my Chianti Girls," Mary said and lifted her wine.

Pizza was her favorite, too, and had been since her first trip to Italy.

Jessie had never been happier than she was in this moment.

Mary and Stella embraced her like they'd always known her, sharing fun and embarrassing stories about themselves.

And they made it easy for her to chime in with her own crazy tales. She could share with abandon.

"Where's the tequila?" Stella asked once they were back at the castle.

"I hid it from you after that first night so we could all stay out of trouble!" Mary said, but she still grabbed the bottle from a kitchen cabinet.

"Olé!" Stella said.

They poured shots and as they drank, their stories became funnier.

Jessie heard about their old boyfriends, Stella's fourteen-month marriage and their silly high school hairstyles from the eighties. She never laughed so hard.

Mary and Stella had been friends as long as Jessie had been alive.

Then Stella brought up Jessie's mysterious letters.

"I hope you don't mind, but I have questions about your stalker."

"Okay," Jessie said.

"Are there any ladies in the office who might have a crush on Charles?"

"Most of the staff is older. They're mature, married women, except for one young assistant. It's her first job out of college. She wants to go to law school but doesn't have the money, so she's doing the admin job to immerse herself in the law environment while earning money. She's really serious and into work. She's kind of nerdy."

"Could she have a crush on Charles?"

"Maybe. He's never had a problem with women liking him. But how would she get the pictures? How would anyone get them?"

"That's the million-dollar question," Stella said. "We have no idea where they went after they left the apartment. When do you plan to tell Charles about this?"

"I don't know. But I'm going to have to. It makes me sick to think about the photos, but especially the dancing."

"Let's think about your time as a dancer," Stella said. "Are there any photos or records of it?"

"No, none at all - well, none that I know of."

"So the dancing confession is optional?"

"She's torturing herself holding in all these secrets," Mary said. "She should tell him everything. They need to start their marriage without lies."

Stella didn't agree.

"Sometimes we do shit we don't need to tell everyone. I'm taking some secrets to my grave!"

"Stuff I don't know?" Mary asked.

"Maybe. Well, probably not."

Stella laughed.

"I was desperate for money," Jessie said. "It was stupid to dance. But I should have been smarter than to let Frankie take nude photos of me because they last forever."

Stella tried to make Jessie feel better.

"Charles knows you're hot. That's one of the reasons he's fallen for you. He surely isn't so naïve as to believe no one ever liked you before him or that you were a virgin. He would think Frankie's a smart guy who happened to be talented with a camera."

"Right," Jessie said sarcastically.

Mary defended Jessie again.

"It was only to be shared between the two of you, and it sounded like you really loved each other. I would've done the same if an old boyfriend asked. Why not?"

"No one ever asked you?" Stella asked Mary. "You dated the wrong guys, or you've got something ugly going on we don't want to know about!"

"Aren't you funny Stella?"

Mary snarled her lip before laughing.

"I think it's time for another shot!" Jessie said.

"Hell yes!" Stella said.

Stella poured three more shots.

"Patrick will get to the bottom of this," Mary said after she'd downed her shot. "He's got time on his hands."

"Too bad he's not better looking. I might be able to get my one-night stand out of the way," Stella said.

"Ewwww. Yuck!"

Mary poked her finger in her mouth.

They didn't stop talking until well after midnight. None of them knew exactly what time they went to bed, but they were all exhausted when their alarms buzzed at 5 a.m.

Jessie had to take the earliest bus from Siena to Rome to catch her flight.

CHAPTER 55

ಐಐಐಐಐ

JESSIE HAD A hard time waking up. The taste of toothpaste was sickening.

As she was brushing, she remembered the last thing that happened in the middle of the night. She had only been asleep a short time when laughter woke her. It was louder than the previous night.

She stepped from her room into the hallway and took a few steps with her head cocked sideways trying to hear where the laughter was coming from.

As she tip-toed along the corridor in the dark, she ran straight into Alex.

She quickly threw one arm across her breasts, because she wore a thin, white tank top. The other arm covered her hips, because she wore skimpy panties.

"Excuse me," she said.

"You okay?" he asked.

"Yes, I thought I heard some people out here laughing."

"Just me coming home," he said.

"Laughing?"

"No, running into you."

"Oh."

She turned her head to listen for the laughter and it had stopped.

"I didn't think you were coming back tonight," Jessie said.

"I didn't plan to, but I wanted to see you one more time. Do you know how beautiful you are?"

She was drunk and could tell he was, too. She didn't say anything.

"I know you have a fiancé, but every time I see you I want to kiss you."

"Oh."

Her lips parted in shock and stayed that way.

Without any hesitation, Alex leaned in and kissed her. She backed up.

"We can't –" Jessie said.

"I know we can't," he said. "I'm sorry. I'm just so...I'm so attracted to you. You're beautiful."

"Thanks, but –"

"But you're in love with Charles. I know you are. But if you ever change your mind about marrying him, please make sure I'm the first to know."

CHAPTER 56

❧❧❧❧

As Jessie faced herself in the morning mirror, thoughts came in a rapid fire.

Alex shocked her with his kiss, and she was attracted to him. But she was engaged, and most importantly, in love with Charles.

She gathered her bags and when she was at the bottom of the steps, she heard Alex call her name.

He was upstairs, so she hurried back up.

He had thrown on sports shorts, but he wasn't wearing a shirt. His hair was going in every direction, and he was beyond sexy.

He spoke quietly and looked directly into her eyes.

"Jessie, I know we were both drinking last night, but I meant it when I said I don't want you to forget me."

He hugged her.

"I've been crazy about you since the day we met," Alex said.

"I won't forget you. But I don't know what's going to happen. I'm -"

He interrupted her.

"I know what you're about to say, but I'm going to stay in touch. Watch for my emails."

"That's safe," she said.

He pulled her closely and kissed her behind her ear.

"You're beautiful," he whispered.

A chill ran through her body.

"I gotta run. Mary's waiting."

She hesitated, but then turned away.

Minutes later she was in the passenger seat of Mary's Fiat. She tried not to think about Alex, and wondered if Mary or Stella noticed that Alex had a crush on her. She decided it had to be brushed under the rug.

This was another saying of Norma's - "Just brush it under the rug, honey. Don't make it a bigger deal than it is."

Stella sat in the back because Mary made her ride along as penance for making them drink too much tequila the night before. If they had to get up at 5 a.m., so did Stella.

Fortunately it was a short ride for everyone. And Jessie figured she could sleep on the bus and plane.

"I'm so glad you came in the gallery," Mary said as they all stood outside her car. "I want to hear what happens about finding your father. And I'm sure Patrick and his friend in New Orleans will get you through the other issue. The next time I see you, you'll have all this behind you."

"I think everything will be all right." Jessie had more to say, but it came out simply. "There was a reason I met you. Look at how much better everything is already."

"It was destiny," Mary said. "You've made our lives better, too."

"We're going to make your paintings the desire of every customer of mine," Stella said. "You're going to be a huge success."

"Email pictures of your new paintings and keep us posted about the wedding," Mary said. "Luca and I want to come to New Orleans, so we'd love to be on your guest list. Stella, too. New Year's Eve could be fun."

"Deal," Jessie said. "Then I'll have guests on my side of the church. I'd love for you to be there."

But she doubted the wedding would happen on New Year's Eve.

The three ladies hugged and Jessie had another passenger snap a picture of the three hung-over Chianti Girls in front of the bus.

Jessie took a window seat and watched as Mary and Stella drove away. She cried as she smiled.

Mary and Stella had truly embraced her without judgment and saw her for everything she could be. They appreciated her warts and all. It was a special gift and she knew it.

On the ride back to the castle, Mary decided to tell Stella about Dorotea's prediction about Mary meeting a lady with the devil on her shoulder.

"It's definitely Jessie, isn't it?" Mary asked.

"No doubt about it. She's a sweetheart but sure is carrying a boatload full of shit."

"I know this isn't the last time we'll see her," Mary said. "Her story has only just begun."

Stella nodded her head.

"Next time we see her, let's not invite that asshole called tequila."

CHAPTER 57

꤮ꤩꤪ꤫

AT LAST, Luca's two-week business trip was over. He got home on Sunday, the day after Stella left. Mary made the same trip to the bus station to pick him up, but this time Enzo joined her. He wanted to see his dad as soon as he stepped off the bus.

They arrived a few minutes early and waited in the car for his bus from Rome. When it pulled in, Mary saw him sitting by a window and her heart fluttered, same as it did the day they met.

"There's *papà*," she said. "Let's go."

Enzo ran to hug him and Mary wondered how many more years he would greet his father like this. He was growing up too fast.

Luca hugged her tightly then he kissed her cheek and lingered so he could whisper.

"I have plans for you tonight after you've toyed with me for two weeks."

She laughed and whispered back, "I hope you do!"

During the ride home, the conversation centered mostly on Enzo's soccer games and answering his questions about the United States.

"Cars are big, roads are wide and everyone dresses alike," Luca said. "And they have terrible coffee."

"I don't drink coffee," Enzo said.

"I know and I am glad we are raising you here. I saw lots of pudgy children who do not play soccer every day like you do."

"Will you play with me tonight?"

"Of course."

Luca had played soccer his entire life, and it was how he stayed in excellent condition. He taught Enzo all he knew and enjoyed practicing with him.

Kicking the ball around was the top priority as soon as they were home. All Mary could do was smile at them. Enzo was a clone of his father, which meant he would be a charmer, too. But Luca wouldn't put the same demands on his sons as his father had done.

Luca had grown up knowing he had no choice but to work for his father's leather factory. So he wanted his sons to follow their dreams. He said he hoped one or both of his sons would want to take over the management of the business, but they had plenty of time to plan for that.

At Luca's request, Mary prepared a fresh antipasto plate and they took it to the patio. Enzo practiced head bounces as they sat on the patio eating the meats and cheeses. This food generated more complaints about the U.S. from Luca. He said the meats and cheeses weren't nearly as fresh and most of the Italian restaurants he tried only featured Southern recipes with lots of red sauce and huge pasta portions.

She ignored him and raised her glass of Chianti.

"Congratulations on five contracts with five distributors!"

"*Grazie!* We will be busy!"

"We're not afraid of hard work," Mary said.

"No, but I still need to talk to Alex to find out why the distributor in Atlanta received two shipments instead of one."

"I think I know. It was right after he and Maria broke up when he shipped them. I bet his mind was on other things."

"Women!"

"You need us!"

"I sure do," he said.

He leaned over and kissed her.

"If you two are going to kiss, I'm going inside," Enzo said, taking his ball to practice in the courtyard.

Mary and Luca laughed.

"I love you," Luca told Mary. "Two weeks was too long to be without you."

While they enjoyed the food and wine, Mary gave him a recap on everything that had happened while he was gone. She ended with the news about the plumbing and electric problems at Cielo.

"Giovanni is probably sabotaging the place, only to prove me wrong for buying it. I don't believe there is a Sardinian curse. The next time there is a problem, I'm going myself so I can see what's happening. Please do not call him for help now that I'm home. I think Giovanni's gone mad."

"It's possible. He's strong-willed."

She didn't mention Jessie's revealing dream because he would likely dismiss it. He was tired of hearing about a "curse."

"And he's as nasty as a wild boar," Luca added.

"Everything else has gone smoothly, and there's some tequila left if you want a shot."

"No, thanks. I want this blood of the earth."

He closed his eyes and inhaled the scent of the Chianti wine.

"This is home," he said.

"Yes, now it is, since you're here. It sure isn't the same without you."

"You'll go with me next time. We need to go in the winter."

"I'm so ready to spend some time in Philadelphia. I'm missing everyone."

She hesitated before she made the next statement.

"And while we're there I think you should consider looking for –"

He cut her off before she could say "your father."

"I don't want to do that," he said.

She remembered what Jessie had said about her father possibly being wonderful like Luca.

"What if your father is someone you would admire who could become a friend. You keep thinking he would complicate your life, but he might be as special to you as you are to Alex."

Luca looked away.

"It's possible," he said. "But it could also be a mess. Giovanni and I are already at odds with each other because he believes I've led a more privileged life than he has. If I bring another relative into this family mix, it could get even messier."

"Or it might not."

"I'm too tired to think about it right now."

"Okay, I won't press the topic, but if your father is like you, he's a fantastic man, and he would be Enzo's only living grandfather."

He smiled and kissed her.

"I'll think about it."

Mary had considered emailing Charles and hiring him to find Luca's father, but she didn't want to go against Luca's will. Still, in her gut she knew his father had to be fantastic.

"Alex will be home in an hour and is staying home all night. Elena's out of the picture, and he's taking his time deciding who to date next. I think he might have been attracted to Jessie, but he was quiet about it since she was engaged."

"I didn't let a boyfriend get in my way," Luca said, flirting with his wife.

"No, you didn't!"

She felt her face get warm. She hadn't been able to resist Luca, even when she had a boyfriend.

"Since we won't be home alone tonight, it's good this old place has thick walls," he said, smiling. "I can't wait to devour you, especially after reading and rereading all those emails you sent me."

She had written three more messages while he was gone: The Car Ride, The Tower and The Costume Party. It was easier to write the naughty letters with a buzz and having Stella around made that happen easily.

"My favorite was 'The Card Game.'"

"Want to give it a try?" she asked.

"Where are the cards?"

She laughed and heat ran through her body as she imagined it.

"You think it's been easy for me?"

She nuzzled next to him and rested her head on his shoulder. Then her hand slipped down his torso. His abs were as hard as they were the first time she touched him so many years ago when she jumped on the back of his motorcycle for a tour of Chianti. A few light wrinkles had shown up around his eyes and mouth, and he had a whisper of gray at his temples. He was as handsome as ever and she melted as their bodies touched.

Luca's second food request was for homemade *pici* in the style of "Cacio e Pepe" - cheese and pepper sauce. She enjoyed making it for him and as she was rolling the pici, Alex came in. After greeting his dad, he washed his hands and helped Mary roll the dough. He enjoyed making pasta as much as she did.

She was so happy to have everyone home for dinner that evening.

During dinner, Luca asked Mary how the writing was coming along.

"I think I have some fresh inspiration," she said. "The young American lady gave me some ideas, and I'm excited to see where they take me."

"I like Charles and Jessie," Alex said. "If they invite us to their wedding, we should all go."

"Alex is right," Mary said. "We need to go to New Orleans."

"Well, it's possible," Luca said. "A distributor I would like to meet is located there."

Later that night, Mary and Luca crawled in bed eager to make love, but Luca fell fast asleep while she washed her face and brushed her teeth. Jet lag and several glasses of Chianti got the best of him, and she knew he would be out for hours.

When she slinked into bed, he rolled to his side and draped his arm across her body. She was so comforted by his warmth.

Roosters woke them at sunrise, and they smiled to be in each other's arms. Neither said a word, but they wanted the same thing. It wasn't playing a card game for sexual favors or having sex against an old oak tree, like the tales in her messages to Luca. They craved old-fashioned lovemaking, heated with the undying, fierce passion that had possessed them since they met on a Tuscan summer day so many years ago.

CHAPTER 58

❦❦❦❦

New Orleans, Louisiana

JESSIE VISITED NORMA the day after she returned from Italy. As they looked at photographs from the trip, Jessie told her every detail. She gave Norma dishtowels with Italian recipes printed on them because Jessie knew it was a gift she would use. Norma liked practical gifts - and sweets. So Jessie brought home some of Dorotea's Amaretto cookies as a gift, too.

"That lady Mary sounds like the kind of mother - and friend - you never had," Norma said.

"No one could replace you, but we certainly formed a tight bond in a short time. She gave me the courage to ask Charles to help me find my dad."

"I'm glad you're doing that, but don't get your hopes up too high. I am not tryin' to be Miss Negative, but I don't want your bubble to be burstin'. I'd hate to see you get hurt by him."

"I'll take my chances," Jessie said. "I have nothing to lose at this point, and it sure would be nice to get my questions answered. Charles agreed to delay the wedding until we get through all this."

The night before, Charles agreed to postpone their New Year's Eve wedding date, understanding the importance of Jessie wanting her father walk her down the aisle.

She had asked Charles if they could pare down the guest list, too, but he said they'd have to make a compromise on that issue to avoid upsetting his parents. If they changed the date, they shouldn't mess with the guest list, he said.

Jessie understood his point and was relieved to have more time.

ℰℭ

In the following weeks, Jessie painted every minute she wasn't working at the coffeehouse. A new energy was emerging in her paintings, and her characters expressed even more emotion and vulnerability.

She practiced the landscape scenes of Italy on small canvases until she was pleased with the colors and textures. Then her first large painting featured Mary.

For the setting she chose a view of the castle from the dusty, white road at the bottom of the hill. She outfitted Mary in a long white flowing dress with her hair blowing in the wind and the pocket watch decorating her neck. The tarot card icon was the Queen of Wands, a nurturing, creative and trustworthy personality.

When it was finished, she hung it in the coffeehouse. It was the first painting in her new series "Trouvé" - French for "Found."

She called it "Bella Maria" - "Beautiful Mary" - the lady who found happiness and the love of her life in Tuscany. It wasn't for sale, so she labeled it "Private Collection."

Nearly every customer remarked about it, saying things like, "She looks like an angel," "I want to visit that place," and "So magical."

Her second piece in the Trouvé collection was called "Tuscan Dreamer." It featured another lady who had found the love of her life - Luca's mother, Anna.

In the painting Anna was waiting in the castle tower for her American lover to drive up the long, white road to visit her.

Anna wore a white dress, too, but had a garland of lavender atop her head. The Lovers tarot card icon denoted Anna's true love for the man. This painting was popular with customers as well, but it was marked "Private Collection," too.

Hopefully Mary and Luca would want one or both of the paintings, and she would gladly give them as gifts.

She created smaller paintings of Tuscan scenes in a series called "Tuscan Love," and they were selling faster than she expected. Nearly every customer who bought one had been to Italy and loved it or wanted to take a trip there.

She'd found a good niche and knew she needed to stick with it.

Her friend Papi who stopped in daily for coffee asked to hear tales of Jessie's trip and see photos. Jessie needed a good friend at home and wanted to become better friends with Papi, but when Jessie invited her to dinner, Papi said she had a busy work schedule. She had some type of senior administrative role with the parish and kept talking about how many hours she was working. Jessie was busy painting when she wasn't working anyway, so she just enjoyed their conversations at the coffee house. Sometimes Papi took notes because she was planning a trip to Italy in the spring.

In the meantime, Charles was hitting a lot of dead ends in his search to find Jessie's father. No employment records existed, and he was trying to find a detective to visit Ashland to conduct personal interviews.

He made a commitment to Jessie to find her father, and if it meant he had to go to Kentucky to do the research himself, he would do it. But his biggest problem was limited time, since his father was bombarding him with cases, forcing him to keep late office hours. He'd come home around 8 or 9 p.m., drink a glass or two of Maker's Mark and barely eat. He was losing weight and getting dark circles under his eyes. He rarely had the energy for sex either, and Jessie was worried about him.

He said it would get better after his dad officially made him partner – and as soon as they set a new wedding date.

This was a bit of a Catch-22 for Jessie because she was relying on Charles to find her father before the wedding, but his job had to take priority.

Each day the situation seemed to get worse for Charles.

She wanted to ask Norma to do a card reading for her, but she knew better. Norma wouldn't do them for her often. She always told Jessie, "You need to live your way into the answer."

So Jessie did her best to be patient and live in the moment.

CHAPTER 59

~

Terzano, Tuscany

On the Sunday morning after Luca returned, Dorotea called Mary and asked her to visit because she had baked Luca's favorite treat – apricot *crostata*. And she had fresh almond cookies for Enzo, too.

It was a pretty morning so Mary made the twenty-minute downhill walk to Dorotea's instead of driving.

Dorotea and Mary sat on the patio catching up on gossip while drinking coffee. She confirmed the Puccis were having fertility problems and didn't have the money for a specialist. And she still didn't know how the Moris paid for the new appliances delivered a couple days earlier. She also said Rossana was going to the doctor often but she didn't know why.

Dorotea was aware of every activity in the area. Her gifts of sugar definitely worked as a bribe to get information from people.

Mary decided it was time to ask Dorotea if she knew why people thought there was a hex on Cielo. If anyone knew, Dorotea would.

"Yes, I'm familiar with the hex."

She nodded her head and appeared to be deciding how much to say.

Mary waited, not wanting to rush her.

"The Sardi lived there when I was a teenager," she finally said.

"Were they kicked out?"

"Yes."

"Were they angry?"

"Very."

Dorotea was responding, even if her answers were brief, so Mary kept asking questions hoping to get more information.

"Giovanni tells me it's hexed, and recently, we had an American guest who had a strong sense of ghosts in Cielo and in our home too."

"Oh, the lady with the tall boyfriend?"

Mary giggled because Dorotea knew everything that happened in the area.

"Yes, Jessie is her name. She said she heard a young man and woman laughing in the middle of the night at our house."

"Do you believe her?"

"I do. She had no motive to lie. Before she went home she told me it happened every night. But she never saw any apparitions."

"It was probably the Sardi."

Dorotea knew more than she was telling, so Mary sat quietly hoping that if she didn't push, Dorotea would open up.

It worked.

"They were kind people," Dorotea said. "But misunderstood because they were different."

"That seems to happen in every culture, doesn't it?"

"Yes. It was disappointing. They were hard workers and never bothered anyone."

Dorotea went in the kitchen and returned with grappa.

"I don't drink in the morning, but today I must. Will you join me?"

"Sure," Mary said, a bit surprised.

After two small shots and at least five minutes of silence, Dorotea spoke.

"I'm old and I doubt I have many seasons left, so it's time for me to tell someone. And I know you always like a good story."

Her eyes twinkled. Mary was all ears.

"I was a young teenager after the war. That is when the Sardi clan settled in the empty villa. The country was different then. It was depressed and many people abandoned those old farms and headed to the cities for work. Sometimes wanderers, vagrants or opportunists like the Sardi would occupy the empty homes. They came to Tuscany seeking conflict-free living, but mostly for work."

Mary had heard this history lesson before, so she wasn't surprised the Sardi might have moved in rent-free.

"Most of the Sardi were shepherds," Dorotea said.

Mary nodded her head. Remembering Jessie's visions of sheep, a chill ran up her spine.

"My girlfriend Patrizia and I would walk through the woods and spy on the Sardi after we finished our chores at home. We had never seen people like them. Their hair was long and dark and stringy. When they spoke, we could not understand them. Only a few words were the same as ours."

Dorotea gazed off before continuing.

"One day, the youngest teenage boy, Brunu, caught us spying, and we were scared. But we soon realized we were in no danger. He and his brother, Fidele, were kids like us, looking for friends. Eventually we learned to understand each other. They were handsome, and as we got older, friendships evolved into crushes and finally into love."

Mary grinned.

"Your first boyfriend?"

"Yes, Brunu was the one I liked. The home you live in now was vacant at the time, and it was where we had our secret meetings."

Mary raised her eyebrows and smiled.

"It's where Brunu taught me about sex!" Dorotea said.

She looked away, recognizing she had shocked Mary. Dorotea tried to stifle a giggle but couldn't.

"I can tell you this now," Dorotea said. "My husband, Antonio, is gone, God rest his soul. Antonio thought he was the only man I ever knew. Bah!"

Mary laughed and so did Dorotea.

"What a relief to make that confession," Dorotea said with a hearty chuckle.

Mary thought she would fall out of her seat laughing.

When they calmed down, Dorotea continued.

"The Cielo property was bought by a wealthy Florentine banker and the family was kicked out. Brunu's father was angry, and whether or not he had the ability to curse the house, I am sure he wanted to."

"You never heard from them again?"

"No, never."

"What about Patrizia and Fidele?"

"Her fate was the same as mine. She married a local boy, but she died about fifteen years ago."

Mary thought for a moment.

"Maybe it's the ghosts of Patrizia and Fidele who meet in our house at night and laugh?"

"Yes, maybe. And someday you may hear my laughter in that old house."

Dorotea laughed.

"I would love to see Brunu again," she said.

Mary smiled, but hated the thought of losing Dorotea. It would be like the loss of Mr. Moretti.

"I wonder what we can do about the curse on Cielo," Mary said.

"Try talking to the father, Austu. Tell him you own the property, and you don't mean harm, but you want him to leave Cielo. It can't hurt. Or tell him he can stay if he removes the hex."

"Do you want to do it with me?"

"No, you know I like to stay home."

She crossed her arms and pursed her lips.

"You will be fine without me," Dorotea said. "But do you want to hear something else about Cielo?"

"Of course!"

"The Florentine man who bought it after the war visited it for many years, but he didn't bring his wife Lucia for a long time."

Dorotea's eyes widened before she continued.

"And when he was here, he didn't come alone. He brought his mistress."

Mary's mouth opened in surprise, then she laughed.

"There sure was a lot of sex going on around here."

"Yes, there was!" Dorotea said. "Do you know why his wife had to sell the villa and move to Florence after he died?"

"Was it too big for her to care for alone, especially at her age?"

"Well, yes, but there was more. Her husband left all his money to his mistress – and their child – so his wife was broke. She could no longer afford it."

"I had no idea. Why didn't you tell me this before?"

"You never asked me."

Mary laughed at her feisty friend.

"Next time I come back, I'll bring a list of questions! No, wait a minute. I have a question now. Is Jessie the lady you mentioned with the devil on one shoulder and angel on the other?"

"Give me your hands."

Mary was pleased Dorotea was willing to answer this. She held out her palms.

"What do you know about her?" Dorotea asked.

"She's a kindhearted lady who seems to have been cast into a difficult life. She's trying to break free of the past, but it's complicated."

"Yes, she's the one. She has a black devil and a lavender angel."

"What does that mean?"

"It's for her to find out. Once she does, life will make a big swing for the better."

"Should I tell her this? I already know her favorite flower is lavender."

"No, no, no. She must learn this lesson on her own. But you'll be involved in it. She can't do it without you."

"She'll be okay?"

"Oh yes, I see a wonderful future. For both of you."

Mary smiled and thanked Dorotea.

As she walked home, she thought about how she wanted to tell Luca what she learned about Cielo, but she had promised Dorotea to keep it a secret.

When she made it back, she handed Luca the *crostata* from Dorotea. He was in nirvana as soon as he took a bite of it.

"They don't make pastries this good in the U.S.," he said.

Then he devoured a second slice.

Mary ignored his comment about the U.S. It didn't matter. She was so happy to have him home.

CHAPTER 60

❧❧❧❧

New Orleans, Louisiana

JESSIE HAD BEEN HOME from Italy for a few weeks when her cell phone rang with a call from a local number she didn't recognize. She hoped it was the call she was expecting.

"Jessie?"

"Yes."

"This is Officer Trudeau at the New Orleans Police Department. I'm Patrick Sullivan's friend. I think you're expecting a call from me."

"Yes, officer, I am. Thank you."

"I'm pleased to tell you you're in luck. We talked to your nomad photographer, and he was highly cooperative with our questions."

Jessie was thrilled they'd found Frankie. She wasn't surprised he was helpful – it confirmed her opinion that he was a good guy.

"We questioned him about the photos of you and he said he was not the one harassing you. Said he'd swear under oath. Then we asked him about who might have robbed your apartment. He gave us a couple of names of guys who were selling drugs. One of those guys is already in jail, and Frankie's information can help us keep him in jail."

"So you know who broke in?"

"I don't have a conclusive answer for you right now, but I'm highly confident we will soon. We've confiscated several stolen items from this guy, and if Frankie's computer is in the evidence inventory, we'll know. I might need you to come to the station to identify your belongings, including the computer."

"Is Frankie going to be there?"

"No, he doesn't have to come since I had him confirm he gave the computer to you. I have some paperwork I need you to sign, but I won't be able to meet with you right away. I have a new grandbaby and he's in the neonatal intensive care unit at Tulane."

"Well, I hope he's not there much longer."

"We think he'll be able to go home this weekend. So maybe I can stop by next week."

"Yes, that sounds good. I appreciate everything you're doing."

"Of course. I'll call before I come."

CHAPTER 61

𐃺𐃺𐃺

Terzano, Tuscany

LUCA HAD TO GO to Florence to file some business paper-work, Enzo was back in school and there were no renters at the Cielo villa, so Mary decided it was the perfect day to visit the hexed Cielo villa.

She did exactly as Dorotea recommended. She stood and faced the front of the villa and looked at it top to bottom. She closed her eyes and imagined it full of migrant Sardinians - men, women and children. She took in a deep breath before she spoke out loud.

"Austu, can you hear me? I want to talk."

Eerily a big gust of wind came and blew across Mary's face.

"Austu, I am the new owner of this home. I traveled even farther than you did to live here, and I love this home like you did. I mean no harm to you or your family, including your sons, Fidele and Brunu. I know they loved living here, too."

Mary walked around the perimeter of the building and came back to the front door.

"Austu, I ask you to leave in peace, and I promise to take good care of this place you once called home."

Another gust of wind blew. Mary heard birds calling and looked up to see falcons circling.

Whether it was a coincidence or her request, the frequent and unexplainable problems at Cielo stopped immediately. They still experienced the occasional plumbing or electrical problem, but it was to be expected in a home several hundred years old.

Eventually Giovanni stopped complaining about the Sardi, and Luca stopped most of his complaining about Giovanni.

CHAPTER 62

൸ൕൟ

New Orleans, Louisiana

AFTER A WEEK and a half had passed since they talked, Officer Trudeau visited Jessie at Java.

"Jessie?" he said as he stepped in the door. He looked her up and down as if he knew her. She knew she'd never seen him before, but there were a lot of men in New Orleans with his same features – dark skin and dark wavy hair with light colored eyes.

"Yes, hi!"

Then she found herself thinking she hoped he'd never seen her dance. If he did, maybe he wouldn't recognize her. The blond wig was a good disguise back then. And she was about ten pounds heavier now.

"Would you like coffee?" she asked.

"Yes. Make it black. No chicory. No milk. No vanilla. No nothin'."

"You drink it like your buddy Patrick does."

"That old boy saved my life in Korea. Did he tell you?"

"No, he only said you worked together in Boston."

"We did that, too. I'll do anything for that old fart."

He sipped his coffee and eased into a seat at one of the old wooden tables.

"How's your grandson?"

"He's better and at home now, but he has some growing to do. He's a little thing."

"I'm glad he's out of the hospital."

"We are, too. Thank you."

"So you have more news for me?"

"Yes, we got very lucky. There was only one Dell computer locked up in evidence that was the same model as Frankie's."

He put his manila folder on the table and opened it.

"If you sign this form, I can give you the computer."

"Okay. So do you know who looked at it and found my photos?"

The door opened and Charles walked in. Jessie's heart skipped several beats. She thought he was in meetings until after lunch.

"Hi, gorgeous," he said.

"Did your meeting finish early?"

"No, we had a cancellation."

He turned to the police officer and extended his hand.

"Hi, I'm Charles Durbridge."

Jessie spoke before the officer could.

"This is Officer Trudeau. He's a friend of the retired Boston police officer we met in Italy. Remember Patrick Sullivan? We're trading stories about Patrick."

Jessie noticed Officer Trudeau close the police report as she spoke. She wondered if Charles saw it. She hoped not.

"Want a Café Americano?" Jessie asked.

"Sure," Charles said.

She went behind the counter to prepare the brew.

"Are you working a case?" Charles asked.

He was never at a loss for words with strangers.

"I'm always working a case," Vic said. "I wish they'd all go away. I'd love to not have a job because then there'd be no crime. But that won't ever happen."

"True," Charles said.

"What's your line of work?"

"I'm an attorney, Durbridge and Durbridge."

"I know the name, but I don't see you in the court room."

"Well, I do patent and trademark law, which doesn't often end up in the local courts."

"Did you go to Tulane Law?"

"No, Duke."

"Oh, one of our public defenders went there. Adele Dupart. You know her?"

"Yeah, small world," Charles said. "She was a year behind me."

"That girl is tough. Makes my balls shrivel just thinking about her. I hear she had a Creole mama and a black papa, just like me. Her family didn't have much, and she had to fight to make it through college and law school. She's tough, kind of like a 'boy named Sue.'"

Vic laughed at his mention of the famous Johnny Cash song.

"I'd hate to have her litigating against me," he said.

"Here's your coffee," Jessie said.

She handed it to Charles in a to-go cup because he rarely had time to sit and drink it.

"That's what I've heard about Adele," Charles said as he blew on his coffee to cool it. "Well, I better get back to the office. What did you say your first name is?"

"Vic. Vic Trudeau."

"Good to meet you, Officer Trudeau. Jessie, I'll see you after work."

He headed out and turned left toward his office.

"That's a high falutin' boyfriend you have, Miss Jessie."

"Nah, he's down-to-earth," she said. "And thank you for your discretion around Charles."

Vic gave a quick nod.

"Well, let's get back to your question. Where were we?"

"Who looked at Frankie's computer?"

"It could have been the thief, but it's safe to assume he never turned it on. It's likely his only plans were to sell it for quick cash, so our list narrows to people involved in the case, like the DA, public defender or paralegals. It could have been any one of them because it was admissible evidence."

"Do you know who worked the case?"

"As a matter of fact I do. The DA was Terrence Navarro and the public defender was Adele Dupart."

"Didn't you just mention her to Charles?"

"Yes, I did. And it was no accident I was talking about her."

"What do you mean?"

"Pat Sullivan told me your entire story, and I have been tryin' to piece it together for you. I believe we have a good old-fashioned case of jealousy. There's someone who wants to keep you from marrying Charles."

"I guess that's good news."

"Yes, it is because hopefully we can make this come to an end quickly. I tell you, jealousy makes people do crazy things. In the police department we see it all. Especially here in New Orleans."

"I can only imagine."

"We can't overlook a very important fact. Your boyfriend is acquainted with the public defender Adele Dupart. I was lucky he happened to walk in because it gave me a chance to confront him myself. That saved us a lot of time gettin' to the bottom of this."

He sipped his coffee.

"Did you notice when I mentioned her name, he didn't want to talk about her? Did you see the way he started blinking his eyes and swipin' his nose when I asked about her? Those are all signs of tellin' lies.'"

"I was making coffee and didn't notice."

"Jessie, I think Adele and Charles were more than friends in law school. It's possible she has a vendetta against him, and you're stuck in the middle."

Jessie waited as Vic scrolled through his phone to find a photo of Adele.

"Look at this," he said. "Have you ever seen her?"

"Oh my God, yes. That's Papi. She comes in the coffeehouse all the time and we talk. As a matter of fact, she's a friend of mine."

"Did you call her Papi? I don't know anyone who calls her that."

"I asked her about the name once, and she said it's a nickname, short for Papillon, her middle name. It means 'butterfly' in French."

"Her name is Adele, and she's no butterfly. She is a ragin' bulldog. She's got a chip on her shoulder the size of Lake Pontchartrain and she takes it out on everyone. I'm surprised she talks to you. She doesn't have many friends."

Jessie was so disheartened. Papi had always been so nice.

"I need you to do something," Officer Trudeau said. "Figure out a way to get Charles to talk about her and see if he'll tell you what went on between them. Then the case might be solved."

She had never considered Papi as a suspect. But Jessie started thinking about the conversations she'd had with her. They had talked a lot since she came home, but she couldn't remember if she told Papi about staying at Charles' uncle's villa before they left. It was likely she had.

"After you talk to Charles, give me a call."

"Okay."

"You understand where I'm goin' with this, don't you?"

"Yes, but I'm so surprised. She's never acted like she knows Charles. And he's never mentioned her."

"There are rumors Adele and Charles dated in law school and that he's the reason she came back here instead of taking a better job in Atlanta. So we have a few facts. She knows Charles, had access to the photos and never told you her real name."

Jessie tightened inside but kept calm on the outside.

"Do your homework and call me," he said, heading for the door.

"Officer, one more question. Do you have a number for Frankie? I'd like to give him a call."

"I'm glad you asked me because I forgot to give you a message from him. He said he hoped you were painting a lot. Said he was still a single photographer on the road."

She didn't know what she would say to Frankie other than "thanks." He had been a guardian angel who stepped in her life when she needed one, but it was long over.

"All right, thanks."

In the afternoon, a middle-aged couple from Indiana stopped in and bought two of her paintings of Italy. They said they liked the soul of her work and would give them to their son who was opening a contemporary Italian restaurant in a new trendy area of Indianapolis. They took a stack of her business cards so they could tell other people about her paintings, too.

The paintings of Italy were selling much faster than anything else she'd ever painted.

CHAPTER 63

꧁꧂

When Charles came home late from work, he said he was more interested in drinking than eating the "Debris" po'boys Jessie had picked up for them at Mother's Restaurant.

He poured a heavy dose of Maker's Mark on the rocks and refilled Jessie's glass with Chianti. It was her third glass of the evening. Since Italy, she'd only been drinking red wine.

Charles sat down on the sofa with Jessie, took off his shoes and propped his feet on the coffee table.

"I sold two paintings today!"

"That's great! Cheers!"

They clinked glasses.

"You can bankroll some money," he said.

"I plan to. I'll need it to quit working at the coffeehouse."

"But you make good coffee," he said.

"That's what Officer Trudeau said today. He was a nice guy." She was trying to transition the conversation to Papi.

"He was nice."

"How well do you know Papi, that female public defender he was talking about?"

"Papi? Who's that?"

"I mean, Adele."

He frowned before speaking.

"We went to law school at Duke, and she's from Louisiana. I saw her in class and sometimes at parties."

"Ever work with her now?"

"Nope."

He ended the subject quickly, and she didn't probe further because she didn't want to make him suspicious.

The next day Jessie called Officer Trudeau and told him she didn't get far with Charles.

"Don't be surprised," he said. "Just keep asking questions."

ॐ

On Saturday, Jessie and Charles went to a Cowboy Mouth concert at Howlin' Wolf with friends, including Charles' best friend, Drew, and his wife, Darcie.

When Jessie spotted Darcie heading to the ladies' room, she joined her. They were putting on lipstick and primping their hair when Jessie asked about Adele.

"Is she still bothering him?" Darcie asked.

"What do you mean?"

"He's never told you about her? My God, men won't talk about anything will they? It's like pullin' teeth to get them to talk."

"What about her?"

"They went to Duke Law together and dated his second year."

Jessie tried not to overreact.

"Oh, really?"

"I heard it got crazy. She was obsessed with him, and he liked her, but he told her it would never work. His family would disown him if he married a half-black girl. They're old-fashioned."

Jessie remembered Charles' questions about biracial dating and his denial of ever doing it.

"Yes they are," Jessie said.

"She stalked him during her last year of law school, comin' here every weekend possible, calling, emailing and texting non-stop. It was crazy. Then she took a job here right after she graduated."

"You're kidding!"

"He hasn't told you?"

"No, he hasn't said a word, but she comes in the coffeehouse."

"She's probably spyin' on him since his office is next door. Does she know you two are engaged?"

"Yeah she does. But she told me her name is 'Papi.'"

"I wouldn't be surprised if she came to the coffeehouse to keep an eye on you, too. That girl is freaky."

"What do you mean?"

"I'm not supposed to know, but Drew told me. She's into that BDSM stuff."

"Wow."

Jessie covered her mouth with her hand.

"You never know about people," Darcie said.

When the two ladies returned to the concert hall, Jessie tried to act like she wasn't upset. Cowboy Mouth's next song was one of her favorites – "Down on the Boulevard." She swayed to the music and watched Charles hanging out with his friends.

She wondered what else she didn't know about him. But in all fairness, he didn't know everything about her, either.

She grabbed Darcie and headed to the bar for tequila shots. Right or wrong, the alcohol would give her the courage to confront Charles later.

They got home around 2 a.m., and Charles started unbuttoning Jessie's blouse as soon as they walked in the door.

She backed off.

"Stop, Charles. We need to talk. Why did you lie to me?"

"Lie? About what?"

"Adele."

He stood still and sighed.

"That was a long time ago. It's over. I don't want to talk about her."

"I do. For some reason you lied to me."

"Jessie, it was a mess. I liked her in law school, but it wasn't going to work. She didn't want it to end, and she followed me here. I avoid her, but you know how small this town is. Sure, I run into her, but it's over."

"Does she know it's over? Or is she still trying to be with you?"

"I don't know."

"You do know."

"She calls. She emails. She stops by the office. I can't control her."

He shook his head.

"Have you told her you're engaged to me?"

"Yes, I've told her, but she won't listen."

"Maybe you're not firm enough."

"I am, Jessie. I am. I only want to be with you, and I don't want to talk about this."

"You can't drop it so easily," Jessie said.

"I have nothing more to say. It's over with her, but I can't make her go away. And now I'm going to bed. I don't want to talk about it."

He headed toward the bedroom with Jessie following him.

"What if she's trying to make my life miserable?" Jessie asked.

"What is she doing?"

"Forget about it. I need to get out of here. I'm going to Norma's tonight."

"You've been drinking. Stay here."

He was right. She grabbed a pillow and blanket and slept on the sofa until the early morning. Then she went to Norma's, planning to stay as long as she needed to get her head together.

CHAPTER 64

𐎀𐎀𐎀𐎀

JESSIE ARRIVED AT the little apartment at 8 a.m. Norma was still sleeping, so she tippy-toed into her old bedroom.

The first thing she did was search the Internet for information about Adele Papillon Dupart. She found some newspaper articles about cases she'd defended. There was one mug shot of a guy she recognized. He'd come to her apartment a few times when Frankie was smoking a lot of marijuana. Jessie thought he was probably the guy who broke into their apartment and stole the computer.

Now she was confident it was Adele who was sending the photos, especially since she started getting them after she began dating Charles.

She thought about the days when the letters arrived – her birthday, Valentine's Day and their dating anniversaries. They were days when she got his attention instead of Adele.

She played through the list of threats in the letters –

- The only way you could attract a rich boy was with your body. He's not with you for your brains.
- One year with that asshole?
- Valentine's Day is for idiots and sluts. You're a slut, so I'm sure you'll be celebrating with your idiot boyfriend.
- Your poor mother has a slut for a daughter.
- Happy Birthday, skanky piece of Tremé shit!

- Your boyfriend is only dating you for sex. Too
  bad your present is his pencil dick.
- You don't get it, do you? You're a slut and
  Charles needs to know about the 177 photos.
- You can't get away from me in Italy. Marry
  Charles and I'll send all your photos to him.

It was definitely the voice of an angry, jilted girlfriend.
Not a man. Not a family member. It had to be Adele.

Jessie kept searching, obsessed with learning everything
she could. She wanted ammunition on this woman who had
slyly inserted herself into Jessie's relationship with Charles.

On the third or fourth page of search results, Jessie's eyes
opened wide. Adele had been a suspect in the mysterious
death of an ex-boyfriend her senior year of high school. The
teenage boy went missing the night after prom and was
found in a bayou several months later. His body was so
decomposed, it was impossible to determine the cause of
death.

In one of the articles, a witness said she saw Adele with
the boy after prom, even though Adele wasn't his date. The
witness said she knew the boy had broken up with Adele
only a week before prom and had taken another girl to the
dance.

Adele was identified as the primary suspect, but was never
convicted. Jessie shuddered as she read it. Adele could be a
murderer.

Vic Trudeau was right about her vicious character.

Jessie slept for a couple of hours, and when she woke up,
she left a voicemail for Officer Trudeau. Then she stayed in
her bedroom until she heard Norma get up.

Now that Norma was older and took more medicine, she
slept later. It wasn't until noon that they sat at the old
Formica kitchen table and had their first cup of coffee.

Jessie had already decided she would tell Norma about her indiscretions. She was always afraid to disappoint Norma, but she knew she needed to confess and ask for her advice.

"I didn't want to ever tell you this, because I didn't want to hurt you. But I want you to know the truth."

Jessie told Norma about the dancing and Frankie's photographs. Then she told her about the stalker and the discovery that it was Charles' ex-girlfriend.

"What have you learned from all this?" Norma asked.

Jessie was surprised by the question. She expected Norma to comment about her embarrassing choices.

"Well, I've learned who I don't want to be, which helps me know who I do want to be.

"I've learned that I get my greatest pleasure and energy from painting, and I want to make a living at it.

"I want to be proud of myself and have successful friends like the ladies I met in Italy. They're full of passion and live wholeheartedly."

"Aren't you full of passion, my dear?" Norma asked.

"Yes, but I'm haunted. It's as if I can't get away from my past."

"You're the only one holding on to it. You're doing the same as your mama."

Jessie leaned back in her chair.

"Oh my gosh. I am."

Jessie closed her eyes and shook her head.

"Honey, you can change it right now, this very minute," Norma said. "The decision is yours. What you did hasn't hurt anyone but you. You weren't a criminal, and you did nobody wrong. You just have to learn and move on."

Jessie nodded. Norma was right.

"If that police officer is correct," Norma said. "You'll be getting' get rid of your nasty stalker soon. Poor lady. She's blamin' other people for her pain. She needs to realize she can make a choice to live a life of love instead of hate."

The elephant Jessie had been letting crush her chest finally stood up.

"If you're worried about Charles tellin' you a lie, it means you care about him," Norma said. "I don't think he was tryin' to be harmful. I think he was only hopin' she'd eventually go away. He was tryin' to move on. Now she's goin' to get in trouble, and I think she'll be gone for good."

"I love him, but when I found out he had this secret, I didn't like how powerless I felt. And I didn't like knowing I was doing the same thing to him."

"Then go home and talk to him. Tell him everything like you told me. If he truly loves you, he'll understand. He may have more secrets. You never know. If there are any that will affect your life together, you need to clear the air."

Jessie hugged Norma and thanked her.

"You always know how to make me feel better," Jessie said.

"How about we make biscuits and gravy for a late breakfast? Then we can get a pot of jambalaya started."

"Sounds good."

Jessie texted Charles and told him she'd be back that night with dinner.

CHAPTER 65

❧❧❧❧❧

JESSIE WENT HOME with a big bowl of jambalaya. It was time to confess. She realized it might bring on the end of their relationship, but it was time to get it all out and move on.

That meant revealing everything, except for the brief kiss with Alex. She never planned to share this with anyone. It was one of Stella's "take it to my grave" secrets.

Charles was clearly shocked by some of her revelations, but he made no comments. Jessie wasn't sure what he was thinking.

She asked him if he had anything else he wanted to tell her in this moment of honesty, and he said he didn't.

For the next few days, it was uncomfortable. They didn't talk much when they were home. It was as if they reset the clock on their relationship back to the beginning, and they were getting to know each other again, but skeptically. Neither was innocent, and they needed to adjust.

In Jessie's heart, she didn't want their engagement to end, and she thought he felt the same, but she wasn't completely sure. Jessie knew if they could survive this, it would be a sign of the relationship's strength.

On Friday of the same week she had to work late because a coworker was sick. After a thirteen-hour shift, all she could think about was crawling into bed. But Charles had other plans.

She walked in the house and noticed a strong aroma. Charles was in the kitchen - and he was cooking!

"The pecorino sauce is ready, and all I have to do is boil the gnocchi. Here's a glass of prosecco to celebrate my first dinner!"

She chuckled before taking a sip of the bubbly wine.

"You? You cooked?"

Her eyes filled with tears.

"I would do anything for you. I would even remember Mary's recipe for gnocchi."

She laughed and threw her arms around him.

"You thought I wasn't paying attention to Mary's cooking lesson," he said. "But I was. I'll warn you, I didn't bake any pears, and I'm not grilling zucchini."

"You crazy guy! This is unbelievable. Thank you. I'm sorry it's been so difficult lately."

"I've been thinking a lot."

He held her tightly.

"You and I had lives – and baggage – before we met. I'd be an idiot to think differently. But now my life is about you and me. And tomorrow it will be about you and me. For the rest of our lives, it's about you and me."

He kissed her and ran his hands down her body.

"I want to make love right here," he said. "But I can't take a chance of burning my cheese sauce."

She laughed until she thought she'd pee her pants.

"I love you so much!" she said once she caught her breath.

Before falling asleep, she told him he earned an "A" for the gnocchi and pecorino sauce and an "A+" for dessert, which was his delicious body.

"I'll take you over a baked pear any day," she said.

Then she nestled into his body for a long night of sleep. She didn't notice it, but Charles didn't fall asleep as easily.

CHAPTER 66

❧❧❧❧❧

SEVERAL DAYS LATER, Jessie emailed Mary and Stella to update them on everything.

She explained the stalker situation and its resolution. Officer Trudeau had to report the offense to Adele's manager and she was asked to resign. Sending the letters wasn't a prosecutable crime, but her job held her to a higher standard.

Her supervisor suggested she get counseling, and the best news was she was going to move to Atlanta. But not until the end of December. Her boss must have suggested she stay away from Java, too, because Jessie hadn't seen her since then.

Jessie recounted Charles making gnocchi and pecorino sauce.

And she told Mary and Stella about her paintings of Italy. She was selling pieces regularly at the coffeehouse, and she was nearly able to buy a car with the profits. Then she could take Charles' old car to the junkyard.

She had also scheduled two art shows. Her first opening was at Java on the Friday after Thanksgiving. The second was in December at a Royal Street gallery in the French Quarter. She invited Mary and Stella to both.

In the two months since Italy, Charles' hadn't gotten any good leads on finding Jessie's father because his own father was making him work regular 16-hour days.

Charles kept apologizing for the lack of progress, but he only had so many hours in the day. It meant they didn't have a new wedding date yet, so she explained this to them in the email, too.

Within a day they had written her back. Mary, Luca and Stella would travel to New Orleans for Thanksgiving and come to her art show opening at Java. Jessie was beyond elated.

CHAPTER 67

ॐ〰〰♋♋

IN EARLY NOVEMBER, Luke Davis arrived in New Orleans alone. He was staying in the same apartment he always rented on Esplanade.

He went to work right away fixing up damaged houses, putting in at least ten hours each day. He took Scout with him on the jobs, and the dog would spend most of his days sleeping in the truck.

Luke settled into a comfortable routine, hitting his favorite restaurants like Port-O-Call and Mother's. Often he'd stop in the Verti Marte for take-out.

Life was simple in New Orleans, and he liked to people-watch. He sometimes found himself in the bars, but he preferred quiet evenings in his apartment with Scout and Jack Daniels by his side.

CHAPTER 68

༚ஐ☙ⓒ☙ஐ

THE WEEK BEFORE Jessie's art show at the coffeehouse, she cleaned the house to prepare for their guests. Unfortunately they didn't live in a castle, so there wasn't room for everyone. Only Stella would stay with them, while Mary and Luca had a room booked at the Omni Royale in the French Quarter.

The second bedroom was Jessie's studio. Stella would sleep there on the futon. The room was small and easily cluttered because it was where Jessie and Charles put stuff they didn't know what else to do with. So Stella's visit forced an over-due cleanup.

Jessie sorted through a few small boxes of clothes stored under the futon and decided they could be donated. Behind the futon, she found a duffle bag filled with her mama's belongings.

Jessie had picked up the items after her mother died. As she held the bag in her hands, she remembered the day she went to Dr. Winn's house to collect her mother's possessions.

The curtains were drawn in the small, lifeless bedroom where her mother had lived for so many years.

When Jessie picked up her mother's pillow to catch one last scent of her, the linens smelled as fresh as a box of dryer sheets. For the first time in her life, she realized how life went on after someone's death.

Today Jessie stifled tears as she recalled how surprised she was at her mother's few possessions. Her work uniforms had already been removed from the room, but in one dresser drawer Jessie found underwear, a nightgown and socks. In another drawer, there were magazines and a book. She looked behind and under the few pieces of furniture in case her mama had hidden anything. Nothing. She looked in the corners of the closets. Nothing.

Now it was time to make some decisions about the bag's contents. Jessie slowly unzipped the bag and took a deep breath before reaching in.

She pulled out the long nightgown and held it close before putting it in one of the donation boxes.

The slippers were tattered, and she tried putting her feet in them, but it was impossible. Her feet were much bigger than her mama's. So the worn slippers were tossed into the trash along with the underwear and socks.

The work shoes were in decent shape, so she added them to the donation pile.

The only items left were three issues of "People" magazine and an old hardback copy of "Gone With the Wind."

Jessie thumbed through the magazines and then put them in the recycling bin.

When she opened Margaret Mitchell's famous novel, she was surprised. The center of the book was cut out and stuffed with tissue paper. When she removed the tissue paper, she found an old Polaroid photo of her mama with a young man. They were in swimsuits at a pool. Written across the bottom it said, "Will & Loretta - Dreamland Pool, Kenova, WV - July 1979."

Jessie's hands shook and she screamed for Charles even though she knew he wasn't home. She ran to find her phone.

"I have a picture!" she yelled into the phone. "I have a picture of my dad!"

"Slow down, slow down," Charles said. "What did you say?"

"I found a photo of my mama and Will in the stuff I picked up from her apartment at Dr. Winn's. He looks tall and has dark brown hair. Like me."

"I can't come home for another hour, but I'll get there as soon as I can. I want to see it."

She hung up, her hands still trembling. She studied every detail of the photo and determined she had her father's bright eyes, height and high cheekbones. It was the first time in her life she felt truly hopeful of meeting him.

She went back to the studio to see if there was anything else in the book. There were no more pictures, but when she un-crumpled the tissue paper, she found a white facial tissue folded into a square, and there was something in it. Carefully unfolding it, she found a simple engagement ring with a small diamond and a wedding band. Her hands shook more.

She remembered Norma mentioning an engagement ring on her mama's hand on the 1979 bus ride. But the gold band was a surprise. She carefully examined it and found an inscription inside – "Us always, Jim & Ruth Price 6/6/64."

She had never heard her mom mention anyone named Price. She did some quick math. If the couple married in their twenties, they would be at least in their sixties now.

She was baffled, but excited. She dialed Charles again to tell him about this discovery.

He took the names and date and said it was the most solid piece of information they had yet. He offered to look for marriage records in Ohio and Kentucky as soon as he could, and said he would be later coming home if he found any information.

The rings didn't fit on Jessie's ring finger so she slid them onto her pinkie and prayed they were the link to finding her father. In a frenzy, she finished cleaning the studio, often stopping to look at the rings.

Charles came home two hours later with a copy of the Price's marriage record.

"Ruth Price was your dad's aunt. She married James, or Jim, in Ft. Thomas, Kentucky, and her maiden name was Reynolds. Ruth had a brother named William Reynolds, and he was a doctor in Ashland, Kentucky, with three children - William II, Richard and John."

"We found him?"

"Yes, William Reynolds II is your dad. He is an M.D. living in Portsmouth, Ohio, born in 1957. He would've been 18 the year you were born. It's him. You found him."

Jessie screamed and jumped up and down.

"Now what do we do?"

"Tomorrow, I'll see what else we can learn about him."

"I can't believe this. I'm excited, but I'm nervous, too."

Her whole body jittered and her hands fidgeted.

"I'm going to look for him on the Internet."

Jessie searched his name and city and found his medical practice. There was a photo of him, but it was obviously from when he was younger.

"Should I call him?"

"That's up to you. Whatever you're comfortable doing. You can call him. You can try to visit him. Or we can have a detective talk to him."

"I'm not sure."

"You'll have time to decide once we get more information."

"Everyone is coming this weekend for the show. This is too much at once."

Charles sifted out the emotion and focused on the tasks ahead.

"Get everything ready for your opening. Enjoy the weekend with your friends. Then we'll take it one day at time with your father starting on Monday."

Jessie nodded her head, but she was a mess inside. Unable to fall asleep, she kept surfing the Internet for information and found several websites with ratings about his performance as a doctor. He seemed to only have average ratings. The most common patient complaint was that he didn't spend much time with them during appointments.

His medical training was good, though. He earned an undergraduate degree from Boston College then got his medical degree from Thomas Jefferson University. His did his residency at University of Cincinnati and returned to Ashland to work with his father for a short time before starting his own practice in Portsmouth.

At 2 a.m., she stopped searching and wrote Mary an email. She felt indebted to her. Her life had become so much better since they met.

Dear Mary,

If I hadn't made the impulsive visit to your gallery, this might never have happened. Because of you and my time in Tuscany, I will soon have the stalker out of my life and have tracked down my father...

She wrote Mary about the discoveries about her father and how she was debating how to contact him.

The next day Jessie stopped by Norma's and showed her the photo and rings. Jessie told her about finding the items in the book.

"That's the ring she was wearing on the bus," Norma said. "What was the book?"

"Gone with the Wind."

"Well isn't that appropriate?"

"What do you mean?"

"The main character, Scarlett, was her own worst enemy, kinda like your mama."

Jessie nodded her head.

"Everything is about to change," Jessie said.

"Yes, it is."

CHAPTER 69

❦❧☙❦

Terzano, Tuscany

MARY WAS AT HER computer editing her manuscript early in the morning. In 150 pages, she had recounted her first trip to Italy and her wedding to Luca, but it still lacked something. She wanted it to be the kind of story she would enjoy reading, and it wasn't. Frustrated, she put it away and checked her email. She was so excited to read that Jessie was one step closer to finding her father. Then she read Jessie's sentence:

> Because of you and my time in Tuscany, I will soon have the stalker out of my life and have tracked down my father.

As she read that line, Mary realized something. The greatest moments in her life, and in so many other lives, happened because of Tuscany. She quickly typed them out:

- I met Luca and now I have adorable sons and a wonderful art gallery
- Alex happily lives and works in Tuscany – he's become Luca's best friend
- Luca learned who his biological parents were because I found his mother's diary and bought the pocket watch
- Jessie met Patrick Sullivan who introduced her to the New Orleans cop who found her stalker

- Jessie became courageous enough to look for her dad, and she is having her first major art show focused on paintings of Italy
- Dorotea found her true love but lost him

Since visiting Tuscany and meeting Luca, a cascade of life-changing events had occurred. People's lives had almost miraculously intersected. Mary realized that if she didn't focus only on her life but included everyone's interesting tales, her manuscript would be much more compelling.

She sent back a congratulatory note to Jessie and logged out of email, eager to return to her manuscript. She began to weave in the stories of those who had set foot on the grounds of Castello di Rondinara, Il Cielo, and Il Ribelli, and how their lives were impacted by their time in Tuscany.

CHAPTER 70

❧❦❧❦

New Orleans, Louisiana

ON THE WEDNESDAY before Thanksgiving, Jessie was busy finishing last-minute tasks for the art opening on Friday. It was her final opportunity to prepare since they were going to Charles' parents' house on Thanksgiving Day.

Charles was putting in a full day of work. He didn't want to work on the Friday after Thanksgiving, so he planned to stay as late as needed to get his work done. He was keeping Friday open to help Jessie prepare for the show.

Jessie knew it would take multiple trips to Java, so she loaded Charles' Wagoneer and made the first delivery. Then she went home for the second load.

When she got back to Java, she saw the light on in Charles' office, so she walked over to see if they were going out later. They had talked about possibly meeting up with his old high school friends who were home visiting their parents.

The front office door was unlocked, and as soon as she walked inside, Jessie heard a familiar female voice.

She closed her eyes and let out a big sigh. She knew the voice, but had to see it to believe it.

She put her hand on the doorknob of Charles' office, took a deep breath and opened it. Jessie didn't know who was more stunned, her or Papi and Charles.

Papi was sitting in the chair opposite Charles' desk in an outfit appropriate for a Bourbon Street strip club.

Jessie played it cool.

"Hi Papi, I didn't know you two were friends until recently."

Papi sarcastically put her finger to her chin and looked up to the ceiling.

"Oh, I'm surprised I never mentioned it," she said.

"So what's going on tonight?" Jessie asked as if this weren't an unusual situation.

"I'm glad you asked," Papi said. "Because we were talking about you."

"Me?" Jessie asked.

"This, this is a complete misunderstanding, Jessie," Charles stammered. "I can –"

"I know how to give him what he likes," Adele said, interrupting Charles. "I always do. Tell her, Charles."

Adele pulled a pair of handcuffs from her purse.

"I was just getting ready to cuff him to his chair."

"Stop it, Adele," he said.

"No! You know you want me."

In a swift move Papi jumped up and cuffed Charles' arm to the chair.

"Take these off, Adele."

"You're funny Charles. I thought you liked it when I got rough with you."

"Adele, that's enough," Charles said.

Jessie tried to back up and leave, but Adele wasn't going to let that happen. She got in Jessie's face.

"You," Adele said. "You naïve little slut. He only became obsessed with you after I showed him your photos."

"The photos?" Jessie asked.

"There's an explanation," Charles said.

"So you're the one sending me the letters?" Jessie asked Adele.

"What letters?" Charles demanded. "What have you been doing, Adele?"

"She's been stalking me for two fucking years," Jessie said. "That's what she's been doing."

"You've been a tough one to scare away," Adele said. "The others were easier. You've got nerves of steel."

"You chase away the women in my life?" Charles asked.

"You know I'm the only one you want," Adele said to him.

"Adele, you're out of control," he said. "Let me out of this chair."

Perspiration was beading up on his brow.

"My father will be here soon," he said. "Put on your coat and unlock these goddamn handcuffs so we can talk about this like adults."

"Oh, Charles. Let's go ahead and tell Jessie the whole story about the photos. I was assigned to the Johnson case, and when I looked through the evidence for information, I realized those photos were of the same lady in the coffeehouse. I showed them to Charles and then he wanted a piece of you."

"It wasn't like that," he said. "I love you, Jessie."

"No, you don't," Adele said. "You love me. You always have."

"Adele, it's over! I'm engaged to Jessie. Do you understand me?"

"You really saw the photos?" Jessie asked Charles.

"Yes, but they have nothing to do with this conversation. I love you, photos or no photos. I want to marry you."

"You're lying right now," Adele said. "You know it's me you want to marry, but your family won't let you."

"That's not true," Charles said.

"Why don't you tell Jessie what happened the night you came home from Italy?"

Charles' eyes welled with tears.

"Oh, Jessie. I'm sorry."

He shook his head, clearly upset. His head dropped.

Adele started laughing.

"Now you know how I feel, Jessie. It's no good when your man sleeps with another woman."

"Charles?" Jessie could barely stand. "What happened?"

"Adele broke into our house."

"You know you wanted me there," Adele said, laughing. "He's caught in his lies. Isn't this great? You think he wants to marry you, don't you? It's all a hoax. He's doing it for his family. They don't want a black daughter-in-law."

"Adele, wake up." Charles said. "You're chasing me. I'm not chasing you."

"This isn't how you love someone," Jessie said.

She pulled off her engagement ring and threw it on the desk.

"Papi, Adele, whoever you are, you deserve him."

"Jessie, I can explain," Charles said. "Please."

Adele wouldn't let up.

"Will you please tell Jessie the only reason your parents love her is because she isn't me? You have to marry someone to get them off your back about me. She's just a whore from Tremé. She's probably like you and likes dark skin, too."

"My life is none of your business," Jessie said. "But I didn't push an ex-boyfriend off a fishing pier into the bayou."

Adele's face turned to rage. She lunged at Jessie's neck.

"You bitch!"

The front door opened, and a second later Charles' father walked into the office.

"Adele! What the hell are you doing in this office? And what are you wearing? Let go of Jessie! I thought we made it clear years ago we never wanted to see you again!"

Sirens raced up Magazine Street and stopped in front of their office.

Charles' dad let out a big sigh.

"Nice work, son. You're going to be written up in the Times-Picayune again. I thought you'd finally grown up. I gave you a job, put you in a house and kept you under my nose, but you fucked up again. Do know how this will hurt your mother? You gotta learn to keep your cock in your pants with this little piece of shit. This confirms it. You're not bright enough to ever take over this firm."

Jessie shuddered at Mr. Durbridge's tone and for an instant felt sorry for Charles and Adele. But unfortunately, Mr. Durbridge wasn't done.

"And pretty little Jessie here isn't exactly what we expected for you, either. We didn't want a daughter-in-law who's an orphan from Tremé, but we accepted her because it kept Adele away."

Jessie's eyes grew huge. She needed to get away from all these people, but just then a police officer walked into the room.

The cop closed the blinds and curtains.

"People are looking in these windows wonderin' what's going on," the officer said. "I want everyone to calm down and we're gonna get testimonies."

"There's nothing to talk about," Mr. Durbridge said. "Just a family squabble. No one is in any danger. You can leave, and no reports need to be filed."

"Does everyone agree?" the officer asked. "If I get a 'yes' from every person, I'll leave."

"Yes," Mr. Durbridge said and nodded his head in way that meant "everyone better agree."

"Yes," Jessie said.

"Yes," Charles said.

"Yes," Adele said.

Free to leave, Jessie walked out and didn't say goodbye to anyone. She headed to the coffee shop.

Vic Trudeau was standing by Java's front door.

"I'm off duty," Vic said. "But I keep my scanner on. When I heard this address for a call, I was worried you were involved."

"Thank you. I'm okay. Just shocked. And single."

"What happened?"

"I caught Charles and Adele together."

She clenched her jaw, too angry to cry.

"I'm sorry. But don't you worry about findin' a good man. You're a beautiful girl and a sweetheart. Some handsome devil will come along and sweep you off your feet."

"I think I just got rid of a devil and his she-devil," she said. "I don't need another one."

CHAPTER 71

ON THANKSGIVING morning Jessie slept late.

Officer Trudeau woke her at 10:30 a.m. with a phone call.

"Did you see the paper this morning?" he asked.

"No, I just woke up. I was up really late. I moved everything out of Charles' house last night and finished most of my show set-up."

"Well, you're on the front page."

"What?"

She panicked.

"No worries. I gave the story to a reporter, and she promised to take care of you."

"What?"

"You are mentioned as a victim in a 'minor domestic squabble' and as an up-and-coming artist who is having a gallery opening tomorrow at the coffeehouse neighboring the crime scene. You better get ready for a crowd. People are going to want to meet the lady who was caught in a love triangle with a public defender and a lawyer from a prominent local family."

Jessie laughed.

"Are you serious? That's a crazy way to get free publicity!"

"Whatever it takes, honey."

"Well, thank you for your help. And thank you for showing up last night. I was in shock and almost don't remember what happened."

"You're going to be all right. Now go eat a big Thanksgivin' dinner."

"I can't thank you enough."

ဆၣ

Jessie and Norma skipped the traditional Thanksgiving meal. They made chicken and sausage gumbo, pressure-cooked green beans, seasoned rice and pecan pie. These were all the comfort foods Jessie needed on a somber, emotional day.

Norma held Jessie when she needed comforting and told her to keep listening to her heart for answers.

But Jessie's heart was broken.

"Time is the only answer," Norma said throughout the day.

CHAPTER 72

ಬಡಾಜುಞಚ

Luke had Thanksgiving off and planned to have dinner alone at K-Paul's Louisiana Kitchen. He took a seat at the bar and dined on some of New Orleans' finest food, including turducken for dinner and a slice of pecan pie for dessert.

On the walk back to his apartment, he stopped in the Verti Marte for some orange juice and a copy of the Times-Picayune.

Then he settled in at his apartment for the night with his bottle of Jack and Scout.

He hated the waste of paper in every Thanksgiving edition. It was full of ads for all the shopping sales, which didn't interest him.

He looked through the entertainment section to see if there were any interesting events on Friday because he wasn't working that day either. He didn't want to visit Santa Claus or do any shopping, but he wanted to see the city. He'd probably go for a walk in Audubon Park and have oysters at the Acme Oyster House.

Then he read a article on the front page that mentioned an art show on Magazine Street. It caught his attention because it was featuring paintings of Tuscany. He'd always wanted to go back to Tuscany and thought it might be nice to see some paintings. He ripped out the article so he wouldn't forget about it.

Then he pulled Anna's photo from his wallet and thought about the last day he saw her. They were in the woods below the Tuscan castle where her family stayed on the weekends. It was the first and last time they made love, and it was the most memorable day of his life.

He took a big gulp of Jack Daniel's.

CHAPTER 73

๛๏๛๛

CHARLES CALLED JESSIE on Thanksgiving night. Jessie didn't really want to talk, but she answered anyway.

"Thanks for picking up," he said.

She stayed quiet.

"I just want a few minutes to explain and apologize," he said. "I owe it to you."

"Okay," Jessie said.

"First of all, I love you more than anyone I've ever met. You are the brightest light in my life, and you make me happy."

Jessie started to cry, but she tried not to sniffle. She didn't want Charles to hear her crying.

"Adele was right. I'd seen those photos once before. She found them on a stolen computer, but it's not why I wanted to meet you. I told you the truth. I needed coffee, and I fell for you when I saw you. Remember I had to talk you into dating me. I wouldn't take no for an answer."

He paused.

"How long did we date before we made love? I waited until you knew you loved me. It's what you asked me to do."

Jessie sniffled loudly by accident.

"In Italy, I loved every minute with you. You were the happiest you'd been since your mom died. I felt like you were back. I craved you like I've never craved anyone. I devoured you as much as I could."

She kept listening.

"I got home from Italy, and on my first day back to work, I stopped in Java for coffee and Adele showed up at the same time. She was surprised I was home early. You must have told her how long we were staying in Italy, because I never told her."

"I did."

"I innocently mentioned you were still there sticking to the original schedule. I should've never said anything. When I got home from work that day, she was waiting for me in our bedroom."

Now he cried, too.

"I tried to resist her, but I'm just stupid. She came on strong, and I couldn't stop her. I didn't stop myself. I'm so, so sorry."

He paused to catch his breath.

"It was the only time I ever cheated on you, and I hated myself. Adele must have seen my weakness. The office last night. Well. I can't even explain. I was working and she showed up in that get-up –"

He broke out into a sob and Jessie did, too.

"I'm not going to try to explain it away," he said. "I fucked up and deserve to be hated by you. I truly love you, and I'm so very sorry. If I only had another chance."

It took Jessie a few minutes to talk.

"I appreciate your honesty, but you know I have a hard time trusting people."

"I know you do."

"Is it true your family only liked me because I wasn't Adele?"

Charles stammered, and Jessie dreaded hearing what he was about to say.

"I had...I had to ask them to give you a chance."

Jessie wasn't surprised by this reply.

Charles cried before he could speak again.

"They did give you a chance, and they learned to like you. They saw what a fighter you are. They like how hard you work. My mother loves your paintings. Jessie, they grew to love you."

She thought about how rigid his parents were. Now she was angry with them for how much they screwed with Charles' life. They had never let him make decisions without getting involved.

"I think you need to get out of New Orleans, Charles. You need to find yourself and stop trying to be who your parents want you to be. Leave this pretentious town and do what makes you happy. Think about joining your sister in Chicago."

"Would you go with me?"

"I can't. I have to be honest. I've been having second thoughts about getting married. I thought it was other things bothering me, like mama's death and finding my dad. But it's more. I need to get out of this town, too. I'm a fish out of water, and I need to spend some time alone. I'm not ready to be married to you or anyone."

"It's not going to be easy without you. I love you so much."

He drifted off.

"I love you, too, but I don't think we're ready for marriage. We have some things we have to work out on our own."

"I think we could do it together," he said. "We're good together."

"We are, but I think it's the wrong time."

"I don't know what I'll do without you."

"You'll figure it out. You're smart. You just need to think for yourself."

"This is killing me, Jessie."

"If we stay together it won't work."

"But we could –"

"The coulds, woulds and shoulds could keep us on the phone all night long. It's not easy, but I think we better hang up."

"Okay."

Now he was crying again.

"Bye, Charles," she said.

It was so very painful, but she had to end the call.

When she got off the phone, Norma read Jessie's cards and told her she'd made the right decision. She also said everything was about to change.

"You're only a victim if you want to be," Norma said.

"I don't want to be."

"Then you have to make changes. Go see the world. Live your life. And know I'll always be here if you need a place to land."

Norma didn't tell Jessie the cards said Charles would be back in her life.

CHAPTER 74

ON FRIDAY MORNING, Jessie went to the coffeehouse early to wrap up preparations for the biggest day of her professional art career.

By mid-afternoon, her paintings covered all the wall space of the coffeehouse, and she featured her two premier works of Mary and Anna on easels in the center of the room. She filled a bookshelf with smaller, simple pieces priced from $25 to $75.

She went back to Norma's to relax before getting ready.

Jessie put on a vintage charcoal gray batwing dress she had bought from Stella and wrapped her waist in a wide tan leather belt. The finishing touch was her signature cowboy boots. Once dressed, she went to the kitchen to have a rum and Coke with Norma.

After Jessie made the drinks, she sat in one of the turquoise dinette chairs next to Norma.

"Cheers!" Norma said and so did Jessie.

After taking a sip, Norma picked up a locket from her lap and handed it to Jessie.

"This was my mother's and now I want to give it to you. You're the only daughter I ever had."

"It's beautiful. Thank you!"

Jessie opened the locket expecting to see photos inside, but instead it was filled with dried lavender.

"I broke off some lavender blossoms from the pots you've always kept for me outside the kitchen window. It should help your nerves tonight. Just open it and smell it if you start to feel tense.

The scent made her think of Tuscany, and an image of Alex in a long-sleeved black pea coat appeared. She wondered how he was, but she hadn't asked Mary recently.

"I'll probably be opening it all night to stay calm."

She draped it around her neck.

"It looks beautiful on you and I wish I could be there, but this old body can't do it."

"I'll make sure to take some photos. Thank you, Norma. I love you and I'll take very good care of this."

"I love you, too."

ℰℭ

At Java, there was nothing left to do but wait for people to arrive. In addition to the free publicity in the morning newspaper, Jessie had distributed invitations to people in the French Quarter and shops along Magazine Street. Her press release showed up in "Gambit," and Jessie had sent personal invitations to acquaintances from her past jobs and college classes.

She knew Mary, Luca and Stella had gotten to New Orleans that morning but had gone to their hotel to rest and freshen up before the opening. Stella was no longer staying at Charles' house but at the hotel instead.

They told Jessie they would arrive an hour early to have some time to catch up before the show started. And they were going to help with last-minute preparations since their Ribelli wine was being served.

Jessie hadn't told them the full story about Charles, and she wouldn't before the opening because her emotions were too fragile. She needed to stay composed until the end of the show.

Stella walked in first, looking stunning. She wore a long-sleeved black maxi dress from the early seventies and glided toward Jessie with confidence and grace.

Then Mary entered in a knee-length black leather coat and black leather boots. She wore a crisp white blouse and a black wool pencil skirt under the coat.

Luca held the door for the ladies, and when he stepped into the coffeehouse, Jessie's mouth dropped open. He was even more striking in real life than in his photos, and she couldn't take her eyes off him. In snug jeans, a white cotton tee and a black blazer, he looked as though he'd stepped off the page of a fashion magazine.

Stella gave Jessie a hug.

"Close your mouth, young one," Stella whispered in Jessie's ear. "The drool is about to run out!"

Jessie laughed and hugged her back.

"Oh. My. God."

It was all Jessie could say.

Stella laughed.

"Do you see now why I'm always looking for my own Luca?"

Mary hugged Jessie after Stella.

"This is impressive! And you look gorgeous in that dress. Great pendant."

"Thank you so much! I can't tell you how happy I am you're here."

Luca approached and Jessie didn't want to shake his hand because hers were now clammy.

"At last!" she said and hugged him. "Good to meet you! Thank you for coming!"

He smiled and kissed each of her cheeks.

"You're even more beautiful than Mary described," Luca said.

Jessie thought she would melt. Now she knew where Alex got all his charm and why Stella was trying to find Luca's clone.

"Thank you."

The coffeehouse door opened again. It was Alex. Jessie had no idea he was coming. He was wearing tight dark jeans, a snug black shirt and a black pea coat.

She was startled.

He hugged her, not wasting a second.

"You look beautiful standing here in front of all this art. You're glowing!"

"Thank you. It's so good to see you here tonight."

Her heart raced, and she realized she'd had a premonition of him earlier when she smelled the lavender.

It suddenly clicked. The scent of lavender was a catalyst for her some of her visions. The visions happened within moments of smelling lavender, like the Sardi vision at Cielo and the laughter in the castle no one else heard.

Lavender had been symbolic for Mary and Luca because they believed it was a sign from Luca's mother. Now it was "talking" to her, too, connecting to the Rusconi's. It wasn't surprising. Jessie felt like she was meant to meet them from the beginning.

Alex whispered.

"Don't forget, I like bumping into you in the dark, too."

She blushed.

"Sorry, I felt like I had to say something to break the ice," he said, smiling.

She was in no condition to flirt with another man, but Alex was an exception. He was so sweet, and he gave her some needed confidence.

She introduced everyone to her boss, Jeremy, and he served Ribelli Chianti to everyone.

Luca wanted to maximize their product's exposure in the Uptown venue, so he had Ribelli-etched wineglasses made as a giveaway for the event.

Mary, Stella, Luca and Alex slowly toured the room viewing Jessie's paintings.

"You've been very busy," Mary said.

"It just seems to flow," Jessie said. "It's as if something takes over my body when I start painting. And I have so many more ideas."

"You did a remarkable job on this one of Luca's mom," Mary said. "The lavender crown is perfect. And the look on her face is one of pure love. I never had the pleasure to meet Anna, but I'm sure she would be pleased if she could see this. You should be proud."

"Thank you, I am. And I'm beginning to think lavender has a special meaning for me, too."

She described her revelation to Mary.

"That's interesting," Mary said. "Anna must like you."

Dorotea had mentioned a lavender angel. It could be no one else but Anna. Mary got goosebumps thinking about it. Then Mary looked at the painting of herself.

"It's not often we like paintings of ourselves, but I love this one."

"Thank you," Jessie said, beaming.

"Won't Charles be coming at all tonight?"

Jessie shook her head and tightened her lips.

"No, we're finished. You won't believe what happened. I'll tell you later tonight. It even made the newspapers. In fact, the reporter who wrote the article is coming tonight. She's going to write a follow-up article about the opening."

"But you're okay?"

"As okay as I can be. There's a copy of the newspaper under the counter. I'll get it so you can read it, and I'll tell you the details later when it's quiet. I don't want to ruin my make-up by talking about it now."

Mary started reading the article and realized Charles and his "friend" must have been Jessie's devils.

But Dorotea only mentioned one devil, she thought. And Charles seemed to love Jessie so much.

She looked at the photos carefully and could see Adele had some features that looked African American.

Mary concluded Adele must have been the "black" devil not only to Jessie, but to Charles. Adele wouldn't let up on Charles until she broke him down - and she did it in a big way.

She wished she could talk to Charles because she was sure he was still in love with Jessie.

As Mary put away the newspaper, customers started trickling in. Soon there was barely room to move. The press Jessie got about the previous night's incident drew more attention to the coffeehouse than she and Jeremy could have ever anticipated. Jessie talked to dozens of people and handed out her entire supply of business cards.

Stella was busy, too, because she had made sure her New Orleans clients stopped in for the show. She was happy to meet them in person and was negotiating commissions for Jessie, too.

Women swooned over Luca, and he charmed them all.

Several perceptive people identified Mary as the lady in Jessie's painting and talked to her about Tuscany. Many asked for travel suggestions, and Mary enjoyed giving them advice.

Charles and his family didn't show up, exactly as she requested, but his mother sent a beautiful bouquet of flowers, wishing her success.

About ten minutes before the show's closing time, the crowd was thinning, and a man strolled in the shop alone. He paused at the painting of Mary for a several minutes and then looked at the one of Luca's mother in the castle tower.

Stella noticed him.

"Look at the blond hunk over there," Stella said to Alex. "He looks older than the guys I usually date, but maybe I'd be happier with someone who's mature."

The guy was tall and muscular, rugged and tanned, as if he spent a lot of time outdoors. Stella wanted to talk to him, but as quickly as she noticed him, he disappeared.

"I always let the good ones get away. Damn it!"

Alex laughed.

"I don't think he went too far, just to the restroom. He's coming back now, heading toward the painting of Mary again."

"I'm going to go talk to him. I'm not letting him get away."

CHAPTER 75

STELLA WALKED UP and introduced herself.

"Hi, I'm Stella, the best friend of the lady in the painting you're looking at."

"Your friend is beautiful. And I think I visited the place in the paintings back in the sixties. I'll never be able to forget it."

"You were in Tuscany?"

He nodded and moved closer to the painting of Anna.

"This painting of the lady in the castle tower is remarkable," he said.

"She's watching for her American lover who was in the U.S. Army," Stella said.

He turned his head and looked directly at Stella.

"Do you know that with certainty?"

"As a matter of fact, I do."

She put her hands on her hips.

"You really do?"

Stella didn't like how he challenged her so she figured she'd met another loser.

"Yes, really. And you never told me your name."

"Oh, I'm sorry," he said. "I'm usually more polite, but these paintings have me shaken up. I'm Luke. Luke Davis."

Stella almost spit out the wine she had just sipped.

"What did you just say?"

He smiled and now he looked at her as if she was the crazy one.

"Um, I just told you my name."

"Did you happen to serve in Vietnam?" she asked.

"Yes."

"Holy Mary, Mother of God! Wait here a second. I need to get my friend and introduce you."

Luke shook his head and watched her hurry away.

Stella grabbed Mary and whispered in her ear. She pointed toward Luke.

"No!" Mary said. "You've got to be kidding."

"No one believes me right now," Stella said and threw her hands in the air before grabbing Mary's arm. "Let's go."

As Mary approached the ruggedly handsome man, she immediately saw the likeness to Luca. He had the same eyes, the same face shape and the same warm smile. Her mouth was suddenly dry. She swallowed hard.

"Hi Luke, I'm Mary Rusconi."

"You're the lady in this painting, aren't you?"

He noticed the pocket watch hanging from her neck and stared at it.

"That looks familiar," he said with a puzzled face.

"Yes. Yes, it is."

She closed her eyes in disbelief. Dorotea told her she would be rewarded for helping Jessie, but this was bigger than anything she could have imagined.

"Let me grab a couple more people to meet you." Mary said. "I'll be right back."

Luke was startled and stayed by Stella's side.

Now they were both speechless, and that was a first for Stella.

CHAPTER 76

❧❦❧❦❧

HE WAS AN OLDER, taller, blond version of Luca.

He was Mary's father-in-law.

He was Alex and Enzo's grandfather.

And he was about to be introduced to the family he'd never known.

Mary came back with Luca and Alex on each side of her.

"Luke, I'm so pleased to introduce you to two of the most important men in my life. This is Luca Rusconi, my husband, and Alex Rusconi, my stepson."

She paused.

"I'm not going to waste another minute of precious time. I'm just going to get right to it. You and Anna had a baby. Luca is your son."

She barely got the words out before she started crying big, happy tears.

"Anna had a baby?"

Luke's mouth dropped wide open.

"Yes, in a convent. She had to leave the baby with nuns for a while."

Mary wiped her eyes.

"But she was able to adopt him several months later. She named him Luca, after you."

Luke reached to shake Luca's hand, but Luca was frozen. Part of Luca's reaction was his practiced Italian composure – his *bella figura*.

Mary, who knew her husband best, realized he was forcing himself to be strong and not to show much emotion.

Luca finally extended his hand to meet his father's. After he grasped it, both men froze.

Luke helped by speaking first.

"You look so much like your mother, but those blue eyes sure are mine. Hers were big, dark pools of prettiness."

Tears rolled down Luke's weathered cheeks.

"Where is Anna?" Luke asked. "Is she here?"

Luca still couldn't speak.

"I'm sorry to say she died at a young age," Mary said. "Luca was only seven."

"She's gone?"

Luke closed his eyes and shook his head. He pulled a handkerchief from his back pocket and wiped the tears from his face.

Luca finally spoke. "She got cancer, and it was aggressive. She only lived a few weeks after the diagnosis."

Luke shook his head again.

"We have her diary, and we read about you," Luca said. "She never forgot you. She and I visited the Uffizi nearly every Friday morning at 10 a.m. I think she was looking for you."

"I met her at the Uffizi," Luke said.

"In front of the 'Birth of Venus,'" Mary said. "She wrote about it in the diary."

Luke took a big sigh before turning toward Alex.

"You must be my grandson."

There was no doubt. Alex looked exactly like his father and grandfather.

"One of them," Mary said.

"I have more?"

"I have a younger brother," Alex said.

Alex's voice quivered as he spoke, then he embraced his grandfather.

"You're a good looking man," Luke said. "How old are you?"

"Thirty. And I'll go ahead and answer your next question. I'm not married."

Everyone laughed.

"Your youngest grandson is home in Italy, and his name is Enzo," Mary said. "He's ten and loves to play soccer. He looks like his dad, but he doesn't have the blue eyes."

She pulled up a photo on her phone.

"Another handsome young man," Luke said.

He kept shaking his head in disbelief.

A few minutes later, Jessie walked up and found the group as they were taking seats at a table. Something wasn't right. Everyone looked happy, but nervous. She didn't know the older, blond man, but he'd been crying. They all had.

"Everyone okay?" she asked.

As Mary explained everything to Jessie, Luke wrapped his thick arms around the shoulders of his son and grandson on either side of him.

Jessie covered her mouth in disbelief.

"You are Luke Davis? Here at Java? No way! Oh my God, these have been the craziest few days!"

Mary introduced Jessie to Luke.

"You're the artist who was mentioned in the newspaper," he said. "I've been coming to New Orleans for years doing Katrina relief work and never knew about your paintings of Italy. But I read about you in the paper today. Imagine my surprise to find a painting of Anna."

"My paintings were only done last month," Jessie said. "I met Mary and Stella in August when I was in Italy. And I met Luca for the first time tonight."

"Some people call this 'kismet,'" Luke said.

"I don't know what it is," Mary said. "But I sure am happy it happened. Where do you live now?"

"In a small town east of Cincinnati that I'm sure you've never heard of called Fayetteville."

"Are you close to Portsmouth?" Jessie asked.

"I am," he said. "Do you know someone there?"

"Maybe," she said. "I'm trying to find some relatives."

"Well, it shouldn't be tough. It's a small town."

"Why are you in New Orleans right now?" Luca asked his father.

"I'm a retired firefighter and paramedic, and I did a lot of volunteer work for the Red Cross after Hurricane Katrina. Lately I've been doing home rehabs. I love this city, and I want to help restore it to its original beauty."

"Everyone here appreciates the work done by volunteers like you," Jessie said. "Thank you."

"I enjoy it," he said. "Especially now."

Luke shook his head in disbelief again.

"It's how Anna works," Mary said.

"What?" Luke asked.

"She has a way of bringing people together."

Mary took off her pocket watch necklace and handed it to Luke.

He held it as if it were a delicate piece of crystal.

"My grandfather carried this in World War I for good luck," he said. "He gave it to me when I left for Vietnam. It's always been stuck on 7:11."

"That's my birthday," Mary said. "July eleventh. Believe it or not, I bought the pocket watch in Venice because it was stuck on 7:11."

"In Venice?" Luke asked.

"Yes, it traveled quite a bit. After you gave it to Anna on your last visit, she dropped it in the tower of our home. But Luca found it one day and gave it to his fiancée."

"Then my ex-fiancé sold it to a jeweler in Venice," Luca said.

"And you bought it," Luke said to Mary. "Unbelievable."

"I'm the one who found Anna's diary in an old cabinet, too," Mary said. "The combination of the pocket watch and the diary helped us learn about you."

"More kismet," Luke said. "Are the little notes Anna and I wrote to each other still in the watch?"

"Yes," Mary said.

"Do you mind if we open it? I'd love to see them."

"Of course."

Luke had a Leatherman tool in his front pocket, and he carefully used it to open the back cover. He unrolled and read them all, and he kept shaking his head in disbelief.

"She was a special lady."

He opened his wallet and pulled out the laminated photo to show Luca.

"I've carried this photo of your mother every day since 1964."

As the photo circled the table, tears nearly flooded the little coffee shop.

"You might want to see this, too," Luca said.

He took off the vintage Timex he'd worn his entire adult life.

"You've got to be kidding me," Luke said. "I had no idea where I lost it."

Luca blushed mildly.

"My mother found it in a wooded spot on the hill below the castle, in the last place you saw her."

Now Luke reddened, too.

"The day when I ran away from your screaming grandfather, pulling my pants up."

"You're lucky he didn't have his rifle," Luca said, laughing.

"I suppose I am! And you've taken better care of the watch than I ever did, so please, keep wearing it."

Luca smiled and put the gift from his mother - and father - on his wrist.

"You keep wearing the pocket watch, too, Mary. I'm glad to know where it is."

Jessie grabbed two bottles of Ribelli Chianti and glasses for everyone at the table. She sat down next to Stella, who had still hadn't said a word since the moment she met Luke Davis.

"Are you married?" Jessie asked Luke.

"Nope. Never married."

Stella's eyes twinkled.

CHAPTER 77

❧❦❧❦❧❦

THE MOST PRESSING question for Luke was about his final promise to Anna – to meet on the last day of January in 1964 at 10 a.m. at the Uffizi Gallery. Everyone knew Anna wasn't there, because she was living with the nuns to hide her pregnancy. But no one knew if Luke had come back to find her.

"I didn't make it, either," Luke said. "I had been saving money to buy a plane ticket to Italy after my discharge from the Army, but an upsetting letter arrived from one of my older sisters and it changed everything.

"My family had been keeping a secret from me. My dad was locked up in jail, and my mother couldn't manage the family farm. She needed to sell it. And I knew I needed to go home and help her.

"Nothing ever seems to be as easy as you think it's going to be. A lot of work had to be done to prepare the house and barns for sale, and believe it or not, it was almost two years before we got rid of that hellhole. Most kids remember their childhood homes affectionately but not me.

"Our 'farm' was really a moonshine operation, and my childhood days were filled with helping dad keep his stills and bottling operations running, living each day one step ahead of the law. Dad drank too much of the production, and he relied on me – his only son – to do all the work.

"I started driving a pick-up truck as soon as my feet could touch a gas pedal. I was a good student, but I became a delinquent. I missed a lot of classes and when I did show up,

I slept. Of course, I thought I was tough shit, but now I know how sad it was. I think the principal finally passed me just to get rid of me.

"But too many run-ins with the county sheriff led to two choices from the local judge after I graduated – go to jail or enlist. Judge Stevens knew it was my dad who was responsible for all my troubles, and I'd never stood a chance. So, he tried to give me a ticket out by enlisting in the Army. I took that option, knowing I'd end up in Vietnam, because I sure didn't want to go to jail.

"My mother was furious and so was her father, the World War I veteran."

"I'm sure she was worried she would never see you again," Mary said.

"Exactly."

"How long did you serve?" Jessie asked.

"Three years. I was a field medic, and it turned out to be a natural fit. All those years working on the farm, my dad and I were always getting injured or dad would come home from a bar all beat up."

He laughed again.

"Sounds pretty rough, doesn't it? On the farm, we had lots of broken bones, especially fingers. And plenty of gashes. He wouldn't spend money for a doctor or hospital visit. And he didn't want to risk running into the law at the emergency room. So I improvised setting bones and stitching cuts. I must have done a decent job because I'm still in one piece. But the Army gave me real training.

"Then, like a lot of other medics who retired from Vietnam, I went to work as a firefighter and paramedic when I got out. It was a good job, and I was able to retire at an early age."

"I'm sure being in Vietnam wasn't easy," Stella said.

She knew firsthand because she had lost two cousins in the war.

"No, but this wonderful country gave back to this law-breaking teenager. I haven't even gotten a speeding ticket since I've been out of the Army, and I only drink alcohol I buy at the liquor store."

"So you never made it back to Italy?" Mary asked.

She had been dying to solve this mystery for so many years.

Luke sighed.

"By the time I could get back, it was three or four years later, and I figured Anna had given up on me. She was such a beautiful lady, and I couldn't imagine someone else hadn't captured her heart. Not a day has gone by –"

He stopped, getting choked up.

"She cared as much for you as you did for her," Mary said. "You'll read about it in her diary."

"Never seeing her again is the biggest regret of my life."

Mary watched Luke study his son's face. Luca so closely resembled Anna that Mary thought it must be a way for Luke to get another glimpse of the lady he loved.

They ordered late-night pizza and drank Chianti while catching up on a lifetime of stories. Jeremy agreed to let Scout in the coffeehouse, and the hound loved all the attention.

With the excitement of the night, Jessie forgot about her woes with Charles. She was glad not to dwell on herself.

As Luke talked about his love for Anna and as Jessie watched Luca and Mary interact, she wished she had the same everlasting, soulful love with Charles. It would take time to get over him, but she knew it had ended for more reasons than his sexual infidelities with Adele.

They finally closed the place down at 4 a.m., but before leaving, Alex asked Jessie if they could have some time together before lunch at Commander's Palace later in the day.

೮ා೦ಜ

Jessie picked Alex up at 11:30 a.m. and took him to Audubon Park for a walk. There she gave him a short version of her break-up story. She didn't want to go into all the details.

"That was just three days ago. Wow! You're doing well, I think."

"Having the show and seeing all of you made the difference," she said. "And Luke Davis stole the show. Can you believe that?"

"I'm still shocked," he said. "He's a great guy."

"He sure is."

"So, when are you coming back to Italy?" he asked.

"Soon, I hope. But it's hard to tell."

"I hope you're alone next time."

He winked, smiled and made her heart skip a beat or two. Then he leaned in and planted a friendly kiss on her forehead. He put his arm around her, like a friend would, and they continued to chat and walk among the old oaks.

She liked how they fit together, but she didn't want a romantic relationship with him or anyone right now. She needed some time alone.

೮ා೦ಜ

In January, after spending the holidays with Norma, Jessie moved to Philadelphia. She packed her art supplies and clothes in the used car she bought with money from Dr. Winn and art sales.

Norma made her go, telling her she needed a fresh start. She told Jessie to live the life she'd always dreamed of having.

She left her paintings in Java and Jeremy agreed to send her checks as they sold. And the paintings of Mary and Anna were shipped to Italy because Mary and Luca wanted them.

In Philadelphia, Jessie moved in with Stella. It was Stella's idea, and she offered her a job in the boutique, too.

Stella's prediction that custom portraits would be a success was right, and it wasn't long before Jessie was making enough money to support herself. But Stella told her not to move out yet so she could keep saving money. Jessie was happy to stay. Stella was easy to live with and made her laugh a lot.

Jessie loved urban living and the access to fantastic art museums on the east coast. She frequently took the train to New York City alone, giving herself much needed time to think, dream and experience life.

She was happy, lonely, invigorated and confused all at the same time. It only reinforced her thought that she needed time alone. She often wondered how Charles was doing and missed his company. But she knew she had to make this journey of discovery alone. She sometimes thought of calling him but always talked herself out of it, thinking it would make things complicated.

She didn't date anyone either. For the next year, it was all about Jessie. She had to "reset her compass," as she read in a self-help book. Her goal was to live in the moment as much as possible and not to overthink everything. She had been living in fear and limiting herself for so long.

Mary and Stella were always available when she needed to share good news or bad. They listened and offered advice when she asked for it. And they never judged her. Eventually she learned not to judge herself either.

On one of her trips to New York City, she discovered a place that carried Ribelli Chianti, so she stocked up every time she went. It helped to keep her in a Tuscan mood when she painted.

It was much colder in Philadelphia than it was in New Orleans, and the only thing about cold weather she liked was the clothes. She built a large collection of boots and coats, vintage and new, to keep herself warm when the temperatures dropped.

CHAPTER 78

‭ಚಿಖಿೂ‬

Terzano, Tuscany

IN MID-FEBRUARY, Luke Davis made his first trip to Castello di Rondinara to visit his family and meet his youngest grandson.

He fit in like he had always been around. He loved the castle and the adjoining properties, and he repaired anything needing a hammer, wrench or screwdriver.

Luke took on the responsibility of repairing the Cielo belvedere after Enzo and Carlo snuck up and fell through the steps. Enzo ended up with broken toes and a sprained ankle, which kept him from playing soccer for months. Carlo broke his tibia.

Giovanni blamed it on the Sardi, but everyone else attributed it to childhood curiosity.

Luke's first aid skills for the occasional blister, sprain or abrasion were valued, too. The farm workers and the kids were always using his services. Sometimes the workers brought their family members to Luke for care. It saved a trip to the clinic.

Enzo decided he was going to be a firefighter when he grew up, just like his *nonno* or grandpa. But he said it would be after he finished his soccer career with the Azzurri.

For Luke, seeing Anna's diary and hearing the rest of her story help mend his broken heart. So did spending time with the family he'd never known. It was the happiest time of his life, with the exception of those four days with Anna in 1964.

He planned another trip at Easter to stay at least a month.

CHAPTER 79

ଔଯ୦ର୍ଔଔ

Portsmouth, Ohio

Before Luke departed for his Easter trip to Italy, Jessie and Stella flew to Cincinnati to visit him. After an overnight stay at his house, the three hopped in "Big Blue" and traveled east about 100 miles.

Scout had to stay home for the day, and Luke's neighbor agreed to feed him and let him out.

They were headed to Portsmouth, Ohio, so Jessie could meet her father. He didn't know she was coming.

After Dr. William Reynolds got over the shock of learning he had a daughter, he had told Jessie's detective he had no interest in forming a relationship with a daughter he never knew existed. He didn't want to upset his wife and kids.

But Jessie was determined to meet him.

She called his medical office and made an appointment as a new patient under the false name of Anna Davis. She lied about her birthdate and address and told the receptionist she'd pay cash for services.

Luke and Stella waited in the lobby when she was taken to a patient room.

After a nurse reviewed her medical history - all fake - Dr. Reynolds came into the room.

He was tall with thick dark hair graying at the temples. Jessie scrutinized his every feature.

They had the same hair color and skin tone. His cheekbones were high like hers and his chin was shaped the same. But his nose was long and thin instead of turned up like hers. He wasn't as handsome as she hoped, but he wasn't unattractive either. He was just the kind of guy wouldn't stand out in a crowd.

"Hello, Miss Davis. I'm Dr. Reynolds."

His voice was deep, and he had a slight Southern accent.

"So I understand you're having stomach problems?"

He stretched his vowels.

"Yes, I don't know if it's a real problem or if it's my nerves. I've been worrying myself sick about meeting you."

He looked up from the medical chart.

"What did you just say?"

"I'm your daughter."

Will Reynolds turned bright red.

"I told the detective I didn't want to meet you."

"Well, I'm not someone who likes to take no for an answer."

Will's eyes were filled with panic, but he didn't say another word.

"I'm not like my mom who was always running away from bad situations," Jessie said. "I guess I turned out to be the fighter my mother wasn't."

"Your mother –"

Jessie didn't care what he had to say. She was there to deliver a message. She interrupted him.

"Do you understand why she ran away from you?" Jessie asked. "Because she was afraid she'd ruin your life. She knew your plans to become a doctor, and having a baby at seventeen would have destroyed your future. That's how much she loved you."

"I never knew Loretta was pregnant."

"I know you didn't, but since she didn't tell you her side of the story, I wanted to make sure you knew it."

"Your mother had problems worse than I knew. The night she ran off, she stole all my money and my aunt's wedding rings. My Aunt Ruth was heartbroken."

"That's another reason why I'm here."

Jessie retrieved a small fabric bag from her purse.

"Here are the rings. She didn't sell them. I found them after she died."

Will took the rings and sighed.

"I never knew what happened," he said. "She disappeared the morning after The Who concert and no one ever heard another word from her. No one. Can you imagine what a mess she caused for everyone who knew her?"

"I just learned a lot of this myself."

"So why are you here? I told the detective I don't want my family to know about this. And I have enough problems of my own with the scandal in this town about pill mills. I can give you money. How much do you want?"

Jessie laughed at this question.

"I don't need your money. I just wanted to meet you in person to see what you look like and hear your voice. Can you imagine what it's like going through life without knowing your father? It's a lonely, empty feeling. But I guess I'll have to get over that."

Will showed no reaction.

"I got my height and dark hair from you, but I must have gotten my niceness from my mama."

She stood up and moved toward the door.

"I postponed a wedding for months to look for you, hoping you'd be the man who would walk me down the aisle. I guess it was a silly dream. But don't worry, I won't ever be back."

She walked out of the room and the tears she had been holding back spurted like a fountain. A nurse in the hallway tried to ask what was wrong, but Jessie left it to Dr. Reynolds to explain.

Luke and Stella jumped up when they saw her and guided her outside.

As Stella held her, Jessie accepted that one of her biggest dreams had just died. As much as she wanted to be surprised by Will's reaction, she wasn't. She was more stunned by her own reaction.

Expecting to sink into a deep wave of sorrow, instead she rebounded. In an instant, she realized nothing could hold her back any more. She was in charge of her life – and her future – and it had taken meeting her father to fully understand that.

Since there was no way Will could find her, Jessie was free of him. She could let go of another excuse that was keeping her from living the life she really wanted to live.

"You ready to ride some more or do you want to stop for coffee?" Luke asked as he patted her shoulder.

"Let's drive for a little while," Jessie said.

CHAPTER 80

୧ଏ৯୨୧ଓ

Buffalo Creek, West Virginia

LUKE BEGAN HEADING to their second destination – Buffalo Creek, West Virginia.

Jessie had her mother cremated so she could bury her at her real home. She planned to spread her mother's ashes over the land where her mother had once lived with her parents and siblings so many years ago.

They drove down narrow, curvy two-lane roads that followed the water and traveled through mountain passages with an occasional hairpin ascent and descent. The only other location Jessie had seen with mountains like this was Italy.

But the West Virginia architecture wasn't nearly as pretty as Italy's. Homes here were small and hugged the winding, narrow roadsides. Many were run down, even though new cars were parked in some of the driveways.

When they reached the small town of Man, they stopped to take a photo of a historic marker about the Buffalo Creek Disaster.

One of the worst floods in U.S. occurred here 26 February 1972, when Buffalo Mining Co. impoundment dam for mine waste broke, releasing over 150 million gallons of black waste water; killed 125; property losses over $50 million; and thousands left homeless. Three commissions placed blame on ignored safety practices. Led to 1973 Dam Control Act and $13.5 million class action legal settlement in 1974.

Jessie had researched the horrible disaster before the trip. At least a thousand people were injured and four thousand were left homeless. Hundreds of homes were lost, damaged or demolished. Being right where it happened was sobering.

Luke turned to drive along Buffalo Creek, and they passed through numerous small towns time seemed to have forgotten. When they arrived in Laredo, they found a pretty spot along Buffalo Creek that Jessie thought would be a peaceful resting place for her mother. Silently and without ceremony, Jessie carefully spread her mother's ashes into the flowing river. The waters had once carried away Loretta's family and now they carried Loretta away, too.

Mama, your troubles are over and you can rest now, Jessie thought as she watched the ashes spin and float away on the current.

It was the first time she felt at peace about her mother's death.

She thought of the words Norma had said so often – "Everything returns to the earth." Jessie prayed her mother's afterlife was better than her time on earth.

Luke drove them to a cemetery where there was a memorial for those killed in the flood, including relatives Jessie never knew. Before coming, Jessie had decided not to seek out anyone from her mother's family. She felt no need to connect with the past. It was time to put it behind her and someday start her own family tree.

She looked at the names on the memorial and didn't see her own last name. Her mother must have made that up, too. She would have a hard time finding family even if she wanted to. Her eyes filled with tears imagining the pain her mother lived with. But she knew she was now in peace.

Jessie, Stella and Luke got in Big Blue and followed the Ohio River back to Luke's favorite restaurant in Portsmouth, The Ribber. It was known for smoked ribs, chicken and steaks.

They sat at a small table by the bar and while they waited for their food, Luke asked Stella if her new shipment had arrived from Europe.

"It's stuck in customs."

"Hopefully it's there when you get back."

"How did you know about the shipment?" Jessie asked.

Luke waited for Stella to respond.

"We talk every day," she said.

Jessie squealed.

"You do? That's great!"

"We have since New Orleans. I'll probably go to Italy with Luke for part of his upcoming trip."

"I can't believe I didn't notice that. I guess I've been selfishly absorbed by my own agenda."

"You've had a lot of healing to do," Stella said.

"That's no excuse."

"Jessie, your mother died. Your promise of a future with Charles ended. You moved to a new city and started a new job. Today you 'buried' your mother and you effectively buried your father, too. You need to be kind to yourself. We don't expect you to be a superhero. You're a passionate Chianti Girl. You feel pain as much as you feel love."

Jessie knew Stella was right. She smiled at Stella and Luke.

"I'm so happy for you both," Jessie said. "I love you so much."

CHAPTER 81

ꙮꙮꙮꙮ

New Orleans, Louisiana

IN AUGUST, Jessie boarded a plane to New Orleans. It was hot and steamy there, and it couldn't have been a worse time of year to visit, but Norma wasn't doing well, so she had to go.

Norma's health had declined to the point where she couldn't leave the house, and she had hired her neighbor Mrs. Jonas to care for her.

When Mrs. Jonas called Jessie, she said Norma's blood sugar was high like her cholesterol and blood pressure. She was losing feeling in her toes and her kidneys were weak. Medications weren't able to control the conditions very well. But the biggest concern was Norma's weakening vision. She wanted to see Jessie before she went blind.

When Jessie arrived at Norma's apartment, she sat in the car for a minute before going in. She dreaded seeing Norma like this.

"There you are darlin'," Norma said when Jessie walked into her living room. "Now I feel like a million bucks!"

Somehow a hospital bed had been moved into the apartment. Jessie couldn't imagine how anyone had moved it up the stairs and into the small space.

Jessie bent over to squeeze Norma's soft shoulders.

"Hi, Norma. I'm so glad I'm here."

"I don't suppose I'm lookin' too good right now."

"You're beautiful."

"Are you tryin' to get something from me?"

Norma chuckled.

"Absolutely not! I'm here to give you some lovin' and spend some time together. Maybe I can make you some biscuits and gravy. I bet no one can make them like we do."

"You can read me like an open book," Norma said. "I been cravin' them, but I don't like anyone else's recipe but my own."

"You never have."

Jessie stayed by Norma's side during most of the five-day trip. She wanted to spend as much time with her as possible.

Since Norma slept late most mornings, Jessie used the time to do errands and shop at her favorite vintage stores. One day she stopped in Java to see Jeremy and collect an overdue check for paintings she had sold.

She parked her rental in front of the coffeehouse, and as she got out of the car, she heard someone shout her name. It was coming from the direction of the law office.

There was a new sign in front of the building – "Durbridge & LeBeau." It made her body tighten. Charles had worked so hard for the partnership, so she could only imagine how difficult it was for him not to get it.

"Jessie! Good to see you," Mr. Durbridge said as he hurried toward her.

Her sentiments weren't the same.

"Hello, Mr. Durbridge."

"Do you mind if we step into Java for a moment? It's like a steam room out here."

"That's where I'm headed."

He opened the door and let Jessie go in first.

Jeremy was excited to see Jessie, but he was surprised to see her walk in with Mr. Durbridge, so he kept his distance from them.

"I only have a couple of minutes, Jessie, but I'm so glad we ran into each other. I owe you an apology – a big one.

You didn't deserve what I said. I was so angry with Charles, and you got in the crossfire. I'm sorry. I'm truly sorry."

"Thank you."

She didn't know if she believed him.

"You were nothing but a sweetheart to Charles and our family, and I was wrong. I hope you will let me explain."

She nodded.

"Charles and I had an argument after everyone left the office. He was furious about the way I talked to you. And he should have been.

"Charles wasn't an easy son to raise. I was always tough on him because I had to be. He was smart, good in sports and girls liked him. But he was lazy and wouldn't grow up. I pushed him hard to make sure he got through college because I wanted him to take over the family firm."

"He worked hard to try to make that happen," Jessie said. "I watched him."

"Yes, but he had to be pushed. I thought I was doing the right thing for him his whole life, but tough love didn't work too well. Now I've nearly lost him. He hasn't talked to me since that night. My wife is heartbroken. He moved in with our daughter, Diane, who's still in Chicago. He's working for a law firm there, and I hear he's let his hair grow long and even has a goatee."

Mr. Durbridge shook his head.

Jessie was surprised to hear this but kept a poker face.

"I don't think it's how a lawyer should look. Anyway, Jessie, I want him back – as my son, not as a business partner. And I think you're the one person who can help. He's lost without you."

"I don't know about that."

"I do. I watched him with you. He loves and respects you – the way a man should love a woman. His cell number is the same. Maybe you could talk to him?"

"Um, maybe."

"Please consider it. Please"

Mr. Durbridge gave her a hug.

"I'm so happy I saw you. You look beautiful. I hope it's not long before I see you again."

Later that night when she sat with Norma watching "Wheel of Fortune," she told her what happened with Mr. Durbridge.

"What are you going to do?" Norma asked.

"I don't know. I sometime wonder how Charles is doing and consider calling him. But I think it would be too hard."

"Well, he was your best friend, too. Don't forget that."

Norma was right. It was the hardest part of breaking up. She lost her closest friend.

"I'm going to Italy next month with Stella, and it's a good place for me to think. I can talk to Stella and Mary about it. They always seem to have good ideas."

Norma smiled and patted her on the shoulder.

"You'll figure it out, Jessie. Don't worry yourself to death. Just believe in yourself. You know, Charles was a lot like you in that regard. He had to learn to believe in himself, too."

Jessie suddenly realized how much she and Charles were the same, but for different reasons. He didn't believe in himself because his family was overbearing, and she didn't believe in herself because she had no family.

CHAPTER 82

𝕊𝕆𝕊𝕆ℂ𝕊ℂ𝕊

Terzano, Tuscany

A FEW WEEKS LATER, Jessie boarded another plane. This one was bound for Rome. She was making the trip alone because Stella and Luke had left a few days earlier. They were organizing their wedding at Castello di Rondinara. They would get married in the same little chapel where Mary and Luca had said their vows. Jessie thought it was so romantic.

Instead of taking the bus to Siena, Alex was going to pick her up from the airport. She was looking forward to hearing how he was doing. They emailed occasionally, and she knew he had a new girlfriend named Mia. This one sounded serious. She was glad for him.

After she got her suitcase from baggage claim, she looked around for Alex, but didn't see him. She walked outside and saw her last name printed on a card. But it wasn't Alex holding it. This guy was tall and muscular with long dark hair and a sexy goatee. He wore a graphic tee with the name of a band she didn't know, and he had on dark, slim cut jeans and leather boots. He clutched a large bouquet of lavender.

Jessie's eyes sparkled as she dropped her bags and ran to him.

"Charles!"

He grabbed her and hugged her tightly before he lifted her off the ground.

"What are you doing here?" she asked.

"I'm your date for the wedding."

She had so many questions.

"But how –"

"Shh. Just kiss me."

When she felt his lips on hers, Jessie melted. She had missed him so much but hadn't known exactly how much until this moment.

"You're so beautiful," he said when their lips finally parted. "You're glowing."

"Maybe it's because I'm in Italy."

"Maybe it's because you're with the man who wants to spend the rest of his life with you."

She smiled and blushed. She loved him so much.

"Come on. Let's go to Terzano," he said. "After we've said hello to everyone, I want you all to myself."

They walked to his rental car arm-in-arm. He carried her bags and she carried the lavender.

During the ride, Jessie found out how he got his invitation to the wedding. After she got home from New Orleans, she had told Stella about what happened with Mr. Durbridge. Then Stella told Mary, and the two ladies agreed they had waited long enough not to intervene. They contacted Charles and suggested he come to Italy for the wedding.

"It was the phone call I'd wanted for so long," he said.

He'd gotten in the day before Jessie did so he had time to get ready for her. Mary and Stella approved his outfit and made sure he carried the lavender for her arrival at the airport.

"Those ladies," Jessie said. "How do they know me better than I know myself?"

"They said something about Chianti Girls having to stick together. They said you'd know what that meant."

"I sure do."

Jessie smiled and held his hand. She liked his new relaxed look, and she could hardly wait to be alone with him. The past was the past and she was ready to move on.

As they caught up on each other's lives, she watched the countryside roll by. It was only her second trip to Italy, and the country enchanted her even more now than it did the first time.

To create all the paintings of Italy, she had studied the countryside's colors and textures. So familiar with them now, she felt like she was home. Once they were off the highway, she asked if they could turn off the air conditioning and roll down the windows.

Charles didn't mind.

Her long hair blew in the wind and her dress fluttered enough that she had to hold it down with the hand that wasn't holding the lavender. Her toes curled in the same boots she wore on the first trip, and she looked sideways from behind her Ray-Bans at Charles. He was biting his lip and his face was flushed.

He caught her looking at him and smiled. He turned on the blinker and pulled off the road.

"I can't drive another mile."

The rest of the world froze as they embraced each other with the desire they had always shared. They kissed, gasped and groped.

"I love you and I've missed you," he said. "This is the happiest day of my life, and I know it will only keep getting better with you."

She smiled, and as the scent of lavender filled the air, she knew right then and there they would be together forever.

CHAPTER 83

৪৩৯৩৩৩

THE WEDDING TOOK place the following day. Stella wore vintage Emilio Pucci and Luke was decked out in vintage Armani. They were quite stunning.

Mary was the Matron of Honor and Luca was the Best Man. And Enzo was the handsome young ring bearer.

Alex brought Mia to the wedding, and she was adorable. Everyone thought they made a really cute couple.

Giovanni and Rossana had been invited, but declined. Giovanni said they'd be intruding on "Luca's life," choosing not to make Luke Davis part of their extended family, too.

For the reception, Mary and Luca set a beautiful table in the center of the castle's courtyard, surrounding it with large vases of fresh flowers and tall candles. After enjoying wine and antipasto, everyone toasted the newlyweds.

Luca stood up first. He had been the patriarch of the little family for so long.

"For so many years, I thought I had the perfect life. I have a beautiful wife, loving sons and this wonderful home. They are all a blessing.

"My goal has always been to give my family the best, and when I didn't think our lives could get any better, we made a trip to New Orleans."

He winked at Jessie.

"In a matter of minutes, our lives changed. I had no idea how much better it could become."

He stopped for a moment to clear his throat.

"Luke, Dad, I know why my mother loved you so much. You're a gentleman, full of strength. And with grace, you have served the world and protected your family. I'm learning so much from you, and I admire the man you are.

"Today you begin a new life with Stella – a beautiful, life-loving lady, and our family grows. You are so deserving of each other's love. May the two of you always be happy and healthy, and may you have abundant time to enjoy each other. *Salute.*"

He raised his glass and after everyone drank, Luke and Stella stood to embrace Luca.

There wasn't a dry eye at the table.

Now it was Mary's turn to toast, but she asked if she could go last.

Jessie sat next to Mary, so she stood up and had Charles get up with her.

"My first toast goes to everyone here for being my extended family and welcoming me into your lives. I'm so glad we all came together in New Orleans, and I thank you for bringing Charles here tonight."

She got tears in her eyes and pulled him close to her. She had a hard time going on because she was so choked up.

"Best wishes to you, Luke and Stella. I'm so happy for you, and I love you dearly. *Salute.*"

Alex was next.

"Here's to my new GRAND-mother, Stella!"

His timing was perfect, and the laughter helped dry everyone's tears.

Stella blushed and waved her hand at him as if she was dismissing him from the table, then she laughed, too.

Once the group calmed down, Stella acted as though she was going to say something highly sentimental.

"Thank you, everyone. I have an important announce-ment to make."

This quieted the group.

"Even though Mary is now my daughter-in-law, I promise to never make her call me 'mom.'"

Everyone laughed again, and Stella hugged her best friend.

"How about you Enzo?" Mary asked. "Do you want to say something to your *nonno* and *nonna*?"

"Do we get to eat soon?" he asked.

"That's a very good question," Luke said. "I'm hungry, too, but I have a few words first."

He stood up, tall and solid. He had one arm around Stella's waist, and with the other, he raised his wine glass.

"Today, I married this gorgeous and exciting woman who I look forward to sharing the rest of my life with. We're going to make our home in Philadelphia. She will keep her successful business, and I will be her, um, handyman."

Everyone laughed at the suggestive innuendo.

"In the last year or so, my life has been a whirlwind of love because of each of you. I was an old, lonely - and probably crotchety - bachelor. Now I am a father, a grandfather, or a nonno, and I am blessed to have become a surrogate father to Jessie. Thank goodness for her exquisite paintings of this sacred home."

He raised his glass.

"I cherish every one of you."

He kissed Stella and said, "You make me so happy. I love you."

The group clapped, cheered and drank.

"Mary has a special gift for each of you now," he announced.

"Thank you, Luke. I'll be right back."

She went inside and returned with a stack of small, wrapped packages.

"If it feels like a book, it is!" she said. "At last! I have a copy of my first novel for each of you, because *you* are the story. While this day is about celebrating Luke and Stella's love, I want to take a few minutes to talk about this Tuscan family."

She opened her arms wide to encompass everyone at the table.

"Wouldn't each of you agree we've been snared in a beautiful web of fate and love none of us were expecting?"

Everyone nodded except Enzo who stared longingly at the cake.

"I began writing this book as a memoir to recount my romantic experience of meeting Luca and moving to Tuscany. I felt self-indulgent writing my story, and it seemed almost cliché.

"One day Jessie walked into the gallery and as our friendship grew, her life became tangled not only in mine, but in Stella and Luke's, too. In a short email she wrote me one day, she reminded me of how inextricably we are linked.

"This home in Tuscany has been a magnet for every romantic soul at this table.

"The title of the novel is 'Because of Tuscany,' and I'm going to read this next part because I don't want to mess anything up."

She unfolded a piece of paper she was holding.

"Because of Tuscany...I found my true love Luca. I now have two wonderful sons and call this historic villa my home. Luca made my dreams come true when he opened the art gallery for me. I love living on this sacred land and cultivating its products."

Luca raised his glass and gave his wife a loving smile.

"Because of Tuscany...Alex has become his father's best friend and a fantastic tour guide, too. We love having him live with us and hope he never leaves."

Luca winked at Alex and they raised their glasses.

"Because of Tuscany...I met Jessie who has become an inspiring friend. I've watched her make some big discoveries and transitions in her life. And by nothing other than a miracle, she was our link to finding Luca's father."

Jessie blew a kiss to Luke and Stella.

"Because of Tuscany...Luke became a father and grand-father overnight and he's quite a spectacular one. It's hard to remember a time without him."

Enzo gave his grandfather a high-five.

"Because of Tuscany...Stella found the love of her life, um, her 'Luca.'"

Everyone laughed as Stella kissed her hunky husband.

"I know they will have a wonderful life together, and I might have to add some new chapters to this novel as their life unfolds."

"And finally...because of Tuscany...let's remember Anna. May she rest in peace as she looks from the stars at this beautiful family she masterfully brought together with the little gifts she left behind. She still gives us signs to this day."

"To Anna," Mary said.

The rest of the night, sultry music by Frank Sinatra, Louis Armstrong and Ella Fitzgerald filled the air, and Ribelli wine was available by the case. Dinner was classic Tuscan with abundant antipasto, bowls of pasta and grilled meats.

Alex and Mia heated and served the food Mary had prepared.

Dorotea made all the desserts, including a wonderful almond cake, but she opted to stay home with Vincenzo.

The wedding group feasted for hours and emptied countless bottles of Chianti.

Enzo went to bed later than usual, but the rest of the group laughed, danced, sang, ate and drank into the wee hours of the morning.

At the crack of dawn, everyone filled their glasses with prosecco and went to the top of the castle tower to celebrate a new day and the adventures ahead.

Mary said a toast to her Tuscan family.

"As sure as the sun rises every morning – and because of Tuscany – we will ALWAYS be together."

CHAPTER 84

༄༅ ༄༅

New Orleans, Louisiana

IN NOVEMBER, a Justice of the Peace married Jessie and Charles in Norma's little apartment. The only other attendees were Charles' parents. After the brief ceremony, they ate a hearty Cajun meal.

Later when his parents were gone, Norma gave them her wedding gift.

"Jessie, you have been the joy of my life. Sometimes I feel guilty your mama wasn't well enough to take care of you. But you know what? I got so much pleasure seeing you grow up day by day.

"For the last ten years or so I have watched you work hard to create the kind of life I always wanted for you. I myself dreamed of leaving this crazy town, but it was all I had in me to visit Nashville one time, you know."

She laughed at herself.

"So I've sat here in this little apartment and watched you. I have always told you we have to live our way into finding the answers to our questions. And we learn by making mistakes. It's the only way. I saw you strugglin' sometimes. I wanted to jump in and save you, but that wouldn't teach you anything."

"Oh, Norma," Jessie said. "Listen to you. You're always so wise."

"No, not always. But I knew you had to be strong and you are. Look at yourself. You're brave, talented and ambitious."

"Thank you."

"No, Jessie, thank you. I fulfilled my life's purpose by taking care of you."

Jessie's eyes filled with tears and Charles wrapped his arm around her.

"I hope those are tears of joy and not sadness," Norma said.

"Some of both."

"Well now here's your gift."

Norma opened an envelope and pulled out a stack of papers.

"Jessie, these are copies of my will and financial documents. You are the beneficiary of everything, including all the money Maurice left to me. I never had much, but Maurice did and he left it all to me. I've only had to use a small amount of it to pay Mrs. Jonas next door. She's doing a good job taking care of me. I probably don't have a lot of time left, and when the dear Lord decides it's my time, you'll receive it all."

Jessie looked through the papers.

"Norma, this is a lot of money."

"Yes, it is. I've had it for years in case of an emergency. Or in case I had to go in one of those nursing homes. But it doesn't look like that's going to happen.

"I could've given you some of this money earlier in your life to make it easier, but I wanted you to learn some lessons on your own."

"Oh, Norma. The money isn't the gift. You are."

Jessie leaned into Norma's big soft shoulders and hugged the woman who had loved her with everything she had to give.

"I hope you don't mind," Charles said. "But I want to join this hug."

He went to Norma's other side and the three held each other.

"You two are one good-lookin' couple," Norma said. "I'm glad you got back together – I always knew you would. And I'm glad you're not living here. New Orleans is a tough place to live. Philadelphia seems to be agreeing with the two of you. Your jobs are good, and I know you're always going to be happy.

"The cards told me this already, but I had to let you find this path for yourself. Now you two lovebirds need to go to Italy and have a wedding in that little chapel and take a lot of pictures for me."

CHAPTER 85

❧❦❧❦

Terzano, Tuscany

TWO MONTHS LATER, on a cold, snowy December day, Jessie and Charles had a simple wedding ceremony in the Tuscan chapel.

It was timed with everyone's visit to Italy for Christmas, and the quaint wedding was exactly what Jessie had always dreamed of.

Luke Davis escorted her down the aisle, and she wore a floor-length, seventies bohemian dress Stella had given her.

Charles wore a relaxed tan suit without a tie and slicked his long hair back.

Jessie knew this wedding was the premonition she had during her first walk in the Ribelli vineyard. Now she could see the beautiful faces of all the attendees.

Immediately after the service, Jessie grabbed Charles and took him to the tower lookout. It was freezing, but she needed to be alone with him in a special place before they joined the group.

"I'm so happy you're my wife, Mrs. Jessica Durbridge. I love you and always will."

"I love you, too."

She closed her eyes and kissed him, dreaming of their years ahead.

"We need to start working on a family right away," he said.

She laughed.

"How about right here?" he asked.

He started lifting the long skirt of her dress but she stopped him and grabbed his hand.

"I took a pregnancy test today."

"What?"

"It was the first day I could do it."

"And?"

"We're going to have a baby!"

Charles wrapped his arms around her and held her tightly.

"Oh, Jessie, I love you so much. This is wonderful! I hope it's the first of many."

"Do you think we should tell everyone tonight? I'm not that far along, but I know they'll wonder why I'm not drinking."

"Why not?"

Back in the house, Mary noticed Jessie wasn't touching her prosecco, but she didn't ask why. She knew the one reason that would keep Jessie from drinking, and Dorotea had predicted it earlier when Mary picked up the cake.

She told Mary the lavender angel still rode on Jessie's shoulder, and she carried another one in her belly.

Once everyone sat down, Charles and Jessie stood to address the group with a semi-rehearsed toast.

"Thank you for coming to our wedding," Jessie said. "It's a special day, and we're happy to be here in Tuscany. But this isn't just a wedding celebration."

"That's right," Charles said. "Our family is growing. We're going to have a baby! I just found out!"

Laughter and joy filled the room. Everyone was thrilled.

Stella screamed.

Enzo clapped.

Mary cried.

Jessie thought it seemed too perfect to be real. But it was real. She was starting her own family tree with the one man she had always truly loved.

As she hugged Mary, Jessie remembered walking into the little gallery on that hot, summer day in August, the day she started the hardest – and the best – journey of her life.

ACKNOWLEDGMENTS

Thank you to everyone who loyally waited for this sequel. So many times I thought it was ready, but would decide it wasn't yet right. I didn't want to take a chance of hearing, "The sequel wasn't as good."

A special thanks goes to these people...

GRIER FERGUSON – A wonderful editor and writer who has the ability to turn run-on sentences into tight ones and place commas in exactly the right place. (I'm, still, learning, how, to, do, this!) Her email: occasionalcliche@gmail.com

NADJA & ERIN – Two ladies who are listed together because they did the one thing I needed most. They gave me honest critique and told me what they liked, and most importantly, what they didn't like.

CRAIG – My husband who once let me read the manuscript to him on a round-trip drive from Sarasota to Miami. He has great plot ideas, and a sense of realism that I sometimes miss.

PATRICIA – My mom who will read draft after draft and never complain, and give me undying support.

MELISSA – My busy niece who read one of the earliest drafts and reminded me that she wanted to read as much about Mary and Luca as possible, even with the new characters.

...and thank you to all these wonderful people who encouraged me to keep writing: Allison, Beth, Bettina, Brenda R, Brenda S, Brenda V, Cara, Carol, Carole, Chip, Connie, Courtney, Dan, Dick, Doranne, Gayle, Janice, Judi H, Judi L, Karen, Kathy, Ken, Kim, Laura, Lisabeth, MariSue, Missie, Nancy, Nettie, Nicole, Pam, Sally, Sandy, Sharon, Stephanie, Steve, Tammy, Tanya, Tracey, and Vicki.

ABOUT THE AUTHOR

AS A TEENAGER KAREN ROSS read an excerpt from Alan Alda's commencement speech to the Connecticut College class of 1980, and remarkably, his words still inspire her. Mr. Alda said to the young graduates, "You have to leave the city of your comfort and go into the wilderness of your intuition. You can't get there by bus, only by hard work and risk and by not quite knowing what you're doing, but what you'll discover will be wonderful. What you'll discover will be yourself." Since then, Karen has challenged herself personally and professionally to live on that outside edge of comfortable and writing this debut novel did just that. Not a classically trained writer, she had a story to tell about life experiences: Gutsy romantic love (something not easily found and often lost), soul-tickling romantic Italy, delectable food and wine (especially Chianti) and passionate living and traveling. So she put pen to paper, not sure of what she was getting herself into. The experience was sometimes easy and often challenging, but it was always exhilarating and satisfying. She definitely traveled outside of her "city of comfort," but it was undoubtedly worth the hard work and risk.

Karen Ross is the granddaughter of an Italian immigrant name Giorgio Rondinara of Vico nel Lazio, Frosinone, Italy. When he because a U.S. citizen he wanted an American name so he changed it to George Egan Ross.

CONNECT

Facebook Page:	www.facebook.com/chiantisouls
Twitter:	@ChiantiSoul
Instagram:	#chiantigirl
Website:	www.chiantigirlpublishing.com
Author Email:	chianti.souls@yahoo.com

AUTHOR'S NOTE about ITALY

ITALY IS A PLACE I LOVE and have explored often, especially Tuscany. As I wrote BECAUSE OF TUSCANY (and CHIANTI SOULS), I needed the locale to specifically suit the tale, so Terzano is a fictitious hamlet that is modeled after a real one in Tuscany. You won't find it on a map, only in the wilderness of my imagination.

BOOKS by Karen Ross

CHIANTI SOULS – An Italian Love Story

Karen's debut novel introduces characters Luca Rusconi and Mary Sarto and their path to finding love, set in the heart of Tuscany, in the famous Chianti region.

On Mary's first visit to Italy, a chance meeting with Luca at a fifteenth-century farmhouse rattles them both, as if their love story continues from another lifetime. But neither is looking for love. Mary is vacationing with her boyfriend Garrett, and Luca is recovering from a broken engagement. Yet their paths continue to cross, and once home Mary's life becomes tangled in lies and betrayal.

It is only when Mary discovers secrets hidden in two mysterious keepsakes found in Tuscany and Venice that her destiny in love is revealed.

Available as a paperback and eBook:

Amazon.com
Barnesandnoble.com
iBooks.com
KOBO.com
NOOK.com

Suggested Reading Group Questions

1) Is Italy another living, breathing character in the book? Are the castle and rental properties characters too? Could this story be set elsewhere and have the same outcome?

2) Jessie and Mary are strongly inspired by Tuscany. What places have inspired you and why?

3) Nearly very character in the book has issues with their families, and Mary states that perfect families don't exist. Why do you agree or not agree?

4) BECAUSE OF TUSCANY is described as "a tale of friendship and love." If you wrote a book about an important turning point in your life (like Jessie's) what would you call it?

5) Could you forgive Charles for the event with Adele? Why? Do you think Adele was the perpetrator of the high school event?

6) BECAUSE OF TUSCANY is told from Mary's and Jessie's points of view. Do you think the tale could have been told from only one point of view and how would the story be different?

7) Do you believe Luke Davis remained in love with Anna all those years? Or was he afraid of something else?

8) What names would you consider for the baby if a girl? If a boy?

9) Jessie and Charles had completely different upbringings in the same city. How were their lives alike? How were they different?

10) Mary and Luca's love grows with time. How often do you think this happens in real life?

11) What do you like about Mary? Stella? Jessie?

12) Norma led a simple life, and was exceptionally strong and nurturing. Do you agree with how she raised Jessie? Do you think Jessie's life was richer as a result of being parented by Norma instead of her mother?

13) Did you feel sorrow or compassion for Jessie's mother? Why or why not?

14) Jessie's meeting with her father was cold and brief. Do you think they will ever talk or meet in the future?

15) If you were going to read a third book about this group of characters what would you want to happen?

16) How are Luke and his father alike? Different?

17) Mary had an older friend in Tuscany and at home in Philadelphia. Why do you believe she has a tendency to befriend older people?

18) Alex and Jessie were attracted to each other. What kept them from getting together?

19) Charles and Jessie create lives. Where do you think they will end up living together?

20) Which character would you most like to meet?